# The Dark Side

# of Forkis

# The Dark Side

# of Forkis

## Death Bringer Prequel

## Zodiac Universum

## Adrianna Biełowiec

ePub ISBN: 979-8-2011968-3-7

Paperback ISBN: 979-8-9859170-4-8

\*\*\*

Written by Adrianna Biełowiec

Published by Royal Hawaiian Press

Cover art by Tyrone Roshantha

Cover Jaguar image by Aldo Dominguez

Black&White content illustrations by Adrianna Biełowiec

Translated by Szymon Nowak

Publishing Assistance: Dorota Reszke

\*\*\*

For more works by this author, please visit:

www.royalhawaiianpress.com

\*\*\*

Version Number 1.00

# Table of Contents

# Vore in Fantasy

Vore is a subgenre of fantasy which is disseminated in the form of prose, graphics, films and animations. It's becoming more and more popular in the international trends, both on portals gathering artists, such as DeviantArt or YouTube, and among the furry subculture. Much of the content of this sub-genre looks controversial and may be disturbing, even disgusting, but some are made quite decently and interesting, such as high-quality fan 3D movies with dinosaurs or dragons (predators in general).

Vore is a fandom abbreviation recognized all over the world, meaning content on this subject. It comes from the word vorarephilia (synonym: phagophilia), which is a conglomerate of the Greek word "liking" (philia) and the Latin word "to swallow, to devour" (vorare). To put it simply, vorarephilia is a kind of paraphilia related to eating. And here are three sub-types: someone fantasizes about being eaten, imagines that he is eating another creature, or enjoys watching such content. There is very little scientific research on this paraphilia, and few documented cases of people talking about it (like the example of the patient referred to as Stephen in the article Vorarephilia: A Case Study in Masochism and Erotic Consumption), but it is attributed to BDSM (bondage & discipline, sadism & masochism). One side behaves dominantly (called pred, from predator - a predator), while the other side succumbs to it (prey, or prey), which is related to the desire to become part of a powerful, admired being. Often vorarephilia is considered a synonym of cannibalism, but wrongly, because in vore the living victim - apart from the hard variety - is swallowed whole. In addition, there are mainly interspecies relationships on the predator-prey line, regarding animals, anthropomorphs and other fantastic creatures, like giants, demons or the aforementioned dragons.

Additionally, ritualism aside, cannibalism is concerned with the consumption or recovery of energy (as with the popular example of a startled female hamster eating its own offspring). On the other hand, Vore is pure fantasy, unreal in the real world, at best exteriorized as a role-playing game in a narrated form. The swallowed live prey usually survives, and how it happens depends on the author's imagination - it may be teleportation, waking up from sleep, or the intact prey travels its way from the stomach to the mouth on its own. Vore is not an Internet invention of recent years, it has its roots in mythology or the Bible - most probably remember stories about Coyote, Jonah or Kronos.

There are many varieties of Vore, here's the list of a few selected examples:

Soft - the "soft" version, the most popular in fantasy, also in cartoons and animations, such as Tom and Jerry or Pinocchio. The victim is not injured in any way, not even a drop of blood flows out during the consumption process. Usually it is swallowed whole, it can breathe in the stomach and stay there for several days (after all, it's a fiction). Predator - prey relationships are mostly friendly, and can also be about love, humor, or fun; the dominant creature often wants to provide for the other safety in your body, for example in severe frost. There is no coercion whatsoever, and both sides agree to consume. On foreign pages of the furry subculture, you can read that in the soft variant, it happens that a terrified prey is eaten against its will, and a happy predator behaves ruthlessly towards it, but this psychological aspect of both creatures fits into the hard category.

Hard - coincides with the term gore as well. The victim is devoured against his will, and the predator often derives considerable satisfaction from its suffering. Mutilations of the body such as biting, crushing or chewing are common, and ultimately the ingested entity is digested. The theme is often used in horror or brutal anime movies.

Macro - the eater is a giant (generally any giant).

Examples are the movies Rampage, King Kong or Jurassic Park.

Micro - one of the creatures is reduced in size and then eaten by other life-size creatures. The theme appeared in one of the versions of the fairy tale about Puss in Boots, when a cat ate a wizard turned into a mouse.

Tiny - a smaller predator consumes a larger prey. In nature, this is evidenced by the feeding of a snake.

Soul - the victim's soul is absorbed, while the left-over body becomes a predator's puppet. An example is Paul Schrader's People-Cats.

After the introduction, you probably already know what to expect in this volume. It will feature story with soft and hard elements, related to the character of Forkis - the greatest criminal in the Zodiac Universum series. The book is therefore intended for adults, resistant to strong impressions. It can be read after Onkalot or treated as a separate item, although in the latter case the reader will come across spoilers, and may not notice a few connections with the Death Bringer trilogy, especially regarding the sciences.

**Pronunciation of major names in Quiché.**

' is a sign of glottalization for the vowels, which are ejective here - air is expelled from the larynx to amplify the sound.

Notation / pronunciation

Characters:

Xajb'a Kej - Shabakai

Q'ualel - Kooalhal

Etznab - Atsnab

Ik - Eek

Muluc - Moolhook

Lolmet Kejnay - Lolhmat Kaynai

Sinaj - Seenai

Places and facilities:

Chiq'aq - Cheekakh

11

Chulimal - Choolheemal

Quehnay - Kooanaii

Che'ab'aj - Chaabai

Tukumb'akam - Tookoombakam

Ajb'atenaja - Aybatanaya

K'otz'ib'aja - Kotseebaya


Other:


achij - achei

Nimja – Namja

# Resurrection of the Monster

## The Terrenic Year 2509

Xajb'a Kej had been traveling through the dense, dark jungle for five q'ijes[1], but he still had no idea what he would do when he reached the border of the territory of the cannibals called Jun Kame, One Death. He slipped out of his city after dusk like a thief

---

[1] It comes from the Mayan word ch'aqap q'ij. Equivalent to an hour among Onkalots.

after a successful heist. However, compared to the looter, Xajb'a Kej was an achij, because such a name was given to warriors-humanoid jaguars from the Chulimal world. The silent escape, avoiding the guard points, was not a problem for him, even in spite of his considerable height and weight. These features distinguished him among the inhabitants of his native Chiq'aq, the Place of Fire. Xajb'a Kej was also the only one to have green eyes. How it was possible - he found out only recently. And from the enemy, not the Onkalots, whom he trusted all his life.

And now he was headed towards yonder enemy. He was hoping to get his partner Pek back. Apparently, she had been kidnapped in the Jun Kame Forest when she had moved too far from border steles in search of rare herbs. The elders condemned her to a loss, they didn't want another confrontation with the cannibals - an attempt to rescue the female would have required a trip of many achijes. Anyway, all the Chulimal tribes were afraid of the demons from heaven who had flown into this world in a terrifying metal pyramid. So, the tribal struggles sounded foolish. Xajb'a Kej understood the reasoning of the elders, their decision to be passive was also reasonable, but his hot, militant blood prevented him from leaving Pek for certain death. He considered that she might have already been dead, but at least he would try to figure it out. Alone, he had at least a better chance of plowing to the enemy territory unnoticed. Although he took an obsidian dagger, bow, quiver and macuahuitl[2], as befited a good achij, it wouldn't have helped much in a fight against even a single Jun Kame member. Fanatic cannibals were considered the best warriors on the planet, and at the same time - the cruelest. Espionage and stealth were advisable this time, although Xajba Kej was disgusted with such a symptom of cowardice.

He went to swamps and wallowed in the black mud, from the whiskers to the tip of the tail, becoming like a rare strain of a humanoid jaguar. He carefully coated in it the weapon and a maxtlatl[3] reaching his knees. The light of the stars and the two moons wouldn't fall now on the bright parts of his mottled fur. The carmine glow of the infravision wouldn't give him away either. In the past, Jun Kame had done at least one good thing for him - Lolmet Kejnay had taught him to suppress the glare of his eyes in the dark by applying a transparent film over them that didn't obstruct vision.

Noiselessly he pushed on, sniffing and listening intently. By contrast, nocturnal animals, proud, dominant males and strong females, were not afraid to announce their presence in the forest by screaming, screeching, roaring, chirping or hissing.

[2] An offensive weapon in the form of a thick shaft studded with prismatic obsidian blades.

[3] A piece of fabric covering the hips, tied with a belt or rope.

Xajb'a Kej had an unpleasant, peculiar feeling that he was being watched. No one in the tribe was likely to follow him, and even if someone had been in the area, he would have picked up their thoughts telepathically. Jun Kame's boundaries, marked by javelins with the skulls of Onkalots on them, were still far away.

His intuition didn't disappoint him, although the part of the brain responsible for logical thinking contributed to it. From one of the trees, a bola was thrown at him, which effectively wrapped his hind legs, causing him to fall on his stomach, measuring his length. The trained enemy acted quickly. Xajb'a Kej noticed two humanoid jaguars jumping towards him - and a macuahuitl heading towards his head - before plunging into Xibalban darkness in stun and pain.

***

It must have been raining, or the enemy dragged him through a wider stream during the transportation, because the first thing Xajb'a Kej felt when he regained consciousness was the wind brush against his fur unglued by mud. He carefully cracked open his eyes. For a traumatic moment he was afraid of losing his eyesight, but fortunately it turned out that his vision was disturbed by the intense glow of the K'ajolom at the zenith. If it had really rained before, the rain had already evaporated in the heat of the merciless star, because no moisture was felt.

The humanoid jaguar glanced at his body with his painful eye. He could see the remnants of mud, practically sand falling as he moved. He assessed that nothing seemed to have been done to him, except for cuts and a few bruises, especially the biggest one on his head. He was lying sideways on the warm, hard ground; of course, all his weapons had been taken from him. His hind and front legs were tied with two ropes. From his awkward position, he looked around at his surroundings. He was in a square paved with gray-beige slabs, about seventy steps in diameter. Apart from the path that had been cut through the trees, he was surrounded by jungle on all sides. At one-point, wooden cages with birds and other captured animals were grouped. Jun Kame achijes were walking around the enclave, busy with weapons, goods or conversations, a few gathered around the fire surrounded by boulders. Xajb'a Kej immediately recognized them by their tall, fit for combat and killing figures covered with bones, stones and feathers. Cahua[4] additionally wore animal skins over their shoulders, also pectoral crosses made of volcanic stones. The achij furs were covered with paintings reminiscent of decay and death, especially the carbon black around the eyes, reminiscent of a skull's eye sockets. Xajb

---

[4] From the Aztec word tiachcahuan - leader; chief.

Kej's attention was caught by solar reflexes. Above the palm tops he could see the tip of a stone pyramid.

He had no doubts about his whereabouts anymore. Tukumb'akam Pyramid, Temple of the Monster. He had been dragged to the outskirts of Quehnay, the city of the cannibals.

"Great," he growled, angrier with himself than concerned with the situation. He had completely failed to take into account that many Jun Kame members were telepaths! It was the dominant psionic ability in this tribe. Those who had it, learned to use it to the nines. They must have picked him up telepathically long before he sensed the intruders. Xajb'a Kej was the only telepath in Chiq'aq, he had no one to train him, he did everything himself. And he was probably far behind with the skills compared to Jun Kame's.

He tried to probe achijes' minds by the fire. He succeeded, but learned nothing useful because they were thinking about unimportant, mundane things.

There was a telepath in the group. Mental noise caught his attention. He reacted with a momentary stupor and lifting of his ears, then looked at the prisoner.

"Look, he's already awake!" He said with amusement.

Another achij, eating meat underdone over the fire, greeted the alien with a bloody smile. Xajb'a Kej knew him too well.

18

Lolmet Kejnay got up from the crouch. Walking lazily towards him, he slipped an obsidian dagger from its sheath. Xajb Kej had once met Lolmet in a forest in no man's land. Back then, the cannibal had been an ordinary achij, now he had to be promoted to a lesser cahua, because he had a pectoral cross made of small predator's tusks around his neck. Xajb'a Kej tried to catch his thoughts, but the latter successfully blocked his mind. He was not a telepath, but like many Jun Kame members without this skill, he had been taught to defend himself against espionage; in a cahua, this ability proved to be particularly useful.

Kejnay leaned over the intruder, eyed up his body, then pushed the tip of the blade to his throat.

"And it's you again," he sighed theatrically. "Do you know why you are still alive?"

Xajb'a Kej didn't answer, still annoyed that despite all the precautions he had let himself be finagled and caught like a kitten with blunted senses.

The cannibal pressed harder the stone blade that almost cut through the fur to the blood.

"Answer me, poor Chiq'aq, when the better and the stronger ask you."

Xajb'a Kej had learned much earlier that psychopathic Jun Kame was no joke. In his position, also with the gallows sense of

19

humor of the cannibals, which in the mildest version ended with biting fingers off, it befited him to cooperate.

"You probably need me for something."

"We'll see. And you are still breathing, because your blood is half Jun Kame, because of your father."

This was unfortunately true. Xajb'a Kej had been conceived during tribal wars, when neither side had wanted to beget a child, and one only had wanted disport itself hard with the victim.

Kejnay pointed to the pyramid with his paw with the dagger. It was there that the Onkalots of other tribes were sacrificed, often in large numbers. He smiled, and smacking, shook his head.

"Tell me, and what am I to do with you now, young man? We came across you while hunting. And there is still a lot of time left to ixiptla, the day of sacrifice. What were you looking for in the wilderness, and all alone?"

Kejnay was joined by two humanoid jaguars from his small squad. Xajb'a Kej saw no reason to invent things in the presence of the telepath.

"I was on my way here to get Pek back," he announced. "Give her back to me."

"Ik?" Cahua turned to the telepath.

"He has told the truth, " he replied.

20

Lolmet got up, looked at his companions, then the three laughed out loud, drawing the attention of the others. Only the two who stayed by the fire and argued, didn't become interested in the new entertainment.

"Who is Pek?" He asked.

"Someone from Chiq'aq," Xajb'a Kej tried to speak as sparingly as possible without thinking too much.

"Oh," Lolmet grinned, "let me guess. This is someone close to you, whom Chiq'aq forbade you to save, so you decided to act on your own paw?"

"And you already know everything."

Kejnay gave him a kick in the ribs. Surprised, Xajb'a Kej was hit in the wound, it hurt him terribly, but he managed not to compromise himself even more and only limited himself to a hiss. If the Onkalots didn't have retractable claws, additional wounds would surely have adorned his chest.

"That's for your stupidity," explained Kejnay. "Nevertheless, you impressed me that you wanted to be a one-man army."

The cannibals started laughing again.

"What did you do with Pek?" growled Xajb Kej daringly. Since Jun Kame cherished bravery and courage, maybe he would achieve something by going this way. "I know you kidnapped her!"

21

"Even if it's so, why do you think we'll give her back to you? Why would we do this? From where such a stupid idea anyway?" Lolmet, still laughing, asked.

He heard a scuffle behind himself. The two youngsters who had been arguing about something earlier, threw themselves at each other like wild cats, and now they struggled on the ground. Kejnay made an arc with his eyes, shook his head, then, without any particular aiming, he swung and threw his dagger at the fighting. The blade hit one of them harmlessly in the thigh, and the humanoid jaguar yelled.

"Enough!" The cahua roared. "It's enough to leave you alone for a moment ..."

"They're bored," said Ik.

"Bored, you're saying ..."

Xajb'a Kej didn't like the look Kejnay gave him after slowly turning his head towards him. Fanatical, hungry, though it resulted from the macabre thoughts of the cannibal. Xajb'a Kej was frightened without showing it in any way when Lolmet leaned over him again. With efficient movements of his fingers, he freed him from the bonds with which he would have probably struggled for half a day. He gave the cannibal a questioning look, sitting and rubbing his wrists and ankles.

"You two, come here." Cahua nodded to those who had fighted. The one with the injured paw, tied his wound with lint, and limped, pressing his fingers against it. When he approached, Kejnay pulled back the material for a moment. "It will stop bleed right away. Wash it with herbs."

Xajb'a Kej completely didn't understand the painful, brutal disciplinary methods practiced among Jun Kame members, although used carefully. It rather wasn't in the interest of cahua to kill his achijes. He disliked even more the fact that he was released. He sensed trouble.

"Let's make such a deal." Lolmet stood slightly astride and folded his arms over his chest. "To save your life, you will have to sacrifice others. If you provide us with enough entertainment, then I will help you with Pek. Perhaps both of you will survive. If you refuse, however, we will kill you and put your skull on the border stele next to Chiq'aq."

"It seems to me that I have no choice." Xajb'a Kej got up. He and Lolmet were of the same height, but Onkalot from Chiq'aq could boast of greater mass and better developed muscles. He knew, however, that if he had wanted to attack the leader of the Jun Kame unit, he would have been quickly pacified by Kejnay, who was older than him, and without the help of his companions.

"And you think rightly so." The Jun Kame member's voice was dripping with venom and irony. A harbinger of cruel fun tailored to local tastes.

"So, what am I supposed to do?" Xajb'a Kej also clasped his paws into the basket.

"Bring the man, Muluc," Kejnay turned to the achij who was fighting with the humanoid jaguar with the wounded thigh.

Xajb'a Kej frowned. He probably had heard this word in the previous meeting with the cannibals. Even in Chiq'aq it had been heard a few times recently.

Muluc drawing group's attention, moved towards the cages. He stood next to one of those closer to the trees, which Xajb'a Kej couldn't see due to the caught colorful birds with large feathers. But when he noticed what achij was dragging out, his pulse quickened, as if he had finished a short, intense run; dazed, he held his breath.

Demon from the stars.

Dressed in a tight robe of shiny material.

One of the riders of the metal pyramid that had settled far from Quehnay and Chiq'aq, but the great distance didn't mean safety at all.

As Muluc led him without finesse, with his hands tied behind his back, Xajb'a Kej was able to get a good look at him for the first time. He had never seen a demon live, only had heard various stories about them that seemed absurd compared to the object viewed with his own eyes. How could something so brittle, pale, without fur (apart from that K'ajolom's ray-colored thatch on the head), mouth, fangs, claws, muscles and tail be a deadly threat to Chulimal?

He realized that the smiling Kejnay must have understood his reasoning, because he replied:

"They themselves are not dangerous, but their things are deadly. We had to pull this one out of a shell, as hard as a hundred armors of turtles, for a long time. Before the Onkalots were on the warpath with people, we had watched them from hiding, we got to know their language a bit. He waved his paw towards the lead. "It's a female. They call them women."

"What did you do ..." This time Xajb'a Kej didn't hide his fear. "They'll kill us all if they find this female!"

"They won't." Kejnay took a small, black object from a pouch at the waist. It resembled somewhat a perfectly polished obsidian plate in the shape of a square block, full of miniature cuts and protrusions. "It's called a transmitter. I don't know how it works, but thanks to it they can talk to each other at a distance, also track each other, although they cannot see or hear each other. I overheard that people call it technology, whatever it is. Man's damaged things are as useless as their pathetic, fragile bodies without armor.

Cahua tossed the broken transmitter under the feet of the woman that was brought. Muluc forced her into falling to her knees, her head down in fear, she wasn't going to raise, anyway.

"Why did you catch her, it will bring trouble!" Xajba Kej, no less scared, already knew what Lolmet would order him to do, but he tried to use any argument to convince him.

"I saw them kill ours. They call it a shooting. She was one of the enforcers." Lolmet grabbed the stranger by the hair and lifted her head. Xajb'a Kej saw fear and resignation in her blue eyes. Having recognized him as a companion of misery, she seemed to judge him to see if he was like the others. "As among Chiq'aq, also amid humans, women are apparently achij." He spat on the ground. In Jun Kame's land, only males could deal with fighting, which was related to greater strength and a stronger body structure. Females, on the other hand, were considered to be smarter and more cunning, although they were not inferior in cruelty to achijes, which is why they were part of the ruling council. "She felt too confident with her luminous, long-range weapon, and one time she plunged into the forest. But we were already waiting for her there. People's weapons also think in some way, work a bit independently of them, but fortunately we discovered by accident that in the presence of ayin volcanic rock, her 'scanners' couldn't see us. The woman must die now. And as you guess it, you will take her life." Kejnay smiled kindly.

All Onkalots in the square became interested in the unfolding scene, as if "you will take her life" was the key slogan ordering to stop the activities performed.

"She didn't do anything to me," Xajba Kej whispered. The line of his senseless defense melted like beeswax in the sun. "And why me?"

"Why not?" Lolmet spread his arms. "Don't be selfish, give our brave achij some entertainment!"

"What guarantee do I have that when I complete this task, I will not lose my life?"

"None, except my word. Even though your blood is tainted by Chiq'aq, it would be still a pity to spill the other half senselessly."

Xajb's Kej growled, showing his fangs.

"If you insult my mother again ..." Two achij pulled out their daggers, the cahua gestured for them to hide them. "What should I do?" asked Xajb'a Kej after a while, wanting to end this nightmare as soon as possible, before he becomes angry enough to attack the cannibals, thus signing his own death warrant.

Kejnay eloquently glanced at Ik, his smile widened. The telepath laughed in an unpleasant way, then nodded eagerly.

"Let him do it. It will be fun!" he said.

More than the silent agreement, Xajb'a Keja was disturbed by the sardonic smile of Kejnay licking, who stared at the woman like a lizard at a juicy beetle.

"Eat her," the Jun Kame member ordered cheerfully.

"What?!" Chiq'aq resident took two steps back. He couldn't go on, because he encountered a wall of few achijes who appeared behind him, it is unknown when.

"What don't you understand?" Kejnay asked innocently. He exserted his claw and plucked out something between the canine and the incisor, which he flicked.

"She's too big," Xajb'a Kej defended himself in all possible ways against bringing the catastrophe down on Onkalots. He also didn't believe Chiq'aq version that the star newcomers were demons - the only fact that added up was that they were from the darkness - but he was smart enough to know that harming someone possessing 'technology' would be fatal. The Jun Kame member didn't seem to notice it or trusted their strength and cleverness too much. "I could eat less than half of her body, and barely."

"Etznab," Lolmet, as if boredly, turned to another achij. "Our guest who has been extinguished by the Chiq'aq tribe, apparently doesn't know what Jun Kame blood gives him. So please show him our capabilities."

"Bird?"

"Let it be a rabbit."

This time, Etznab approached the cages. He chose the right one and cracked open the door. He slipped his paw with outstretched fingers inside to grasp the fold on the neck of a defending, large rabbit. With some kind of control over the terrified animal doing little donuts in the air, he returned to Lolmet. He didn't even care about being scratched by the claws of the rabbit's hind legs.

Kejnay playfully put his arm around Xajb'a Kej, pressed the side of his head to his and whispered:

"Look closely now."

Xajb'a Kej's heart began to beat faster, and in the underbelly appeared a long-undetectable pressure, having something to do with the horror of fascination, when Etznab lifted the rabbit with its mouth towards him and opened his drooly mouth wide. The animal began to thrash in full panic, but even waving its claws in all directions, it had no chance against the much stronger, larger predator.

Onkalot put the head of the senselessly fighting rabbit into his mouth and began to move it towards the moistened throat. He pressed the animal's forelimbs against the fluffy brown torso.

Xajb'a Kej was sure that this was some kind of sick joke, supposed to throw him off balance, and it would end when he achieved his goal, when he watched to his stupor Etznab's jaw tilt more and more as he pushed the enormous body into the stretchy esophagus. For the first time, he observed in a humanoid man that the lower jaw and bones of the skull weren't fused together, but tied loosely with joints and ligaments, so that they could slide apart at impressive distances. Chiq'aq couldn't do that. Other tribes probably neither. Chiq'aq ate half plant food, while the meat obtained from fishing and hunting was ground up and then processed with fire before consumption. Eating it raw, or even consuming whole living creatures, was forbidden, because this way of consumption was considered unsanitary, primitive and barbaric. Apparently reconciled to their nature, Jun Kame didn't have such dilemmas.

In Xajb'a Kej something started to wake up, like a parasitic larva in a broken egg. An old feeling that was stuck somewhere under the weight of tuns[5] came to life.

He remembered that when he was a kitten, once during a training of little ones in the field, he had watched a snake eat a huge frog tearing loose. The animal literally devoured it whole. It was an ambivalent feeling, because repulsive, but also exciting.

[5] Sidereal Year on Chulimal.

30

Q'ualel who had looked after them had come and of course, had had to ruin everything. He had taken Xajb'a Kej, slapped him on the head and forbidden him to admire the reptile's way of feeding. It couldn't have ended otherwise than with the awakening of a secretive inquisitiveness in him; Little Xajb'a Kej hadn't understood why many Chiq'aq had considered something natural to be a crime. But he had always thought a little differently from the rest, had been culturally resistant. He had tried to understand the nature of the serpent by secretly eating alive first insects, then rodents. He had pulled out their mandibles, teeth or claws so that they wouldn't hurt him inside. He had liked it madly as the living, terrified contents had wandered down his esophagus, and then for a while had delightfully squirmed in his stomach. Some beetles had endured all day, mincing and tickling, before finally dying in the gastric juices. For Xajb'a Kej it had been like unconditional domination and a sense of power.

Time and new life challenges had stifled these inclinations. Chiq'aq had raised him according to their social norms, wanting at all costs to destroy in him everything related to Jun Kame which they had hated.

The section leading to Etznab's stomach turned out to be very flexible, and the absorption of the large prey was also possible thanks to the bones of the torso sliding apart. Helping himself with his paws, the humanoid jaguar pushed into himself with little

31

difficulty the whole rabbit, moving as far as the squeezing muscles of the esophagus allowed it.

"He won't choke?" Xajb Kej asked, fascinated. The feeding of cannibals reminded him of the snake.

Kejnay, who had moved away from him earlier, guessed straight away that it was about Etznab.

"Jun Kame, while absorbing large pieces, can hold their breath for a long time."

Etznab closed his maw and swallowed the last contents with slight resistance. The entire rabbit, still alive, ended up in his stomach. The moving belly of the satisfied humming humanoid jaguar, who licked his lips with delight, was slightly convex.

The Jun Kame seemed to be enjoying the reactions of Xajb'a Kej, whose perception of the world had been reduced to Etznab's stomach and the animal squeezed inside. Fighting more and more weakly. "What a terrible death," flew through his head.

"You're all crank and insane," he said.

"You can't deny you liked it." He shuddered as Lolmet, wagging his tail, roused him from his delightful numbness with that announcement. Xajb'a Kej would have gladly taken that horrible, cute smile off his mouth with his fist. Indeed, he couldn't deny that there was something exciting about this ruthless, horrible rabbit show.

"You can do that too. Now it's your turn." Kejnay pointed his claw at the woman, of which all show courage flowed out, revealing her pure, animalistic, primal fear like in the previously devoured lagomorph. "If you want to defeat your enemy, you have to kill his females. It's worth remembering."

"And the bones?"

"It takes a long time, but we also digest them. If you don't have a fight, escape, or anything else that strains your body in the coming days, you can eat something like this and then rest. Now get to work."

The beast within him wanted to try. The civilized part of his identity forbade him from doing so. The father's genes fought against the mother's. Nature with upbringing. He cursed Jun Kame for what it had done with his psyche.

"This woman is your enemy," Kejnay continued to sip venom into his mind with a hissing, indoctrinating voice. "They'll kill us all if we don't stop them. We are just vermin to them. They will unscrupulously inflict pain, suffering and death on us, even if we submit to them. Jun Kame, however, doesn't humble itself before anyone, humility is shameful, it is the domain of victims. Now do with her what Etznab did with the rabbit."

Xajb'a Kej glanced at the humanoid jaguar squatting, his stomach didn't move anymore.

"Come on," Lolmet continued.

Xajb'a Kej fell to his knees in front of the tiny woman. She looked up at his jaguar face. He saw in her blue eyes a high intelligence, almost divine, and therefore disturbing. These people had drifted down from the stars here, so it was possible that more would also come. Onkalots knew so little about them. On the face of the woman there was fear, sadness, but also reconciliation with fate, he didn't notice a hint of regret directed at him. She understood perfectly well that he was part of the sick play, and so was she.

The achij untied the rope binding the victim's hands and stripped the clothes off her, leaving her completely naked, ineptly trying to cover herself with her hands. Ik barely brushed the skin of her forearm with his paw, and right away a scratch formed there and blood began to ooze, the same red as that of humanoid jaguars. Xajb'a Kej couldn't understand how the gods - he didn't really believe in them, but he used to fill the gaps in his ignorance with them - could create something so powerful and delicate at the same time. Fish and frogs had firmer skin, and they were among the most delicate creatures on Chulimal. Nevertheless, one thing constantly troubled him - Onkalots and humans were in many ways very similar. In Chiq'aq, it was forbidden to eat intelligent beings.

He eyed up the woman's body. He was over three times heavier than her.

"She won't come in," he spat the words out almost with obnoxiousness.

"She will come in," Lolmet replied dismissively. "If her head passes through your mouth, and it will pass for sure, the rest also will be able to handle it."

Xajb'a Kej lowered his head.

"I can't..."

"I can see you're still fighting like that rabbit." Kejnay crouched next to him. There was the obsidian dagger in his paw again, which he waved in front of him. "Are you stupid or you were hit in the head too strongly?" He asked impatiently. "I told you what will happen if you refuse to cooperate with me. Shall I describe it in detail? Okay. If you wash out, I'll gently cut that female's throat - he touched her chin with the blade and lifted it slightly, "and trust me, I know my stuff very well. We will make you watch at least for two q'ijes as she dies in front of your eyes, her life drains from her drop by drop. This will turn out to be so frightening that you will watch your own future. And then Pek will probably die as well, since there will be no one left to save her. Kill the woman and you both will survive."

Mischievously he stroked the fur between his ears and stood up.

"Exsert your claws," the woman said in Anglo-American.

"What is she saying?" Xajb'a Kej looked at the achij.

"I have understood the word claws."

Kejnay put the dagger in a leather case.

"She wants you to exsert them," completed Ik.

"What for?" Xajb'a Kej asked. "And how do you know what she says?"

"It turned out that Jun Kame's telepathy also works on people. I see their thoughts in the form of pictures. I don't understand much of their heads, but some images are universal.

"What do she need my claws for?"

"She knows she's going to die soon. She wants to feel as much as possible as if a great animal was killing her. It is difficult for her to accept the fact that she is treated in this way by other intelligence."

"Enough of this farce." Lolmet waved his paws. "You drag it out forever. Let's roll!"

The eyes of the woman and Xajb'a Kej met again. As she asked, he pulled the cat's claws out of his fingers. She nodded gratefully to him. She raised her arm and touched his fur on the left side of his muzzle, stroked it with her fingers, bending his mustache. Xajb'a Kej narrowed his eyes, tilted his head slightly in this direction and placed his big paw on the woman's hand. Contrary to Ik, who bettered him several times in skill, he couldn't read anything from her mind. But he could still sense her fear with the predator's senses, which she tried to control and which she was doing quite well. They looked like friends saying goodbye now. He decided that he would try to be as gentle as possible. He would help this, in his opinion, innocent creature to move to the other side in peace. He looked at her delicate throat. For a moment he was tempted to attack quickly and in two breaths to end the suffering of the woman with his fangs, and thus the fun of the Jun Kame member.

"Don't even try." Of course, Ik had to follow everything that was going on in his head.

"More and more irritated, Kejnay took a coconut mass bottle from someone, pulled out the cork and put it under Xajb'a Kej's nose.

"That's for the courage, because otherwise you probably will never start."

"Drink." Onkalot took a few gulps of spicy alcohol made from cactus and other succulent leaves. He didn't think it would help for his dilemma, but it might have brought him a little relief.

He felt a pleasant burning sensation in his mouth, esophagus, and finally in his stomach. From the inside, soothing warmth quickly began to spread through the body. Some brave thoughts also emerged immediately.

He wondered what the best way to calm this woman down, to make her mind groggy so that she could bear her end better, and he came up with the idea that he would do what mothers did to the mischievous kittens who didn't want to go to bed in the evening. It was also useful in the case of females frightened by their first intercourse with their partner. It worked on Pek. Xajb'a Kej hoped that the substances contained in his saliva would also have an effect on humans.

He approached the woman. He stuck his tongue out and dragged it along the side of her face, brushing the soft skin with the hot breath, and when she reacted with a slight surprise rather than disgust, he repeated the action on the other side. She tasted of the salt and the wood of the cage, also of the sweetness of a fragile flesh. He put her hand in his mouth and sucked it for a moment. He lowered his head, touched her belly with his warm tongue, moving it up between her breasts, to the top of her neck. He moved behind the woman, grabbed her shoulders with his clawed paws and began to lick her back. The method seemed to work, because she was starting to relax. The same emotions, similar reactions, telepathy acting on the mind, stupefying with substances contained in saliva - Xajb'a Kej had no doubt that humans and Onkalots, although they were divided by stars, somehow had to be related.

She closed her eyes as he licked them with his wet tongue as big as her entire face.

Ignoring the laughter and taunts from around him, he crouched down, grabbed the woman by the shoulders and brought her close to his mouth. After a short hesitation, he touched his forehead to hers.

"I'd like to know your name," he whispered.

"Jenny."

He moved his head away and looked at her in surprise. This foreign word with unknown meaning, but sounding beautiful, could indeed be a name. He wondered if that was the case and if so, if woman had learned a few basic phrases in Oncalock, or she had guessed what he asked her.

"Nice name. If I ever have offspring, I will persuade my partner to call the female that way. In memory of the brave woman of the stars. At least this is what I can do."

She surprised him even more when she wrapped her arms around his neck. He hugged her back. He was completely lost in all this; the situation was so abnormal that he couldn't find an adequate word for it. To save one female, for pure entertainment, he was ordered to eat the other, and the victim, without resenting him due to her fate, cuddled up to the hunter who was about to kill her. But who was he to judge the behavior of the star creatures?

"It's time," he said, stroking her cheek. "Forgive me, but I can't do otherwise. We are both their victims."

She understood the message, but not the words. She nodded firmly, biting her lips to keep them from twitching.

Xajb'a Kej opened his jaws and put Jenny's head into his mouth, he felt her rapid breathing on her tongue and the pulse raging in her throat. It wasn't bad anyway, because she could scream and struggle like that poor rabbit. His heart was going crazy too - from anxiety, deep regret, shame ... and from this damn excitement. Whether he wanted it or not, the primeval predator had awakened within him. He no longer had to defend himself and lie to himself that it was otherwise - he enjoyed eating an intelligent being alive. It was a bit of a pleasant feeling, as if in a one-on-one fight he had knocked down a worthy foe or had forcibly appropriated enemy lands. He felt exactly the same as in the case of insects and animals in childhood.

Xajb'a Kej continued to do it as Etznab had showed him with the rabbit. He pressed Jenny's arms against her torso and began to slide her leisurely with his paws into his throat. The Jun Kame member briskly commented, gave directions, laughed and clapped, as if watching a good, bloody duel in an arena. Onkalot tried to forget about their existence. He concluded with amazement that was happening exactly what Kejnay had told him - his skull and lower jaw moved away from each other as if in a full-blooded Jun

Kame member. Just like in a snake. The woman had a smooth body, without the uncomfortable creations of the epidermis, such as horns or ruffled feathers, and the additional moistening with saliva made it even more conducive to its movement into his viscera.

The head easily entered his dilated esophagus, and the rest of Jenny's naked body began to slide in behind it. Xajb'a Kej clearly felt her nervous ticks and jerks not stronger than vibrations, because she was squeezed by his muscles and had little room for maneuver. He tried hard not to think what the woman might have felt now, in the dark, damp and claustrophobic cramped space, listening to the impending doom sounds of his gut. He took into his head that it was why predators had long fangs and strong jaws - to kill their prey prematurely and spare it from going through the worst nightmare of its life. To the nightmare of the victims, some hunters had unfortunately broken out of this pattern.

He was brushing her belly with his teeth, and soon his fangs were touching Jenny's thighs. He felt her head slide into his stomach. For the time of consumption, as announced by the Jun Kame members, he didn't breathe, but he didn't feel any discomfort because of it. He had never devoured something so enormous without tearing it apart and chewing it; his peristalsis didn't cope well and it would have failed if Xajb'a Kej hadn't supported himself with his paws. He realized that he was nervously

41

sweeping the slabs of the square with his tail. Left to right, left to right.

Finally, Jenny's feet found themselves on his tongue. He clenched his teeth, trapping the victim definitively in his body. The eyeballs went deeper into his skull as he swallowed hard and loudly.

The whole woman reached his stomach, he could feel her in the embryonic position, the pressure against the folded walls. Gods, she was moving there! It seemed to him that she was pressing from the inside with her hand his enlarged abdomen, he placed his paw there. The claws were still extended on all limbs, so he retracted them into his fingers. He wanted to believe that Jenny felt a little better knowing she had been eaten by something like an animal.

The body began to demand replenishment of air; Xajb'a Kej was panting heavily through his mouth, with his tongue hanging out. He slumped to the side. Earlier, he hadn't noticed how much he was tired of this consumption, especially mentally. He remembered that he wasn't alone there.

Kejnay applauded nonchalantly, staring at him from under his tilted head.

"And? Don't say it wasn't great and you don't feel heavenly."

"May you die in agony, and the Xibalbans play ulama with your skull ..."

Unfortunately, he felt comfortable with what he had just done. The term 'heavenly' fit perfectly here. That's why he wanted to lace into cursed Kejnay for telling him the truth in the face. He could at least make an excuse to himself by bringing the culprit to the fore - Lolmet resurrected in him his dark side from his early youth. Regardless, Xajb'a Kej felt sorry for Jenny. The star strangers hadn't stepped on his toes, he didn't resent them and he had to pay for someone's animosity.

After the gruesome performance was over, some achij returned to their activities. It became cloudy, from the dense gray clouds began to drip rain, which quickly turned into a tropical downpour. Behind the Tukumb'akam pyramid it flashed with white and blue, a mighty thunderbolt swept over the enclave almost immediately.

Kejnay knelt by Xajb'a Kej, holding the fruit taken out of the pouch in his paw and nibbling on it.

"Speaking of skulls," he said, "you'll give it to me in the morning." Cattle tying poles protruded from the ground nearby. Muluc pulled a thick rope to one, while Ik put a thick collar around Xajb'a Kej's neck made of gold, an ore that was abundant in some parts of Chulimal.

"You said you wouldn't kill me!" Xajb'a Kej shouted.

"Not your skull!" Lolmet indicated his belly. "Her skull. You should make a cast by morning."

The return of undigested remnants happened in Onkalots outside the Jun Kame community who ate hard parts such as nut shells or epidermis with a valuable meal. However, Xajb'a Kej didn't understand what he was to return, since he had eaten perhaps the most easily digestible meat in his life, and the bones were supposed to dissolve as well.

Another bolt of lightning struck. The bones.

At the mention of them, Xajb'a Kej felt as if he had been hit from heaven by the anger of the gods. Focused on the traumatic situation and the victim's feelings, he didn't think about the fact that he would soon have the large skeleton inside him.

The downpour soaked the fur of the Onkalots more and more. Most of those who had been in the square had already gone towards the city or disappeared into the forest. The cages were removed, the fire flickered out.

Xajb'a Kej realized that he was able to walk away from the pole only three steps. However, it was enough to hide under a wooden shelter with a cattle feeder, which he hadn't done yet. Sitting on the ground in the streams of rain gave him that little peace he needed so badly. The objects that were captivating him looked solid, and even in a wild frenzy he wouldn't have had a chance to break the collar apart or tear a heavy pole out of stone slabs.

"What's that supposed to mean?" He asked aggressively. "Give me back Pek! Bring her here now since I complied with your stupid request!"

He got up. He didn't feel particularly heavy with the woman in his belly, but he had to forget about long jumps and fast running for a while, if he ever left this area alive. He felt empty and depressed as he realized that the contents of his stomach were no longer moving. "But it's better, he thought, "to fall asleep calmly from lack of air than die, bleeding out of their throat on the rocks." Was devouring really such a terrible form of death as it had seemed to him before? Perhaps the best, in warmth, peace and, in a way, a sense of security?

Kejnay spread his arms.

"We don't have any Pek." He chuckled.

Xajb'a Kej lunged at him, but choked when the hoop tightened on his throat.

"You tricked me! You are monsters, but apparently truthful! This is your only feature that I've appreciated!"

"I didn't lie to you. I said I would help you with Pek, not that I would give her to you. And I will help in such a way that you will survive and will be able to look for her. There is no Pek with us. We don't sacrafice females, and we don't need slaves for work now."

"You don't even know who she is. You've never seen her." During another flash of lightning, Lolmet looked with his ghastly paintings on his head as if he had been a dark inhabitant of Xibalba, the realm of death. With his wet, slicked-back fur, he looked like a decaying corpse.

"No slave or victim," he explained, "is anonymous here, although it probably seems so to everyone from the outside. Remember that Jun Kame is a tribe of telepaths. If I were you, I would look for Pek among star friends. Our achij, they have already killed. Give me the skull tomorrow and you'll be free."

Soon Xajb'a Kej was alone in the rain. Wet to the last tuft, he finally hid under the wooden logs.

When the lightning area moved to other parts of the forest, Onkalot curled up into a ball and tried to fall asleep. The emotions that bombarded his mind, regarding both melancholy and culinary fulfillment, didn't allow him to do so for a long time.

***

He was awakened by the sounds coming from his gut, as if mud had been plopping there. Three loosely walking stags, nibbling at the grass from the pasture, also paid attention to them. For a moment they looked at the humanoid jaguar with interest, lazily grinding food with their jaws. It was no longer raining from the cloudy sky; It seemed to Xajb'a Kej that it was much brighter than when he had been nodding off.

"Hey, I have to go to the forest!" He called to a group of mature cannibals who stood bored near the trees, watching the youths beating each other with shields and macuahuitls. When something happened to any of them, for example someone bruised his knee after being kicked, the teacher called his names sharply and told him to quickly get back to the fight. The youngsters did just so. Among Jun Kame members, weakness was despised. A student didn't feel sorry for the other student, they didn't show friendship, fighting in pairs, they behaved as mortal enemies.

Xajb Kej was ignored.

The presence of cattle and its manure proved to be beneficial. When it seemed to the humanoid jaguar that no one was looking in his direction, he added in something and then covered it with a large amount of grass.

He was still very sleepy, too tired to succumb to the tormenting influence of thoughts or to see the nuances of his body. Soon he plunged into non-existence again.

He dreamed that at a crossroads he was talking to a human skull hanging on a tree and showing him the way.

\*\*\*

This time he was awakened by the Jun Kame member prodding him with a javelin, who, out of curiosity, came to check the stranger's viability. K'ajolom hung quite high in the cloudless sky, but wasn't yet hot enough to fully dry the puddles. The cattle were taken, and the waste was cleared away; Xajba Kej was angry with himself for having slept through those moments. achij should have always been vigilant. He blamed the alcohol, which was also handled with care, by the way, because it dulled the senses. Kejnay must have deliberately given him something strong, seeing what mental state he had been in.

The Jun Kame member with the javelin left disappointed. Xajb'a Kej yawned widely and reached towards his belly with his paw. He checked with his pads that it was much smaller than when Jenny had been eaten, and the previously doughy bumps had disappeared. Now he felt a curved hardness, and a lot of space between them.

He sat up abruptly, as if on command to go to war.

The gastric juices had already managed to digest all human flesh; this was what he had expected due to its delicacy and low fibrousness. But it wasn't over. The energy-intensive process still kept Xajb'a Kej's heart rate high, he was hot, and his internal organs were enlarged.

A few Jun Kame members were walking around the square, none of them paid any attention to him. Ignoring flies getting into his fur, Xajb'a Kej lay down on the slabs with a loud sigh. He ran his fingers over the skin of his stomach, trying to recognize the protruding bones. He easily felt the one Kejnay wanted. Jun Kame was crazy about skulls, it loved them. They built walls called tzompantli from them, kept them as trophies, placed them on the borders of territories conquered by force, used them for betting, sports games, and wore fragments in jewelry. Xajb'a Kej suspected that Lolmet needed a human skull for something specific, but for some reason he preferred to get it with someone else's paws, not even involving his own achijes in getting the trophy. And instead of doing it quickly, with the most ordinary, painless, honorable decapitation, he decided to have fun at the expense of Jenny and Xajb'a Kej, humiliating both of them.

Lolmet soon appeared, accompanied by Muluc, Etznab, and Ik. Xajb'a Kej had no idea why Etznab needed a charred javelin, and the telepath a cotton sack that smelled of burning, burned in some places.

Kejnay, on the other hand, approached him with a club. He pressed it against the belly of Xajb'a Kej who was being held by Muluc and contentedly tapped the sphericity just next to the cardiac orifice, before the paw of the annoyed humanoid jaguar, which broke free from his grip, knocked off the wood.

49

"Perfect." The Jun Kame member looked at the stone slabs for a moment. "I'm impressed," he said after inspecting it. "I was expecting a huge bone vomit here, but it turned out that your digestive system is stronger than I thought. However, you still had to sleep for two days. It was nice idea to shit onto cattle dung. Maybe you would like to join us after all?"

"Screw you, Kejnay."

He shrugged.

"As you wish. Here you are, drink it." He tossed him a corked coconut bottle, which Xajb'a Kej grabbed in flight. Muluc released him from the collar and pushed him closer to the cahua.

"Do you want to get me drunk again?" Xajb'a Kej muttered. "Or maybe poison this time?"

"Poisons are used by cowards." Lolmet folded his arms over his chest. "Drink."

Xajb'a Kej knew that if he hadn't obeyed the order, they would have poured this liquid into him brutally, and he would probably haven't endured another humiliation. If they had wanted to make him do something by force now, he would have attacked to kill, no longer caring about the consequences.

The drink smelled sour. Xajb'a Kej brought the spout of the bottle closer to his mouth and looked at the cahua suspiciously.

"Bottoms up." Kejnay smiled.

The plant-derived fluid tasted sour, too, and was fairly bitter foul.

Grimacing, Xajb'a Kej managed to take a few gulps and he felt terribly sick, as if he had actually been poisoned.

"Stand back." Lolmet pushed a little Muluc with his forearm, and the other two took a few steps back.

Xajb'a Kej fell on all fours, contracted immediate, strong cramps of the abdominal, diaphragm and chest muscles. His head was just above the ground. He opened his mouth, began to snort like a cat struggling with swallowed hair. Thick saliva ran down his tongue. The stomach was ready to eject the partly digested bones, but their size and shape made it difficult for it.

Onkalot thought he was going to suffocate when the stomach finally opened enough to allow the powerful muscle contraction drag out the nearest contents.

He tossed out of himself her skull plastered with hair, followed by a part of her spine. The skull rolled a bit and stopped on the crown, still swaying. With successive contractions, several smaller bones got out before the unpleasant paroxysm finally subsided. Everything was covered with mucus, saliva and gastric juices.

Onkalot thought he was going to vomit again, but this time without any cannibal specific. On all fours, he fell into a stupor. He

51

was panting with his mouth slightly open. He couldn't take his horrified eyes off the skull still swinging on the square slab. The view was macabre, stunning, terrible, but also - in some sick, worthy of Jun Kame way - fascinating. Xajb'a Kej had just seen this woman alive, hugging him, stroking his head, forgiving him for the act he had been forced to do.

Kejnay's as if muffled voice came to him: "Great. I've already thought it would be necessary to kill and cut." Xajb'a Kej changed the object of observation only when it disappeared in a bag, into which it was carefully carried with the charred javelin, whose pointed end was inserted into its eye socket.

"Now run along." Kejnay threw him his dagger, then started waving his paw towards the jungle. "The scouts won't hurt you. Good luck with Pek." The last words sounded ironic.

Xajb'a Kej tried to probe telepathically what they wanted a human skull for, but as he had expected, he hit his psionic ability against mental barriers.

"I had more weapons!" He called as they began to head towards Quehnay.

No one was interested in him anymore, so with a huff of irritation, he moved to the jungle.

The first thing he did was slake his strong thirst in a found pond, he washed oneself in it almost morbidly, especially focusing on the inside of his mouth.

He wasn't rushing back to his hometown, depressed, lost in thoughts that mostly focused on Jenny and - why should have he lied to himself? - pleasant sensations when he devoured her.

Of the most terrible meal of his life, there was no trace when, two days later, he saw the glow of a torch in the darkness at the outer pyramid of Chiq'aq City.

\*\*\*

The four achijes, who went to Xajb'a Kej for the skull, entered the House of Five Females. Soon they stopped in front of the council members seated on stone thrones. achijes bowed their heads in respect.

"Done?" Kejnay was asked by the highest Onkalot in the council, colorful from decorations like a quetzal in the mating season.

"Yes, lady." He picked up the burnt sack.

"That's good. Did you make sure that only the traces of the Chiq'aq humanoid jaguar remain on the skull?"

"According to our knowledge, great ruler."

"Then finalize our plan. Needless to say, no one can notice you. Best of all, let only two achijes go."

"It will be so."

Kejnay bowed and turned, as did his companions. In the outer courtyard, using fish-bladder gloves, Lolmet drew Xajb'a Kej's bow and, from a distance of several dozen paces, released a Chiq'aq arrow with a characteristic fletching. It hit the skull protruding from the sack, which Etznab had previously placed on the ground, piercing the frontal bone.

*\*\*\**

Dr. Twist had had enough of staying on the Bear shuttle for the second week by Lieutenant Sunder's warrant. From the moment when relations between the Earthlings and the humanoid jaguars from the planet H14 deteriorated, the scientific nature of the expedition in accordance with the procedures became military, and Twist lost his sovereignty. The crew, on the other hand, lost six men before the airlock was closed for good; The fate of Corporal Jenny Bengtsson was still unknown. Sunder's soldiers retaliated by killing every Onkalot that came near the ship. The doctor's research was limited to looking at the bodies of anthropomorphs brought to him.

The hunger for knowledge gave him no respite. Especially since the newly discovered planet turned out to be a phenomenon on the scale of the entire cosmos. The local flora and fauna were almost half composed of terrestrial species, and the highest evolutionary creatures, apart from the fact that they descended from the jaguar and shared more than sixty percent of genes with humans, also spoke the languages of the ancient Aztecs and Maya, although distorted. Their technolithic culture and Indian customs were also similar. No one had any idea how such phenomenons could have happened.

Not wanting to end up with depression, the doctor broke the warrant and walked out through the maintenance door. Before that, he had put on sufficient armor to protect himself from primitive Onkalot weapons. He wanted to see at least the local star live and the plants closest to the shuttle, collect more samples. He walked a bit on a solar terrain burned-out by a cannon, previously prepared for the landing of the Bear. He stopped dead as soon as he looked towards the jungle. There was a human skull placed on a pole, and an arrow ended with exotic birds' feathers protruded from its forehead.

"Jesus Christ!"

"Dr. Twist, are you serious?" Outraged Lieutenant Sunder, commander of the platoon assigned to the expedition, went out right after him. He was speechless. He cursed at the sight of the skull, consciously placed in plain sight. "It must be Corporal Bengtsson ... Well, unless there are other people on this goddamn planet, which I doubt." He connected with one of the soldiers on duty in the cockpit via communicator. "Sergeant Rodriguez, scan the area for fauna."

"No more than twenty kilograms of fauna within a few hundred meters, sir," the report arrived soon. "Only animals. But please remember, sir, that these pissants have learned to use rocks with strong ferromagnetic properties to mask their presence."

"They probably discovered it by accident," said the scientist, as if the remark had been to in any way minimize the damage done by the indigenous peoples. "Their civilization has no idea about digital technology. It's zero point two on the Kardashov scale."

Three subordinates joined Sunder. When they became able to obey orders again, the lieutenant ordered them to hold their barrels towards the forest, while he himself approached the gruesome gift. He grimaced, looked to the side, wanted to return the breakfast.

"It's Jenny's skull, unfortunately," he whispered to the doctor, who followed him like a scared duckling. "I recognize that dent above the socket. On one mission, the corporal was hit by shrapnel. She didn't want to correct this, saying that scars added value and character to a soldier. Without looking at what he was doing, he tucked the glove under the skull and grabbed it from underneath.

56

They started to get back on board.

"Now no one is supposed to go out anymore," muttered the lieutenant sharply. "I'll shoot like a dog before those bastards do it. Doctor, please take the head to the lab and examine it, but don't let the girls see it ..."

"What are we not to see?" One of Twist's assistants stopped on the stairs next to the maintenance door. She squealed at the sight of the skull, pressed her fists to her mouth, then started screaming again before escaping into the board.

Sunder returned to his cabin. There he could already throw off that uncomfortable mask of a composed guy with a soulless face - he fell heavily on a chair and hid his head in his arms.

An hour later, the doctor called him to the lab. Twist was pale as linen, close to the color of his smock. He showed the officer the results of his analysis on a holographic screen.

"This poor girl was eaten up by something," he began unprofessionally. "Every millimeter of bone shows signs of digestive juices working."

"What do you mean by eaten up by something? Please be clearer."

"Microbiological and chemical studies show that one of the Onkalots did it. The skull must have been in his stomach for two days. I even figured out which tribe it came from using the data that research drones had given us at the beginning of the expedition - those the size of ping-pong balls that your soldiers laughed at - before the natives had started knocking them down. We cataloged cats based on their memory portraits and scanned biological materials. It's Chiq'aq, sir."

With his deadly face, Sunder raised an arrow pulled out of the skull.

"Jun Kame is responsible for Jenny's death," he said, turning the object.

"How can, you be sure?"

"Chiq'aq wouldn't have done so. They fear us too much, at least for now. Jun Kame must have realized that we can identify it, though of course it doesn't understand how we do it. It also understood the essence of disinfection. It slipped him a crewman skull with ostentatiously added clues to make us think he was killed by a rival tribe. It wanted to trick us into its goals." The lieutenant threw the arrow onto the table.

"The situation has become critical; we are no longer safe. The humanoid jaguars are smarter than we thought, they are as intelligent as we are, and they are outstripping us in cruelty. We only live because they are stuck at the level of tribal culture. They will never want to work with us. Due to the new circumstances, the scientific expedition is definitely over, doctor. According to the procedures, all decisions are now up to me."

"Sunder, what are you gonna do?" Twist asked confidently. The lieutenant didn't answer, walked out of the lab and headed down the corridor towards the bridge. After an argument with the civilian officer who had been in charge of the "Beer" owned by Space X, he ordered the soldiers to take him out of the room.

Sunder first connected to the two shuttles still on their way, sent with the Bear on the H14 expedition. Due to a strong magnetic storm in space, which was avoided by the Sunder shuttle, the trip of the two was extended by an on-board month. 'Bear', on the other hand, had problems with navigating and locating dangerous objects, which resulted in rubbing against a comet, damage to space panels and fuel tanks, and leakage of precious fluid. Therefore, the ship couldn't leave the planet.

After describing the threat and canceling the landing of the shuttles, Sunder contacted the commander stationed on the Proxima Centauri e.

"We have code 71," he informed his captain. "An terrestrial planet ready for colonization. Aggressive natives brutally murder our people. We need air support. I recommend an aerial attack."

"You confirm code 71, Sunder?" Thanks to satellites porting signals, dropped in space along the way, there were no great delays in communication.

The lieutenant thought for a moment.

"I confirm, sir. And please send me some extra fuel."

# Only the dead were witnesses

## The Terrenic Year 2511

The sun on the planet Aj reached its zenith above their heads more than four hundred times before Q'ualel and Xajb'a Kej finally managed to activate the porter of Nimja - the divine ancient ancestors - and return to Chulimal. As two primitive humanoid jaguars, they had no knowledge of interplanetary travel, and they managed to complete the return portation by trial and error, vaguely remembering what steps they had taken at the Tonatiuha temple when they had accidentally moved from there to Aj. Then the opposing Onkalots simply beat on the ground of the sanctuary and hit the structure, we don't know how, initiating the procedure of transfer.

And also, of the rescue.

The process was high-energy, so the moment they were thrown from the porter on Chulimal, the whole mountain began to shake. The port's stone frame exploded, hurling boulders and debris in all directions. Q'ualel was hit in the head by a projectile, losing consciousness on the spot. Xajb'a Kej slung his friend over his shoulder and began to head rapidly towards the exit through the temple, as dark and chilled as if no one had looked into it for a long time. Eternal, holy fire didn't light his path for the first time, so the Onkalot had to use infravision.

He didn't take Q'ualel off himself until he reached the nearest trees, beyond the reach of an avalanche of earth. He himself dropped on the grass to catch his breath. The ground vibrations soon stopped. Xajb'a Kej found it difficult to estimate the full damage, but he could see that most of the main entrance had been blocked. If Nimja had ever used the stone porter to travel between worlds like Chulimal and Aj, they would have had to do so competently, without undermining the stability of the mountain, and thus the temple within it. Unless time had weakened the foundations, but it was more likely that both Onkalots couldn't use the mover, which had apparently been lost forever. Probably the Great House could repair it, but its representatives had departed from the planet into the unknown thousands of tuns ago.

Xajb'a Kej started to look around. The jungle, gilded with K'ajol's rays, looked normal, just as he had remembered it: leaves rustled, branches swayed, a fearless animal squawked again and again in the depths. Exactly, animals - maybe that was the problem? The Chulimal forest before the portation to Aj had been constantly jumping with the spontaneous sounds of the fauna, different at any time of the day, and now everything was disturbingly quiet. In addition, none of the achijes or acolytes guarded the Tonatiuha temple.

Q'ualel moved, grunted as he touched the bloody fur where he had been hit with a stone.

"Are you alright?" Xajb'a Kej asked.

"Probably not. My head is a little throbbing and I'm also a bit dizzy. At most it's a slight concussion, I've experienced such states many times before, it should be normal soon. Thanks for getting me out of there."

"You're welcome. We made it, brother." The larger humanoid jaguar smiled at him victoriously.

"Yes, finally!" Q'ualel smiled back, then both of them laughed even goofily.

"If you are all right, let's go to Chiq'aq as soon as possible," Xajb'a Kej announced soon when Q'ualel's minor neurological symptoms wore off.

The Tonatiuha Temple wasn't far from the Place of Fire, where there were three more pyramids, traditionally in the open.

As they headed for the tribal city, Xajb'a Kej grew more and more perturbed by the feeling that something was very wrong. Disturbing gloom hung in the air like poisonous vapors above the swamps they passed. They noticed bones slightly protruding from the mud, making them difficult to recognize, not seen in this area. Too numerous for a random animal to perish here, they were more like the nightmarish remnants of some fight or execution. Xajb'a Kej looked at his companion and noticed that he, too, shared his fears - especially when they sensed the stench of corpses in the final stages of decomposition.

They didn't sense the presence of the guards, always present somewhere on the edge of the city. The worst thing was this traumatic silence, as if almost all life had disappeared from the jungle.

They stood frozen and terrified as they found themselves on the stone slabs at the edge of Chiq'aq. All the wooden houses had burned down long ago, some of the brick houses had turned into rubble, and the rest had solid traces of damage. There were bodies everywhere - skeletons covered with scraps of cloth and mottled fur. Only the pyramids seemed untouched by the paw of gruesomeness, which must have happened here dozens of kins earlier: always majestic, always enduring, always indifferent. Although not quite - looking against the sun, Xajb'a Kej noticed that a ceremonial temple at the top of one of the pyramids had collapsed, something huge had also destroyed the stairway. It must have been done by a force that could have been generated by at least an avalanche of boulders or an above-average earthquake. The stone sidewalks had holes and burn marks.

"No ..."

Panting with anxiety and despair, Xajb'a Kej began to run across the square, from one body to another. Q'ualel stayed where he had stood - he was shocked and could only stare in disbelief.

With his heart pounding like that of a victim about to brutally die at the paws of a Jun Kame member, Xajb'a Kej ran towards the house where his mother Baji's and his young sister lived. The former, he found in a condition as bad as that of the rest of the humanoid jaguars, outside before the threshold. The body had been chopped from the air; it was arranged as if Baji's had rushed

65

to get inside. But she hadn't made it. As achij, she died a shameful death - unexpected, degrading, not in an honorable fight.

Xajb'a Kej fell to his knees beside her, put his front paws on the ground and started to cry.

After a while, as if in a trance, he went to examine the ruins of the house. There he found an even more horrible sight - his little sister had died in a children's lair, crushed by a fragment of the roof.

When Xajb'a Kej stepped outside, he roared in pain and anger so powerfully that he probably scared away all the birds that remained near the Chiq'aq plunged into death.

He knelt on the ground for a long time, staring blankly at her and remembering his family before depressed Q'ualel found him. Upon seeing Baji's' remains, he sadly turned his head. He sat down next to his friend.

"My little sister, too," Xajb'a Kej said to him mechanically, only moving his jaws. "I'm so sorry, Kay. I checked both temples. The priests are dead. Only we are alive in Chiq'aq. But some of the inhabitants managed to escape."

"And they were surely caught in the woods. Be realistic, Q'ualel." Xajba Kej turned. His green eyes boiled with such an anger, not seen in Q'ualel before, that he himself began to fear him. "People attacked from the sky," he said, alarmingly calmly. "Who wasn't killed by ship fire, was shot dead by small drones that could fly anywhere. I already saw it before we moved to Aj. As we fought to get back to Chulimal, the humanoid jaguars fought for life. She was so tiny ..." Xajb'a Kej rubbed his nose. He got up and looked at the dilapidated sanctuary at the top of the pyramid. He clenched his fist tight enough that partially protruding claws pierced his fur and skin. "They have to pay for it. Not only those who came to Chulimal, but all of them. We have to annihilate these monsters."

"Xajb'a Kej." Q'ualel stood up. "Cool down, please. I know we've suffered an unimaginable loss and my heart is bleeding too, but we can't help it. We are much weaker than the enemy. We also don't know how many Onkalots survived."

"You say that because you haven't lost anyone. Your parents emigrated to unknown place and left you in the temple to be raised by acolytes when you were a kitten. You've never had anyone close. What can you know about loss?! Xajb'a Kej growled at him, sticking out his fangs.

"All Chiq'aq was my family. And I know what losing a loved one is. Just because you haven't experienced something, it doesn't mean you are ignorant in this area, someone inferior in that category. And my blood is exactly the same as yours. And you shouldn't direct your anger at me."

"My blood is slightly different than yours. You have always been passive, Q'ualel, though you have the achij body and agility,

67

the priestly half is stronger in you. I remember what you taught the kittens. When there was a fight between them, you told them to look for peaceful solutions. You said that when the enemy is stronger, you should withdraw and not irritate him, you told the stupider to yield. You taught the youngsters to be a meek victim, avoiding strife and competition. Always passivity. Always cowardice. Always that damn melancholy of yours."

Q'ualel forgave him for this insult only because he knew that Xajb'a Kej had always dealt with trauma, looking for someone to blame and directing his anger at those around him. He also didn't intend to start a row in front of his house, where the tragedy had taken place.

"Because revenge is not a good solution," he said, "and especially not against an enemy who can travel among the stars." Q'ualel waved his paw skyward. "If we let it go, they will continue to spread death elsewhere."

"We? What do you want to do? With a scream and the obsidian dagger, attack their drones and ships?"

"I'll figure something out. Maybe we can summon other tribes."

"As long as they don't have problems of their own. Anyway, it had already happened before the trip to Aj, and as you can see - the reconciliation ended tragically.

"We have to check what the situation looks like. But first ..." Xajb'a Kej's voice broke, "let's gather everyone in one place and burn the bodies. We can't leave them like this ..."

"Hold off." Q'ualel grabbed his arm just as he was about to move. "There may be a plague here now. We may already be infected. Better to come when the bodies ... completely ..." He looked sadly at Baji's.

"You don't have to finish," Xajb'a Kej broke free from him. Despair, he tried hard to mask his anger. "You're coming with me? It is necessary to find out what happened to the other tribes. Maybe we'll meet someone from Chiq'aq in the jungle."

"Yes, we can go now.

"Wait for me in the forest, I will join you soon."

Q'ualel reassuringly placed his paw on his shoulder before walking away.

Xajb'a Kej was watching over the bodies of his mother and sister for a little longer.

"I promise they will pay for it. I would so much like to have the power that would allow me vendetta. So much ..." Expressing his wish with enormous passion, he bowed his head and shook it. He had heard somewhere that when you sincerely want something, in the end the will is fulfilled, 'the word becomes matter'. He would have very much liked it to happen, but he didn't believe that verbal pleas and prayers had any power.

He sobbed again.

He knew deep down that Q'ualel was right; a friend like him, enjoying the privilege of loneliness, wept on the edge of Chiq'aq, with his forehead pressed to the ground.

They reached Quehnay at night, not because they were concerned about Jun Kame's fate, but because the city was the closest. They didn't enter its territory, because they could see from a distance that people had done exactly the same with the cannibals as with Chiq'aq. Above Quehnay also hovered even physical aura of death and despair. Xajb'a Kej, however, didn't feel sorry for the fate of the wild people. The cruel one had finally come across the more cruel one.

When, after two days of fast travel, they found exactly the same in the territory of the Che'ab'aj tribe, meaning the Stone Tree, they already knew that the massacre on the part of the people was global. Even more it undermined the hope in their hearts that they hadn't met any escaped humanoid jaguar on their way in the jungle.

Amok was building up in Xajb'a Kej. It might have seemed that the extra energy passed to him from the increasingly moody and broken Q'ualel. The smaller humanoid jaguar spoke practically only when asked.

Exceptionally, the first broke the silence when they made a stop in the woods next to the ruins of an old temple:

"I give up." Ashamed, Q'ualel looked down. "The will to fight is no longer in me."

The companion, sitting under a tree, opened his muzzle in amazement.

"Are you serious? You're not leaving me now, are you?! We should stick together!"

"Leaving with what?" The ex-priest-warrior instinctively looked his interlocutor defiantly in the eye. "We're not doing anything anyway."

"I'm thinking. I'm trying to figure something out. For the two of us!"

"Enough of this." Q'ualel rose nervously. "I didn't want to tell you this earlier, so as not to plunge you into despair even more, but so many kins have passed that I think it's the right time for it. Let's be honest. I thought what you were doing was temporary, and once you cool down you would let it go. But the fatal passion is still as powerful in you as it was on the day you entered Chiq'aq. It's consuming you as much as regret. This, however, is nothing more than a form of defense against reality, a desire to do anything just

71

for the sake of doing. There is nothing we can do, Xajb'a Kej, and besides, there are only two of us. It's just like we want to fight the gods!"

Xajb'a Kej also stood up, looked down at him as if Q'ualel had challenged him.

"Exactly. And where are your gods anyway, huh?" He talked back aggressively, wagging his tail. "You prayed to them so earnestly most of your life. Why do they allow their followers to be murdered?"

"Not for me or you to judge them. Who are we to understand them?"

"Or maybe they just don't give a shit about us? Or they don't exist at all? Have you ever seen your beloved Tonatiuh live? Ruling out herbal delirium support, of course."

"Stop blaspheming," Q'ualel said softly, sighing. He no longer had the strength to resist the madness of Xajb'a Kej more vigorously.

And he continued, having the counterirritant to explore:

"Why are you telling me what I should do? Have you gotten rid of arguments? Why did the gods allow this?!" Into his voice, in a clean, swift stream, burst despair, which he tried all the time to hide under the guise of rage.

"I don't know ... And did you come up with something?" Q'ualel changed the subject.

"Nothing by now. But I will definitely do something about it."

"I don't advise you, however, to go where people have settled. They will definitely kill you. We're lucky they haven't tracked us down with their objects yet."

"I conclude from your words that our paths will separate?" Xajb'a Kej asked more rhetorically.

"I can't live like that, Kay. Forgive me."

"What are you gonna do?"

"Survive, just this."

Q'ualel started walking as if beaten towards the jungle.

"And you were supposed to be a Chiq'aq warrior-priest?" Xajb'a Kej shouted to him, making nervous gestures with his paws. "The great Q'ualel who defeated me in the fight to be the leader! Where is he now? You know what? Go away and die somewhere in bushes under a rock, you damned coward!"

Q'ualel stopped for a moment and tilted his head slightly.

"You have no right to blame me for my choice. I don't see any sense in what you are doing, especially since you are still in the heat of passion."

73

He crossed the ford of a stream and soon vanished among bushes and foliage; no word was said between the old friends, though they were both suffering.

Xajb'a Kej began to wander restlessly by the shore. Out of anger, he swung his paw and hit a trunk so hard that he broke a claw; his tendon stung.

At least one thing had come out of the breakup, maybe not good, but allowing him to shake off the shackles - he could stop pretending to be tough and determined. He fell to the ground with his back and lay staring half-consciously at the firmament until the K'ajolom were driven out by the stars.

\*\*\*

Throughout the next day, he felt chewed, consumed, and expelled by despair. Loneliness only increased his depression and anxiety, which he had managed to keep in check with Q'ualel. But he didn't have to flaunt anything now, at least in that respect he was free. He was lying practically constantly on his back, sometimes turning to his side, blindly watching the rustling palm leaves or the clearing of the changing sky. He ignored the insects wandering around his fur, eagerly trying to get to his nostrils and mouth. He thought that he had no one else close to him; he was completely alone. As soon as he drowsed away, his mind began to play colored, macabre scenes from the city of Chiq'aq, as well as generally about the extermination of Onkalots, which Xajb'a Kej hadn't witnessed during his forced stay on Aj. His whole body often shuddered like in a person dreaming about falling, bringing him back to full consciousness. He alternately cried, fell asleep, lay still and dolefully as a condemned man sure of imminent death, depleted of his strength.

And now he needed it so badly.

His thoughts began to circle Jenny. Had the girl been exactly the same monster as the rest of the people, and only the situation and loneliness had made her temporarily become the victim? Had she really deserved his pity? Maybe Jun Kame had been right from the beginning, and mankind deserved only cruel treatment? There were mathematicians among the humanoid jaguars who created precise astronomical observatories or pyramids that could survive, perhaps, of the Onkalots themselves. They argued that when a certain examined group of random creatures behaved in a particular way, the entire species was exactly the same, with exceptions. Could Jenny be such an exception among the murderers of humanoid jaguars?

Another wasted evening full of blues came.

\*\*\*

He couldn't remember when he had fallen asleep in the position of a floater pulled out onto the shore. As he sat down, he noticed that the stars above had also moved to the ground. The ugly skins of lichens, during a day attached to everything in the environment, including tall branches, at night turned into natural works of art. Immature diaspore balls glowed blue, those ready to breed were red, and used ones turned green. The area had once belonged to one of the piedmont tribes, Xajb'a Kej had no reason to visit these areas, therefore he admired the phenomenon unknown to him. Had he been here in normal circumstances, it would have certainly brought him more joy. But it was still something to look at, he could at least for a moment forget about the nightmarish demons. Onkalot thought it would have been nice to have such a multi-colored fire that could have been used in the city instead of the traditional one.

But he didn't have his city anymore.

Not only the lichens delighted with an interesting, bioluminescent effect - luminous beetles gathered at the banks of the stream. Xajb'a Kej stepped into the water up to his thighs and followed the current like a route marked with garish colors.

Not far away, deeper on land, he saw another light source, more intense this time. He reminded him of a friar's lantern or a great magic flower Azal Uoh, in which chemical reactions also took place in the dark, but their effect was a rainbow, not a golden color...

Xajb'a Kej stiffened as if he had seen a compressed, poisonous snake step away.

In Chiq'aq, there were legends about an immortal golden mouse which was a gift from the Great House to the humanoid jaguars from Chulimal[6]. An animal, yet an artifact the color of the beloved ore of the gods. Some claimed that it revealed its presence only in great need, others believed that it appeared by accident.

The golden mouse was said to had once saved his mother Baji's from death by Jun Kame. At least she had firmly believed it when she had told her son the story from the tribal wars. He himself had encountered the mouse in the jungle before the humans arrived on Chulimal, but at the time he had found it to be simply a phenomenon of its own kind, like a black humanoid jaguar among a multitude of spotted brothers. An ordinary rodent, nothing more, because of its rarity, burdened with the myth.

Fascinated by the phenomenon, Onkalot didn't care how much true was in it. He stopped believing in gods and myths, and legends with the passage of tuns, he also began to consider nonsense.

[6] What alien artifacts really are is explained in Mission Rebirth and The War with Kandrok.

Nevertheless, the enchanting artifact that stood on a stump and wasn't afraid of the giant predator at all, had to have some effect on him. Xajb'a Kej wanted to take it into the paws, keep it for himself, possess it as a precious treasure.

He walked cautiously towards it, but when he was within arm's reach of the golden mouse, it jumped off the stump and disappeared into the bushes without haste.

"Eh ... Why would that be easy?" Xajb'a Kej growled.

Artifact - if it really had something to do with Nimja - didn't run away like a victim terrified by the presence of the hunter. It looked more as if it had been leading Xajb'a Kej in a certain direction, quickly moving through tunnels of high underbrush, but also stopping so that struggling Onkalot could easily catch up with it.

He followed the mouse for a long time through the forest, intrigued, feeling somewhat relieved that he was finally doing whatever was the seedbed of his intentions. With his infravision, he didn't lose sight of the target even at great distances, especially since it glowed more like fresh volcanic coke than a living organism.

He reached the city of Quehnay in the early morning hours, specifically he found himself in front of the formidable Tukumb'akam pyramid, where the artifact entered through the main portico. This city had always terrified Xajb'a Kej, especially now, cluttered with the fur-coated skeletons of its former inhabitants. Overwhelming fear, heavy depression and a deadly odor hung in the air, their quintessence seem to move on the wings of flies, active even in the dark. In Quehnay, as in Chiq'aq, no lights were on. Xajb'a Kej wondered what sounded spookier: the screams of the murdered victims, once frequent in the city, or the current ubiquitous murmur of the wind, whispering imaginary words about helplessness and death.

Onkalot shuddered, got roused from his torpor and, with the dagger in his paw, plunged into the dark corridor leading to the center of the pyramid. All its internal architecture and paintings were associated with macabre and death. From the reliefs depicting mostly bones and demonic inhabitants, Xibalba shifted his gaze to tzompantles - a lot of the skulls had been gathered here.

The Mouse stopped in the very center of the pyramid, in the middle of a burial chamber, full of rectangular stone blocks. After lighting a found log with flint, Xajb'a Kej wondered why they ended up exactly there. He believed that the artifact led him to the nearest sanctuary where hecatombs had been performed; especially on the day of sacrifice, the captives fed abundantly their blood and hearts to the eternally hungry, evil gods. The mythical artifact came from the gods. So it could be about drawing power from the closest source. At the top of this pyramid had died also a lot of Chiq'aqs. Xajb'a Kej began to consider whether he was ready to receive help from the place associated with unimaginable suffering and terror. Was this the price to be paid for the revenge of one humanoid jaguar? If anything happened at all - he might as well have followed a stupid rodent with a hair anomaly.

He decided to try, however.

There was always a chance that he had misinterpreted something. After all, his head was overwhelmed with the memory of the unfortunate events. Besides, that gloomy place wedged in it, like a priestly blade between ribs.

"Come on." He stuck his clasped paws out, the pads up. The mouse jumped on them as if it had been a tame pet. Xajb'a Kej lifted it close to his nose and began to examine it. He felt like a fool, stroking the artifact on the head, hoping that anything would come out of what was starting to crystallize in his mind. It is possible that he was indeed the only idiot on Chulimal - however angry he was with Q'ualel, he couldn't call him a fool.

"What are you ..." he thought aloud, letting the mice roam over his paws and shoulders. "An organism, a machine, a psionic device?"

All he knew about the Great House was that their civilization was based on mental power. This might make sense, since the humanoid jaguars had inherited their psionic abilities from them. The people of the stars who so easily defeated Onkalots took a completely different path - they developed a civilization based on digital technology. But their minds were weak and empty. During guerrilla stalking with the use of ayin stones or successful single attacks before the Aj expedition, Xajb'a Kej had learned to read people's minds freely. Then he had realized that they had had no psionic abilities.

He closed the mouse in the clasped paws, creating a cage with his extended claws.

"Alright, what's the harm?" Even if his wish echoed off the walls of the chamber, he would at least relieve himself with the words. Often praying Q'ualel claimed that they were said to have great power. The priest-warrior, however, pleaded and bowed down every time. What if you were to demand something from the gods? Perhaps they hated weakness and humility, and that is why they so seldom bestowed their grace on godly followers? "I want to become human!"

It would have been a pretty good plan. People referred to this strategy as the Trojan Horse. Xajb'a Kej would have crept into their lives pretending to be one of them, would have later styled himself as a savior - and attacked them when they least expected it. However, he needed allies united by faith and idea. Lots of allies. The tyrant himself was useless, indoctrinated subordinates always worked for him. As he had expected, nothing happened. The situation was so idiotic that he began to laugh. It's good that only

81

the dead priests and dignitaries in the tombs witnessed his clownery.

"I want to become human!" He exclaimed, this time confidently, when he calmed down.

The echo of his baritone wandered along the adjoining corridors, repeatedly carrying the demand around the sanctuary.

He felt a pleasant warmth radiating from inside, as if from good alcohol, which he associated with a natural increase in blood pressure when someone is suddenly amused by something. He quickly realized it was more than that as the warmth turned to sickly heat, engulfing his whole body. This rarely happened, because humanoid jaguars' fur had the property of cooling in heat and warming during colder days, maintaining optimal body temperature in healthy individuals. Xajb'a Kej frowned, instinctively worried. He felt a tingling sensation in his limbs. He stood on all fours; the mouse jumped out of his paws, ran off a bit, did a handstand and began to move its mustache vigorously.

"What's going on, by all the monsters of Xibalb..."

His eyes widened in astonishment - the bones began to move! With a roar, he fell on the sand-strewn ground, twisting like a damaged larva. Initiated by alien technology, accelerated transmutation, the essence of which (with his zero knowledge of the cosmos) Xajb'a Kej wouldn't have been able to comprehend, was launched in full force, according to the guidelines of the unconscious operator.

The transformation was not particularly painful, but unpleasant and terribly shocking, especially for someone skeptical about the supernatural. The coat began to contract, as did the tail and claws, changing into bare skin, tailbone and nails. As if matter had been thickening and falling in. The paws and fingers grew thinner. Overall, every section of the body began to shrink, including the muzzle. The teeth looked like the same pebbles - the smallest possible. They weren't actually the same, but with the long fangs and powerful bone-crushing incisors that the humanoid jaguar had previously had, it made no difference. The weakness effectively pressed him to the ground.

After what people called a quarter of an hour, he was lying on the floor of the pyramid as a man in the maxtlatl a little too loose, with the pouch and obsidian knife at his belt.

Grimacing, he sat up, shook his head, and something black began to tremble around it. Surprised, Xajb'a Kej caught it with his paw ... or rather with his hand. From his neck-length hair, he immediately shifted his gaze to those small, pale pork sausages, ended with tiles as if of thin glass.

He tightened the maxtlatl stripes. When he got up, he had no problem with walking - the hind limbs of Onkalots and humans were shaped similar, except that the latter had a heel that belonged

83

to the foot instead of a cat's high joint. The living artifact stood on a stone nearby and waited patiently for the operator's next command. Xajb'a Kej was swaying at first, but soon mastered walking on delicate feet covered with thin skin and devoid of hard pads. It was terribly inconvenient and strange, the terms 'failure', 'bald' and 'naked' came to his mind. He could clearly feel all the unevenness underneath, and to suffer, it was enough to step on any blunt stone or groove between the slabs.

"Now I understand why they constantly wear shoes." His voice was similar to his native form, he still spoke in the baritone. The transformation didn't seem to be entirely successful, he had been misunderstood or that was the assumption of the artifact, because he had retained his infravision, although at the fading log, he saw twice as badly as usual.

After the first shock had passed, Xajb'a Kej felt more and more satisfaction as he began to realize what had just happened. Shouting and laughing, he ran around the sarcophagi and statues in the chamber. He waved his hands, jumped, testing his new incarnation. He absolutely wanted to see what he looked like in all his glory, he peered into the ceremonial pond, but saw mostly a black silhouette outline in it.

He went through the corridor beyond the pyramid to the sunny weather of the late morning. He wandered to the bank of a lazy river where he stood in the shade of a tree. He leaned down and started to look at himself in the water. The artifact had turned him into the about forty-year-old man with an athletic build. Despite being over two meters tall and weighing over one hundred kilograms, he was much smaller than in his feline form, the effect was even more pronounced by the naked, fair skin devoid of fur enlarging it. Mosquitoes mercilessly clung to it, the skin was already beginning to itch, and in addition it stung in the tropical K'ajolom rays shining through the leaves, and the star was still far from the zenith. He noticed with little regret that his eyes were now brown, not green. "Too bad," he thought, much worse things he would have to accept.

Xajb'a Kej hadn't taken into account a few issues, such as the fact that humans lived, on average, seven times shorter than Onkalots (the fact that such a short-lived creature had ruined the humanoid jaguar civilization was particularly irritating). He wondered if his body would be subject to the same biological laws as human from now on. As a precaution, he could plan everything so to accomplish his revenge within decades of man's time, but he didn't even want to think about it. After all, he had the artifact that, according to the myth, could fulfill two more of his wishes, however absurd it sounded.

"So, immortality?"

He smiled at his face, twitching in the water circles formed by insects, and saw the fangs. The canines were too far apart from the

85

rest of the dentition. He began to investigate what else was inhuman in him. As he checked the edges of the lower jaw with his hands, he realized that it still had an earlier structure. This meant being able to eat large chunks of food without chewing - in short, swallowing them whole. Fortunately, in humans there was such a thing as transhumanism, that is, technological and biological modifications of the body, sometimes so intense that a person could resemble an animal. It wasn't Xajb'a Kej's nature to lie, he loathed it, but he could leave room for interpretation, not denying or confirming anything. So he liked transhumanism - let people think that he was modified.

There was also the issue of telepathy.

As in the jaguar form, also now he was unable to test it on frogs, birds, or fish in the vicinity. It worked only on creatures with a brain structure similar to his - so he had to find a human.

He looked back and saw that the artifact had followed him from the city of the cannibals.

"So now another wish." He crouched down and took the mouse in his hand. There were many more things he would like; it would have been best for him if the entire human race had died in an instant. In this way, however, Xajb'a Kej couldn't have enjoyed his vendetta, moreover, the artifact's field of operation was limited. Perhaps even the gods, if they had really existed, wouldn't have been able to kill an entire species suddenly. Instead, he came up with a different idea. He got up, glanced toward the distant pale mountains where the transporters should have been stationed. "I want to gain ever higher power, climb the social ladder. I want to be successful in everything. I want people to follow me. No one to be able to stop me! I want an army! I want to be the most powerful man!"

He chuckled as he realized he was talking with increasing passion. The urge to retaliate for the destruction of his species seemed to blind him more than he had supposed. Perhaps he made too many requests at once, unless the mouse took it as one long request. Nevertheless, he knew that his fate would rest in his paws anyway ... well, now in his hands. He plunged into madness, probably impossible, but he preferred madness, action, rather than hiding in the mud, under leaves like Q'ualel.

"It would be better if no one else used your power," he turned to the mouse, stroking it. It froze, only its whiskers was twitching; it was staring at him sharply with its golden eyes. "Because how do I know how exactly you act? Someone might try to stop me, assuming, of course, that my crazy scenario came true. Thank you for what you have done for me. The rest, I have to handle myself."

If the animal had telepathic abilities, perhaps it took advantage of them, or the most ordinary animal instinct integrated with the artifact was triggered, for it stiffened when a crazy thought formed in Xajb Kej's head.

The artifact that had existed for thousands of years had to disappear here and now. It was too dangerous in the wrong hands - his, for example. The human considered asking the mouse for immortality, but let it go. It was not known if this would have worked at all after the litany of his wishes, and he would have felt bad if paranormal forces had been to do everything for him. Or alien technology, as humans would have probably said.

How, however, was he to get rid of the artifact that had existed since the time of Nimja, so that there would be no trace left? Is it possible to destroy anything created by creatures with the power of gods? If he kills the mouse, there are bones left. If he burns it, ash will remain. Could the ash also be used by someone?

He realized he was hungry.

Why not exactly? He will check his pathetic teeth at the same time.

The artifact didn't react like an ordinary animal, it just stayed alert when Xajb'a Kej brought it to his face and licked it on its back, wanting to taste the prey before eating it, as he had done in his feline form. His sense of taste had deteriorated as well, but at least he recognized that the mouse fur tasted like any other.

He parted his jaws and placed it, perfectly still, on his tongue.

It wasn't as bad as he had suspected before. With a strong clench of his teeth, he managed to kill the animal quickly and painlessly the first time. Sweet, hot blood ran down his mouth, trickled down his chin, dripped onto his chest. It is possible that also in the case of the mechanics of the jaws, he had a lot of an Onkalot left, and an ordinary man wouldn't have been able to kill a rodent in this way. People probably didn't even do that - he would have to learn a lot about them. The smell and taste of blood didn't turn out to be as intense as in the case of animal organoleptics, but Xajb'a Kej was ready for the sacrifice and ordeal in this weak body to achieve his goal.

After chewing for a short time, he decided to keep the femur pulled from his mouth as a souvenir. He slipped it into the leather pouch next to the obsidian dagger; maybe he would make a pendant with the trophy. He managed to swallow the rest of the shredded mouse at a clip. No way, he wouldn't give up such a way of feeding, even if he was forced to practice it in secret, so as not to arouse disgust and suspicion. And to think it all had started with damned Kejnay. Initially, Xajb'a Kej had hated the customs practiced by cannibals, but when there had been a conflict between people and humanoid jaguars, his views had changed and he had started using his barbaric practices on captured intruders. Killing them had helped him deal with enormous stress and maintain a meager sense of patriotic fulfillment - that he could do anything about the tragic situation at all. Male flesh had turned out to be hideous, so he had eaten only the more delicate and tastier female flesh when the occasion had arisen sometimes. He began to do exactly what had scared him not so much earlier. Among the tribes of humanoid jaguars, the killing or kidnapping of females could indeed lead to the extinction of the tribe.

Now he had to go to the people.

After washing off the blood, he headed towards the nearest alien abode, half a day's walk from the Tukumb'akam pyramid.

All the anger from the cuts, abrasions and wounds inflicted on him by insects and forest plants vanished immediately when, upon reaching the destination late in the evening, he saw a growing human enclave. Xajb'a Kej stopped short, rested his hand on the trunk of a palm tree and surveyed the unimaginable changes. A huge part of the jungle had been completely liquidated by logistic orbs, which in an incomprehensible way had completely wiped out the biomass. The area prepared in this way had been leveled for development, something resembling rock in the hardness had been poured over it, although probably much more durable. The silvery buildings most often looked like coconut halves, they grew alarmingly fast, made by busy machines with arms. Several hundred people were walking around the settlement under construction, others were probably in space shuttles stationed on the sidelines, surrounded by numerous military machines. Garbage was scattered all over the region.

Xajb'a Kej learned a bit about people before he was moved to Aj. He also learned the basics of their Anglo-American language and a lot of neologisms. However, it was still not enough to blend in with the crowd without arousing suspicions. People had flown to Chulimal in great numbers, but one man must have known the other at least by sight. Procedures unknown to Xajb'a Kej also had to be in force between them. He considered going down into the valley and playing a fool, but he quickly dismissed that idea. No matter how he hated humans, fools weren't likely to be brought to a foreign planet, or so he thought.

When he finally decided to take a risk and improvise, he found out how wrong his assumptions were.

He entered the construction site where the newcomers worked with machines and androids. He scooped up a bottle of alcohol on the way, standing on a table made of a huge cut tree trunk, and took a few gulps to add himself energy and credibility. He was surprised that hardly anyone paid attention to him, and when someone did, raised his eyebrows in surprise not at the sight of Xajb'a Kej, but of his clothes. He really stood out - the rest of the builders wore drill pants, were naked from the waist up, and those who were teased by the heat, were sporting only shorts and hats.

A balding pyknic foreman with a holonote in his hand, surrounded by a group of workers, glanced at him. After a moment he looked at him again, first in amazement and then in irritation. He dismissed his subordinates, and he himself headed towards Xajb'a Kej.

"Great, another one," he set the ball rolling. He smelled alcohol from the newcomer. "We also drink while working."

Xajb'a Kej only understood the word 'working'. He didn't know how to behave or what to say, but luckily the Earthman completed the script himself and took the initiative, showering him with questions:

"You're also from the Jacobson handyman and they didn't give you health and safety training? What are you wearing anyway, man? Where do you have your assigned clothes?" The foreman raised the holonot higher and shifted it close to Xajb'a Kej's head. "They sent you out into space without an entraser?! I will lose my shit right away!"

The former Onkalot assumed an innocent face and shrugged. He completely forgot that in his previous incarnation he had been a telepath. He tried to enter the man's mind and see what he was thinking. And ... it worked! Fortunately, the artifact had transferred his psionic ability to the new body! Xajb'a Kej breathed a sigh of relief in spirit, it would make his life much easier. The foreman imagined some people, probably workers, and among them an equal to him worker from another group, a certain Jacobson. He didn't even know he was being probed, his mind wasn't protected by any consciously sustained barriers that were Xajb'a Kej's torment in dealing with Jun Kame. So it was still working the old way.

"I can't believe it ..." The foreman, with the help of his personal assistant, called Jacobson. After two minutes of arguing over the drunken people, mess and three-ring circus, he again turned to the newcomer. "You will report to the infirmary right away, you will get an entraser. You will wait a few hours after it and go to mix birclone[7], understood? As always, they need hands to work there. And dress normally, man." Although the man ostentatiously made a face, Xajb'a Kej saw in his imagination that he envied him his height and stature. "Just because we're in the woods, it doesn't mean we have to dress like savages. Give me your identity, I have to sign you up for chipping."

This question, Xajb'a Kej understood without rifling through the foreman's head. Right, in all the confusion, he had forgotten to give himself a human name. He only knew four, three of which belonged to soldiers and one to the woman he had eaten. He didn't know if among people, achijes and workers had any specific names, characteristic of a social group, and he didn't want to piss off this man even more, who would have probably thought he was mocking him if he had given him the wrong identity. Xajb'a Kay's telepathy worked in such a way that he only knew what a person was thinking at a given moment, so he couldn't check what the names of people around him were. Though he was lucky, one of the

[7] Material for road construction. Obtained from synthetic and environmentally friendly plastics mixed with clay.

93

colonists thought about a girl named Athena, but it didn't help anyway.

His gaze fell on a candy bar synthetic wrapper, wandering on the ground in the gusts of wind. He also knew the earthly letters well enough to read part of the capitalized text: 'For Kids'. The paper caught on a stone and bent in such a way that one of the letters was obscured.

"Forkis," Xajb'a Kej replied in a hurry.

The foreman wrote something down in an electronic notebook.

"And surname?"

"I don't have."

The man thought again of something well known to him. He looked at Forkis suspiciously.

"Are you from the in vitro breeding? Did you do something wrong and they disinherited you? Or maybe problems with the divorce and wife whose surname you took? Looking at your stature, menacing staring eyes, and stern face, I guess it's probably the last one. You couldn't keep the chicks off you and she was jealous," he made Forkis' biography with the skill of a writer. He sighed broodily and looked at the area beyond the nearest space shuttle. "That's the way it is, women like Spaniards. Although you look a bit Indian, your complexion is unnaturally pale. I used to go through it with women too ..."

Forkis smiled kindly. Too late he remembered not to part his mouth too much, so as not to show his fangs and make himself an even bigger freak at this stage.

"Aaaah, you are a transhumanist!" The foreman, who turned out to be a talker, took this fact without surprise. "Hence the unnatural phenotype. So, you must be rich since you modified your body. It's a bit strange that you ended up doing colonization works ... But wait ..." He narrowed his eyes and waved the holonote in front of Forkis' nose. "Are you serving your sentence? I already understand; I can see that you are a very talkative character. Well, that's not my business. But there is rather no such a bastard to send us serious criminals to help us. After three Terrenic months, however, the team will be sent back to Earth anyway. I gotta go, it was nice to talk."

The foreman must have liked him because he shook his hand goodbye, then walked away, leaving amazed Forkis in the middle of the construction site. So far, everything had been going very easily for him, as if he had been flowing with the current of the river, and not fighting it, as he had imagined blending in an extra-planetary society. Could the reality created by the artifact begin to unfold? If so, the mysterious object from the past, in the form of the living animal encrusted with gold, must have been very powerful and dangerous. Forkis had risked a lot, destroying it so thoughtlessly. Or maybe this is how the essence of the artifact had passed onto his body? How little of all of this he understood ...

The aliens didn't turn out to be like the gods he had taken them to be just because they had flowed from the stars. Quite the opposite - they had a total mess in their ranks and thought about matters as mundane as bored Onkalots did. Drinks, fun, sex, sex, sex, girls, sleep, rest, party, sex again. Forkis inclined to suppose that perhaps only automated, intelligent equipment that thought for the operators had allowed them to win the war against humanoid jaguars. If he himself had been to create a perfect society, he would have begun to shape it, starting with total discipline and order based on achij. To ponder it, was a pleasure for him. Having your own nation - that was a pretty cool thought. He always wanted power. Had he not lost the public duel with Q'ualel, he would have been perhaps the new leader of Chiq'aq.

He went to the indicated building, and after a long time of admiring the interior, he found himself in the brightly lit infirmary. His nose was tickled by intense smells he felt for the first time in his life. He was ordered to sit on a silver-white chair. The doctor who had been waiting for him, injected something into his neck with a thin, long needle, just below the occiput. It turned out to be a bit unpleasant, but it didn't hurt at all. After the injection, he was ordered to lie down on a couch, where Forkis quickly fell asleep.

When he awoke after a few Terrenic hours, he was surprised to find that he knew a lot of different things about building new cities and settlements. However, it wasn't the most shocking thing.

"And how are you feeling, Forkis? Your health parameters are normal, you can return to your tasks," said the doctor pleasantly. "The entraser is already nested in the frontal lobe, the information transfer should be complete. This is a permanent version, harmless to the body, but if you want to have it surgically removed, a simple, low-invasive procedure using a needle will only take a minute. We could also inject you with a bionanite that would pluck out the entraser, pass the blood-brain barrier, and head into the excretory system."

Forkis understood every word and context as if he had learned Anglo-American from birth as an Earthling. He also understood human social structures, terms for all inventions, machines, colonies, planets, moons, professions ... everything!"

"Thank you, doctor." He smiled kindly. "For now, the interference is not needed, I will think about it later. Now let me go get my drill pants and go back to work."

"Of course, Forkis. Have a nice day."

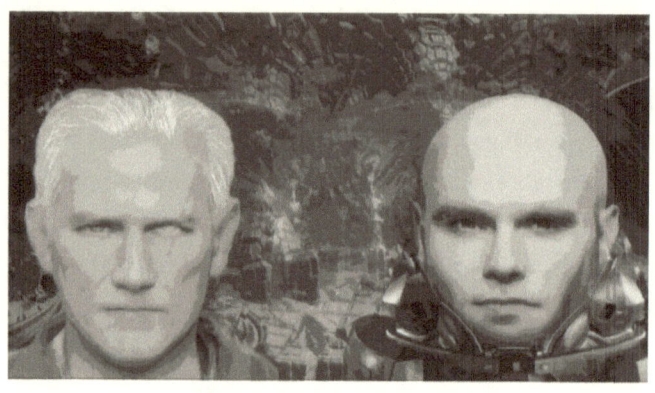

# The Wolf and the Girl in a Red Uniform

## The Terrenic Year 2681

Space storms were rare; they were discovered in the 24th century, when the population of Earth began to colonize exoplanets. This was the colloquial definition of very fine matter in the area of strong CME[8] activity, usually pieces of rock crushed into sand, with strong radiation and magnetic properties. It was made of destroyed celestial bodies with a specific chemical composition. The cloud rushing through space had different mantle sizes, it could reach the length of a planet, but there were also huge ones that stretched across several star systems. The latter usually occurred near hypernea and black holes.

Returning from a survey of the recently discovered iridium-rich planet, the Kiritians didn't expect to fall straight into the heart of a huge cloud upon exiting the subspace tunnel. Calculations with the use of the Alcubierre drive didn't take into account rare phenomena at the end of the journey, which were within a very low probability of occurrence, and therefore were ignored. Small pieces flooded a corvette, armored personnel carrier, and several fighters like a desert storm wanderer in the Sahara. Visibility behind the portholes decreased almost to zero, due to CME the navigation was also broken, including it was impossible to catch signals. In 2681, the Kiritians became the dominant nation in the cosmos, currently only rebels could defeat them in combat, but neither one nor the other side had such shields so that they could protect the machines against destructive cosmic phenomena, such as a combo of matter from destroyed planets and CME.

---

[8] Coronal mass ejection of a star.

"It's good," Forkis thought "that our squadron[9] machines are protected by dhurnsteel armor, and the cabin covers and portholes are made of ultra-hard puronax. So, the cloud can't do more damage than a little scratch." With this in mind, the man began to contemplate the striking spectacle from his armchair located in the center of the corvette's bridge. Many filings opalesced, shining their own light; the effect was reminiscent of living silver floating in space.

In front of Forkis, there were positions taken by captains Kiret "Necron" Biffter and Velkee Vandringen, also known as the Warfighter. Officers tried to talk to the pilots from the escort, but there could hear little amid the crackling noises. The immortals ended up communicating in Morse using external lighting. However, the machines must have come very close to each other.

"General," the voice of the gray-haired Velkee, skiritianized in his sixties, roused Forkis from his meditations. "Forgive me, but ... I don't know where we are," he added angrily. "Certainly, somewhere in the Fish Universe. The on-board capripods had to detect the threat and the automatic course correction system was activated, which ignored the manually entered destination

---

[9] In Kiritian aviation, several machines of different types, usually half a squadron.

coordinates. And due to the cloud disrupting its calculations, our squadron was thrown into the center of the eye of the cyclone."

"We are practically flying gropingly," completed Kiret, with the shaven head, immortalized at a much younger age than Vandringen. "I propose to turn off the equipment completely, stop the squadron and wait it out."

Velkee immediately turned his face towards him.

"I refuse. This is an area of rebel activity. They will kill us if they track us and find that we are drifting. We will be like a stationary shield for them. In such a number, we will surely lose."

"How will they track us, if the electronics don't detect anything inside the cloud?"

"It is not known how long this phenomenon will last. It might fly by in a few minutes and we'll be in a black...unknown."

"And by flying gropingly, we can go straight towards the enemy."

Forkis closed his eyes. He was used to rivalry between the captains, or to be more precise, it was lively Velkee who usually attacked conversationally calm Kiret. The Kiritians, as a forming military nation, temporarily settled on CD4G5 because it turned out that the planet didn't live up to their expectations. Forkis wielded a supreme authority among these people, he was called a dignitary, autocrat, but preferably a general. When they found a new, better home - and it should have happened soon - he planned to move Kiret onto a high, civilian position, so that this jostling with the Warfighter ended. He also intended to give himself a specific, so far unknown title.

"What's your decision, General?" Velkee asked. Opening his eyes, Forkis saw both captains staring at him.

"It's always better to do anything than to stand in the middle and surrender to fate. So, let's fly, but carefully. We need to get beyond the cloud's acting area." Kiret was his friend, but Forkis this time supported the more sensible idea of the Warfighter.

So, they flew. Officers were constantly working to establish the location of the squadron.

Watching the work of his men, Forkis turned with his fingers a metal capsule hung on a chain around his neck. The golden mouse bone locked inside became for him a kind of relic, a symbol of his power. Not being harassed by reports of his subordinates, he once again devoted himself to meditation. He had to admit that he was proud of his Kiritians, also referred to as the Immortals or the Infected. He no longer had any intention of getting rid of them after taking his revenge, as he had planned to do in the creation of the nation. They were his faithful achijes, devoted to the last drop of blood; out of attachment and a sense of duty, he felt responsible for them. One hundred and seventy Terrenic years had passed since he had underwent an accelerated transmutation into human and allegedly joined a team of workers on Chulimal. As the foreman had announced then, after a few months he was sent back to Earth, where he began to observe and study a human being. Promoting telepathy - which was perceived as a form of transhumanism that was practically impossible to create - only in a small group of services and the police, he worked on the selection of criminals and state enemies for the Visegrad Group. He was disliked as due to only one person it was possible to lock the building and fire almost all the staff[10]. However, Forkis didn't care at all, the important thing for him was that he had the job and money. Big money. When his path crossed the paths of a deserter from the New Order Army, formerly the European Union Army, Kiret Biffter, and Dr. Maximus Figam, they created a secret laboratory together. They hired trusted people to help, which was easy with the abilities of the former humanoid jaguar. There, Figam created a super virus immortalizing body. Forkis attacked the headquarters of a global government in London and created Kiritian. Then fights against the ANO left after the collapse of the

[10] Robotization of workplaces increased in the 21st century, but it turned out to be ineffective, mainly due to hacking and the co-evolution of electronics inhibitors. Moreover, in order to prevent society from becoming unnecessary, the role of machines was limited to supporting, not crowding out, humans.

global government began. The war from Earth moved into space, onto more and more distant Earth-type planets. The ANO in space turned into rebels.

And so, it had been for two centuries - the fight for domination over humanity between the Kiritians and the rebels, in which various colonies had been hit with a ricochet along the way. So far, no one had definitely gained the upper hand, though the Immortals had become a technological power; for ordinary people outside the nation, called oderses, they were like gods.

As a powerful shock unexpectedly swept through the corvette, Forkis felt for a moment as if he had been about to be shot out of a chair along with a chest protector.

He looked at the control panel and saw Velkee lying with his forehead on the console. The captain wasn't injured, it was just the way he wanted to vent his irritation.

"Lieutenant Robert Milles flew in our a... The transporter bashed us vehemently," he said contrary to the regulations. "Due to the lack of navigation, the pilot remained far behind us, he only wanted to accelerate slightly and he turned on the impulse drive instead of the plasma drive."

"But the situation is under control," Kiret reassured.

"Breakdowns?" Forkis asked, rubbing his right side.

Biffter glanced at the list from the analysis completed by AI.

104

"Corvette armor damage. But the board is already secured and there is no risk of decompression. In addition, a crushing of four protective field generators. A burst of the orbital cannon base. Also, a burning of the antenna."

"So, in other words, the combat potential went haywire, gentlemen," muttered Forkis. It wasn't that bad, however. If the corvette had been hit by a medium- or small-class enemy combat machine, a dhurnsteel armor would have crushed it into a harmonica. It would have been different if two Kiritian units protected by the same materials had collided by accident, but such incidents practically didn't happen.

"General, I think I have something ..."

Velkee and Forkis turned their attention to Kiret, with his arm raised.

After the series of clicks, indeed a male voice could be recognized on the civilian channel of universal communication. It didn't belong to anyone in the squadron.

"gg..t nge... ..rse by sevent... ...ees, course ze... ...rds ...tar..."

The warfighter frowned, trying to understand something.

"Who you are? We can hardly hear you, repeat," he ordered. After a few minutes, the message finally sounded correctly:

"At your current speed, I suggest you change your course by seventy degrees, course zero toward Antares. Unless you want to stop, you still have time."

The captains and the general looked at each other in surprise. Forkis slid open the chest protector and walked over[11] to Vandringen's station to look over his shoulder at one of the holographic monitors. Aside from the rebels ostentatiously despising them, probably everyone was afraid of the Immortals. Certainly no one would have dared to speak to them in such an arrogant manner.

"Who's speaking? Introduce yourself," Velkee demanded.

"He sounds like some drunken civilian," commented Kiret. "It may be that the cloud is getting weaker or we're nearing its end."

"I advise you to change course or you will run into us," said the mysterious man again. "It's not too late. There are twenty-nine point seven minutes to the collision, if you keep your current speed."

---

[11] More about Kiritian technology - in this case, enabling walking on the boards of craft and battleships in space - you can read in the Death Bringer trilogy.

"This is the Kiritian Captain Kiret Biffter speaking. It is you who should change course. We will follow the designated trajectory."

"I refuse. It is impossible. I suggest you change your course by seventy degrees, course zero toward Antares."

"They're definitely not rebels," Forkis muttered, with his hands clasped at the back of his neck.

The entire squadron listened intently to the exchange of views - the communication began to slowly return, although the visibility remained terrible. There could be seen lights on of the fuselages of distant machines, and a tiny blur of what was probably the nearest yellow dwarf, perhaps a blue main sequence star, or a sub-giant - it was difficult to tell anything in such conditions.

Annoyed by Kiret's ineffective, gentle talk, Velkee took the communicator from him.

"This is Captain Velkee Vandringen. In our squadron there is flying a corvette, battleship and a group of fighters. We won't change the route and either you will do it or there will be a firefight."

"We have no way of stopping or changing the course," the anonymous interlocutor continued recklessly. "If you don't do it, you will all die and you can also send many innocent people to the grave."

Finally, Forkis, amused so far, lost his patience. He hadn't experienced anything like that before. He leaned in beside Velkee to access communicator.

"This is General Forkis speaking, commander-in-chief of the Kiritian army and the nation's dignitary at the same time. Better get the hell off the route, beggars, or only your people will bite the sand. And I know you are not rebels." That only they might have endangered the Kiritians now, Forkis, of course, couldn't say.

"I see," the other side said irritatingly and impassively. "So at least change your course by ten degrees in either direction, because then if you hit the planet, no one else will get hurt."

Forkis was speechless.

"Who the hell are you? What planet?"

"I'm Lindgreen, third generation android from Space Dream. The operator of the spaceport tower of the Mirphak settlement. You're headed towards Atla."

The faces of the general and his officers were so eloquent that any comment turned out to be unnecessary. One of the fighter pilots couldn't stand it and started laughing stupidly. They experienced the greatest disgrace in the history of the Kiritian nation. And in a thousand years, jokes will be told about it, and they, as immortals, will listen to them - unless they die in some battle beforehand and are exempted from it.

Forkis wanted to smack his forehead against the instrument console, like the Warfighter had done before, and stay so for a few minutes.

They managed to slow down before Roche's border.

The cloud was slowly fading away.

Before their eyes appeared a freshly terraformed Earth-like planet with three moons and a purple surface color as a result of refraction of light.

\*\*\*

The landing near the small spaceport took place without major problems. Even though the first wild plants were planted on Atla, the naturalized atmosphere was functioning properly enough to allow to breathe freely, like on Earth. Air pressure and humidity also proved to be bearable. The globe's mass was four percent greater than that of the Blue Planet, but in a short time the human body could adapt to it. Especially when someone often traveled in space and was used to the systematic change of environmental conditions.

It was night in the hemisphere, which is why the Kiritians had difficulty seeing the planet's surface. They left the machines and began assessing the damage.

"How long will it take to repair them?" Forkis asked.

"It depends, sir, on the equipment they have in the spaceport hangars," the mechanic technician replied.

"Okay. Check it out right away."

"Of course, sir."

"Shit, I didn't even know there were settlements on Atla." Velkee, with arms akimbo, began to look around at his surroundings. Forkis followed suit and quickly realized why the existence of Mirphak had eluded their attention. They landed on a hill with a good view of hundreds of hectares of land. The small enclave with buildings was surrounded by rocky desert. The spaceport, along with its tower, which was home to the fearless android, was about a kilometer from the nearest houses. Adjacent to the air station was a small, characteristic square, now empty, where intra- or interplanetary trade of essential goods took place. Forkis noticed a lot of serpentine astroplarns near town, intended for food farming. So, it looked like Mirphak was practically self-sufficient and minimalist. This resulted in little movement over the settlement in the cosmos, which in turn meant a low energetic and thermal signature to be captured in deeper space. In any case, the estate didn't flaunt its existence.

The Kiritians landed without anyone's permission, and apart from the android, nobody contacted them. It was similar on most of the colonized planets and moons - few were eager to cause difficulties for the Immortals. Only on the spot did a group of mercenary soldiers assigned to the colony approach them. After a short conversation, Forkis learned from a local lieutenant that the homogeneous agglomeration, which had existed only for a few months, was inhabited by more than four thousand civilians plus two hundred mercenaries. The dignitary knew from experience that this was a terrible protection in the event of an attack from space, and the small size of the army, in addition mercenary one, could only mean one thing - Mirphak got along with the rebels. It is possible that they paid them regularly to ensure themselves protection against other nationalities, gangsters or pirates from space.

"If you inform the opposition," addressing the mercenary commander, Forkis, as usual, used the method of firing cannon at a mosquito, "that we are here, we will call for our own backup. And that means you can expect then a battle in your streets and over your heads. We don't want to hurt you, we will only repair the damage and fly our way. We don't care about your planet."

111

"Of course, sir." The pale officer calmed down, at least in terms of safety. The Kiritians were considered a cruel nation, but they were famous for their truthfulness, which was part of their scrupulously obeyed creed.

Forkis read with satisfaction from his thoughts that they had indeed been in contact with the rebels, but for fear of complications, they were not going to inform them of the arrival of the Immortals. So at least it would be quiet here. He looked at the corvette and the damaged orbital gun that couldn't be slid into the landing gear recess. In case of problems, a shot even from the lower atmosphere would have been enough to annihilate the entire colony, but even without that the Kiritians would have dealt with the indigenous people with the help of fighters if the mercenaries had made their units take off.

Some of the Immortals stayed at the machines, the rest, including the captains and Forkis, headed towards the estate. The homogeneity of small colonies consisted in the fact that people with the same views or needs gathered in one place, the law was established there, and the authorities weren't elected. The order was kept by the army or other uniformed services. It even worked well, but always for a time. Eventually there were disputes and divisions - Forkis knew from experience that humans couldn't function differently. Even though he owed much of his success to the artifact, he was proud of himself that he had managed to create inhuman Kiritians who followed him like sheep follow their shepherd. Or a wolf that terrifies them and because of it, is admired by them.

In front of the houses resembling puffballs, there was a square with an archaic, Medieval-style Diamond Geyser inn. The two-story, quite large building was built of synthetics, visually indistinguishable from wood.

As the light-armored Kiritians stepped inside, the conversation broke off, and all looks, surprised and terrified, turned towards them. For long seconds one could hear only fire sizzling on logs in a great fireplace. The clients sat frozen as Immortals ignoring them, took the empty tables; Forkis, Kiret, and Velkee sat down together. Only the little girl, who came to dinner with her father and her sister a few years older, broke the pattern - she approached Forkis' table with enthusiasm and a naive smile. She grabbed a corner with her hands and started jumping, waving up and down two blonde pigtails on the sides of her head. Sweat appeared on her father's forehead. Kiret smiled at the girl and waved to her.

"Everyone, get out," Forkis snapped at the guests of the inn. And everyone in a hurry began to leave their places. The dignitary gave the little girl an icy look that softened slightly.

"Where's your mom?" He asked.

"Joint!"

He checked her mind, and as he thought, it was about a job, not a prison. The woman looked after one of the plant sectors in the astroplarn.

"The girl and the family can stay," he said, looking at her father. The Kiritian raised his hand as the latter was about to get up.

"Relax, just sit back and finish your supper."

The man, still concerned, nodded. He had no choice but to carry out the order of the dignitary with a disastrous reputation, not wanting to annoy him, and for the comfort of his own nerves. He would feel uncomfortable all the time, but at least the meal they had scarcely gotten, wouldn't be wasted. His older daughter showed more courage than her parent and approached her sister. Looking apologetically at Kiritian, she grabbed her armpits.

"Mika, come on." She pulled the little girl away from the table, then both returned to theirs.

Velkee walked over to the bar. He looked around the dining room, then, resting his hands on the tabletop, turned amiably to the silent, worried host:

"Really nice shack and its look was a great idea. Besides, traditional service, without machines. Your business is surely booming. We take it over in full for three days, including food. Please don't worry about financial losses due to the lack of clients. We pay in advance, triple."

114

A synthetic bag with several grams of painite landed on the counter - the Kiritians manipulated the value of this mineral, controlling all its found deposits. The astonished host opened the pouch more and began to touch the contents uncertainly, as if for fear that it was only an immaterial projection. But no, the painite was really there. Out of the back room, looked an equally confused blonde female worker.

"As you can see, we are not such monsters oderses think we are. Sometimes it is enough just to be nice to us."

"Velkee smiled factitiously, glancing at the girl who blushed. "I think there won't be any problems?"

"Of course. No problem," the owner of the building replied meekly. "Call me Ramaphosa."

"Captain Velkee Vandringen. If there are customers upstairs, throw them out. And don't worry, this building won't lost even a splinter. We will leave it in the same condition as we found it. Now make us a nice supper."

The blonde replaced the host behind the bar - glad to be able to glance at the aged but attractive Warfighter now - and Ramaphos went into the kitchen to correct the team so that no one would screw anything up. Trying not to look in the direction of the Kiritians, the father and his daughters took care of the meal, in the breaks between bites the man talked to the older one about the school. achijes from the fighters and the transporter also engaged themselves in a lively discussion. Three of them went outside to smoke tumbaku, a popular drug at the Zodiac Universum.

"Well, Necron, what else interesting do you have there?" Forkis asked Biffter as Velkee returned to them. Far from their achijes, they could talk more freely. "During the flight, you spoke about one more candidate."

"Oh yeah." Kiret placed a chestnut-sized projector on the table, and the holographic image appeared immediately.

"This is the last planet from the presentation that would be suitable for our headquarters," described Necron. "Rocky, terrestrial type, of course. About five hundred and forty-five light-years from Earth. Three moons. It orbits a yellow dwarf, but it is the last globe in its system, which means that the star has little effect on it and is hardly visible to the naked eye. However," he held up a finger, "a few light years from the planet there is a red supergiant Betelgeuse and it acts as its main star, has a significant impact on the climate and the earth's crust. The planet is seismically and volcanically active, so we would have endless sources of free energy for processing. The threat to us would be zero. It is nothing that we wouldn't be able to cope with with the current state of our technology ..."

"Sir." Sergeant Ivester, who had been smoking tumbak outside, approached their table.

"Yes?" The achij, with a small pony at the back of his head and a slightly crooked nose, seemed embarrassed. "A girl came to you. She wants to see you."

Forkis leaned back in his chair.

"Seriously?"

"What girl?" Velkee asked.

"Some from town, sir. I mean, she came from the wilderness. She looks, talks and acts as if depressed. We scanned her for bomb, chemical or microbiological threats. She is completely clean. And healthy. She has no gun. It looks as if she came here of her own free will, with no relation to other people."

The three looked at their commander, curious about his decision. The inn's staff brought them food and beer and set them on the table. Forkis wasn't afraid that some poison had been poured there - telepathy was a versatile, powerful tool for surveillance of oderses. If anyone had wanted to harm them, they would have probably be thinking hard not to make the slightest mistake, thus being a readable card for Forkis' skills. They wouldn't have been trying to do differently to keep their mind in a tabula rasa state. The suspicion that the Lord of the Immortals was a telepath, to his amusement, still existed among the oderses as a conspiracy theory - one of thousands about him. Telepathy worked most effectively when Forkis, focused, had a probed object in the line of sight and at a maximum distance of several dozen meters, but he was also able to catch thoughts through thinner walls, especially non-metallic ones. That is why the employees in the kitchen, sometimes wandering around the room, couldn't hide anything from him. In addition, almost everyone was afraid, so there was no question of messing up the dishes and poor service. Several people cursed the Kiritians mentally, which was nothing new, and no community had any penalties for negative thinking. Only the blonde, setting the plates in front of them, was interested in Velkee, giving him discreet glances when he didn't see it. Once she didn't manage to look away and they looked at each other. The captain smiled meaningfully, and so did she.

Forkis picked up his silverware and said to Ivester:

"When I'm done eating, bring that girl over here, Sergeant." The achij was slightly surprised.

"Are you sure of that, sir?"

The dignitary took his eyes off the unattractive contents of the plate and stared at him sternly.

"Haven't you understood something, achij? You have just made it clear to us that she is not here to assassinate me."

"Sorry, sir. And of course, I'll bring her in here..."

"Let it be a quarter of an hour." Forkis waved his fork at him and started to appraise the meal further. "Where's the meat?" He asked the blonde scouring the counter with a cloth. Little Mika left the table again and walked eagerly towards the armed soldiers in cool armor.

"We don't have it, sir. Only vegans live in Mirphak."

Velkee laughed, began to play with a date tomato, rolling it between his fingers.

"We already know what the homogeneity of this estate is about. Damn, I won't be full after eating it," the dignitary grumbled, shifting the elements of the salad with his fork. It was comforting, though, that the mushroom and vegetable croquettes of the local traditional cuisine were covered with a lot of caloric fat.

"I wonder what this girl is about and what she wants." Necron started with a mug of beer. "I'm surprised you just didn't blow her off, Fork. You have to respect your status."

"A little entertainment won't hurt us in this hole," replied the dignitary. Starting with beer, and in fair amount was indeed a good idea.

Kiret looked at Mika, who was pressing her upper teeth against the tabletop, slobbering it, and smiling cheerfully as she watched the Kiritians. The man reassuringly raised his hand as the nervous father was getting up to take his daughter.

Mika grabbed the corner of the table with her hands, started jumping up and calling:

119

"A fairy tale, a fairy tale!"

"Come on, Velkee, tell the little one a fairy tale," Forkis suggested, slightly amused.

"Once upon a time," Warfighter began to say, busy with his plate, "there was a pacifist Oder who wanted to be a gardener. However, the global government ordered him to go to the army in the ANO. He didn't want to, because he said he would die there and he doesn't like weapons. However, he couldn't do anything. They sent him on a mission where he got a bullet in the head. The end."

"Was this supposed to be funny?" Kiret said to him.

"Forgive me, but there are guts and dead bodies in all the stories I know," the captain replied with ironic seriousness, between bites.

"You probably came up with it offhand."

The warfighter gave Biffter a gloomy look.

"You know what is the biggest educational mistake among oderses when it comes to children? That from birth, they don't tell them the truth about life, but only come up with some talking animals, the magic power of friendship, Santa Claus or claim that there is no death. Then a kid grows up, and a poop comes out, a knockout right in the face. You practically have to learn life anew because of this nonsense that is supposed to protect the mind of a toddler. And if it was differently, all would be known from the beginning and not scary, thanks to the method of gradual dosing of reliable information. I know what I'm saying because I had several sons, then I educated their offspring. And they all grew into tough people. As kids, they were scared for maybe a few days and that's it. It is better to teach scary but real things when a kid still encompasses emotionally little."

"If you think you can do it better, you can tell a story yourself, Kiret," Forkis suggested.

"Come on." Necron spread his hands, smiling friendly. Mika, contentedly and without fear, allowed herself to be put on his lap. He knew how to deal with the little ones, it got tough only with teenagers. The captain had to admit that Velkee was somewhat correct about instilling sweet gentleness in the children, so he opted for an educational story.

"It happened quite recently, on the planet Proxima Centauri e," he began to tell. "Once upon a time there was a young man, quite rich, because his parents earned a lot and willingly shared their property with their children. He also earned well, but it didn't give him happiness. Even though he was a good man, he constantly experienced some unpleasantness from people. He came to the conclusion that this wasn't his reality, because he was different, he didn't belong there and he felt bad there. He learned that there was a sect called lycans that became his inspiration.

121

"Careful, she might understand something of this," Velkee interrupted, not caring that his confidential comment was heard by the achijes, amused by the hilarious sight of the captain telling Mika the fairy tale.

Kiret noticed that the room was as quiet as when they had entered the inn, and everyone was listening, including the blonde behind the counter and Miki's family. The father obviously didn't mind his younger daughter hearing the story, or he himself was curious about the stories that circulated among the Immortals.

"It's okay, go on," Forkis encouraged him. "Don't interrupt, Vandringen."

"The man decided to go and live somewhere in a strange forest, away from the city, so that the change of surroundings and the de-stressing neighborhood would do him good. He also wanted to change. He used his money to undergo a strong cosmetic and genetic transmutation and become like a wolf. It worked, he was made into a creature like a werewolf: with a mouth, fangs, claws, fur and tail, but with his old human mind. The wolf lived in the forest, he was indeed happy, away from people and their chaotic, sad world. However, with time, the transhumanist began to feel lonely, because he preferred it to joining the sect of lycans, where others were similar to him, he would have then ceased to be special, he would have become a troublemaker. More than once he watched a girl in a red uniform fly on a skulak somewhere to the edge of a nearby town. After a few hours, she returned the same way. This happened regularly, so the wolf remembered this cycle.

One day he decided to accost her. Just to greet.

"Hi," he said cordially, leaving the woods. "Where are you flying?"

The girl looked at him contemptuously, critically. For she didn't tolerate alterity.

"To my grandma," she replied, then set off on her skulak.

The wolf felt sad. When another time he wanted to try to talk to the girl when she was coming back from her grandmother, she threatened him with a weapon.

The wolf hated people. They teased him when he was a good, conciliatory, and meek man. They didn't like him as a transhumanist. It was just human nature, he realized, and they mistreated others for no reason at all. But he also understood that he didn't have to put up with it and remain passive.

He decided to change and release his dark nature. Wolf one. Because why was he supposed to be good?

Long before the girl in the red uniform went to visit her grandma again, he ran along the road through the forest. He reached a lonely cottage on the edge of a clearing, away from the town. As the grandma was a trustful person and no one in the area teased her, she had no monitoring or other security measures at her house.

The wolf had lived in the forest for a long time and learned to sneak noiselessly. So, he attacked the grandma by surprise while she was working in the garden, he stunned her, tied her up, and hid her in a shed. The woman was one hundred and forty years old, but she was still lively and healthy, so he was not afraid that something would happen to her. Initially, he planned to eat her, but gave it up. Human nature spoke in him, saying that in the end the grandma did nothing to him, moreover, after devouring her, there wouldn't have been enough room in the stomach for the girl in a red uniform. So he put on the grandma's clothes and hid under a quilt in bed.

Kiret paused for a moment to take a sip of his beer. Everyone was still listening to him, but Forkis seemed to be most absorbed in the story, moving the empty mug on the table. Propping his head with three fingers, he was focused, serious, and a little absent.

"The girl," continued the captain, "came as the wolf predicted."

"Hi, grandma, I'm home!" She said behind the threshold, put down her uniform jacket and gun holster.

She headed for the bedroom. She immediately noticed that the quilt was very bulged.

"Grandma, are you okay?" She asked.

"Hello, sweetie, of course I am," the wolf croaked. "It's a bit cold today and I took some extra layers."

"Why do you have such a strange voice?" The girl walked over to the bed and stretched out her hand to fold back the quilt.

"It couldn't be better," rejoiced the wolf. He grabbed her hand and pulled her screaming towards him. He opened his mouth and quickly ate the terrified girl. Then he lay down in bed to rest.

"So, without bising to piecies?" Mika asked surprised, with sincere interest.

"Yes, without biting to pieces," confirmed Kiret, smiling good-naturedly.

"Why? Did she fitz in the beiy?"

"She's smart. She's so little, and she doesn't let anyone tell her a whopper," commented Velkee.

"Because it was a very big wolf," Necron completed, ignoring the captain. "So, the wolf fell asleep. However, he didn't know one thing because he hadn't been in this area before. The sector was regularly patrolled by a forest sentry drone. Not long after the wolf ate the girl, it flew over the grandmother's cottage. It scanned her property from above, and as the drone's rays easily passed through the walls, it saw three living beings: the grandma locked in a cell, the transhumanist and the girl inside him.

The transmission from the drone was immediately picked up by a young officer of the forest service, who was happily in the area. Soon he ran into the cottage, kicked open the bedroom door and aimed the barrel of a multi-mode rifle at the wolf, who had been awakened by the noises.

"Free the girl!" He demanded sharply.

"I'm not able to do it!" The terrified wolf replied. "I could swallow her, but I won't throw her in that direction. It is impossible."

The newcomer fired a sleep dart at the transhumanist to keep him from moving during surgery. He himself with a surgical light knife taken out of a bag, which every forest officer was equipped with, began to cut open his belly.

"And the miss didn't suffocate?" The girl asked another question.

"She is actually intelligent," Velkee said.

"As I said, it was a big wolf and he had a lot of air inside," Kiret explained hesitantly, not wanting to tell the child that it was just a fairy tale, and in them there was a lot of illogicality. "After a few minutes, the terrified girl emerged from the wolf's stomach. The officer sealed the transhumanist's abdomen with molecular glue. Then he called the gendarmes to take him into custody and for trial.

A moment later, the man released the grandma from the shed. The elderly woman and granddaughter were very happy that everything turned out well. The girl, after she had washed and changed clothes, started kissing the officer in the garden, and then ... Anyway, irrelevant." Kiret smiled. "As this is a fairy tale with a moral, you will now go back to your daddy and talk about who the real beast was here: the wolf or the people who contributed to his condition."

"And did you knol that my bother was also eatem by a wolf?" The girl announced something that she didn't really understand, but once had heard.

Miki's embarrassed father turned pale, stood up immediately to finally pull her away from the Kiritians.

"I'm so sorry for her, gentlemen," he said humbly.

Forkis frowned, pressed his fingers to his temple and entered his mind. The carefree confession of the little girl triggered a number of unpleasant memories in the locals. This was before Mika was born. Forkis saw a boy bitten to death by dogs on someone else's property. Among the gathered people, the desperate father howled, threw himself on the ground, was at his wit end. Some tried to help him, sometimes forced to hold him by force, others stood aside and looked at him with sympathy. The dogs were finally taken and euthanized, the owner of the plot went to jail.

In the mind of the tipsy dignitary, the dog turned into a fairy-tale wolf, which in turn became Onkalot.

"I'll better go," said the father, holding his daughters' hands. "Thank you for entertaining Mika. And sorry for the inconvenience again."

"Good luck," Forkis said, looking at him impassively.

The man turned. Seeing piercing, keen gaze of the dignitary, he only managed to nod. He had the unsettling impression that the Lord of the Kiritians knew perfectly well what had happened in his past.

As they left, the satisfied girl waved to the achijes from another table, and they bid her farewell in the same way, sending her smiles.

Kiret noticed Forkis sitting at the empty plate, thinking unnaturally for him.

"Are you alright?"

"Do you think it was cannibalism?" The dignitary moved the spoon between his thumb and forefinger. "You know. A transhumanist is like a wolf, he has a wolf body but a human mind."

Velkee and Kiret were intrigued not by the question itself, but by the questioner.

"This beer isn't that strong," Biffter remarked, looking at Forkis' empty mug. The dignitary glared at him.

"It's just a silly fairy tale," replied the other captain. He looked at Necron. "Anyway, Mr. Kiret Biffter fluffed it. Your version is completely pointless."

"Why?"

"The transhumanist dude was from Mars, he had to move out urgently because he had problems with the law, and Proxima Centauri e seemed the best option, and they hate Martians there. These were once economically and settlementably competing planets, and attempts were made to palm a lot of expensive houses off on the colonists. As for the communities themselves, at the time of the fairy tale action, this guy was also about contempt and xenophobia for his religion and appearance, which is why he hated the new colony. He gave up after many years of persecution and no reaction from the authorities. So he began to conduct lynch crusades. With time, he got mad, he developed a dual personality - human and wolf. As a wolf, he ate the old woman and her granddaughter, which took him a month.

"The kid wouldn't have understood it, and had restless nights for the next years."

"But who lycans and transhumanists are, maybe every four-year-old already knows it? And she wouldn't have relieved herself in bed at night, if everything had been conveyed to her properly. You wouldn't have needed to go into details about the gradual depriving these women of their body parts."

Forkis didn't concentrate on exchanging the last sentences.

"But what do you think, Velkee?" He asked. "Was there cannibalism in this fairy tale or not?"

"Psychologically I think so, but biologically no," Biffter said, accepting the explanation that the dignitary had gone overboard with the beer. "I think so. A wolf's body, but a human mind."

"I don't know." Looking at the bartender and listening to the conversation with half an ear, Velkee finished the rest of the hot tea that had just been served with dinner.

"And if it was the other way around?" Forkis continued. "Let's suppose that a very intelligent animal was changed into a human in the laboratory, and that human would feed on human flesh, but had a mind of a different species."

"Where did this sudden need for philosophy come from?" Velkee asked with a smile.

"I just thought so."

"These are questions from the paradox of Theseus' ship category: if we start to cyborgize a human being, when they become one hundred percent a machine, will they still have awareness or it will disappear."

"They will still have it," replied Kiret. "This is a case known to science. This is how androwolves are made."

Forkis freed himself from his thoughts and turned on the communicator next to the strobilus of his helmet.

"Sergeant Ivester, bring this girl."

The called out achij entered immediately, as if he had constantly been guarding at the door, awaiting orders. Ahead of him walked uncertainly like a deer, a delicate, petite woman - seeming to ponder whether she had been right to come here - visually no more than thirty years old. Had it been not for a soil stain, her dress would have been creamy; on her shoulders hung an oversized coat resembling a cape. Her hair, reaching her chin and dyed a matte purple, she had combed to the right side, only the roots were bright. Her big green eyes and, for the sake of contrast, a tiny chin gave the arrived innocence and girlish look, and the effect was even more pronounced by her eyes fixed humbly on the pseudo-wood floor.

Forkis propped his head up with his fist, placed his right foot above his left knee and, like the achij, followed the girl with a curious glance as she passed the tables. Contrary to the constantly scared, lonely oderses, the presence of the Kiritians didn't turn her into an incoherent bundle of nerves, the girl seemed to be in a world of her own thoughts - Forkis hadn't bothered to check it out yet. He preferred the traditional face-to-face conversation, explaining the whole matter, which had always been soothing to the human psyche, and the newcomer clearly looked to be in need of help. Her every movement and body position indicated that she was mentally broken, the expression of resignation and reconciliation with the inevitable fate was visible on her sad face.

Her face changed only when she stopped a step in front of the dignitary's table and looked up at him. She sucked in air through the slightly parted lips, she looked now at him with fear and with a fascination he knew well. He had seen a similar look in women a thousand times, so it didn't make the slightest impression on him.

"I heard you wanted to see me." He looked at a piece of lettuce picked from between the incisors.

"Yes," she replied after a moment.

He spread his arms for a moment.

"So, I'm listening."

She looked uncertainly at the table where non-commissioned officers sat snickering and whispering.

"I came here ... for you to kill me."

Once again that evening, the inn would have been dismayingly silent, if the fire, as indifferent as ever to human matters, hadn't been popping.

And then the achijes started laughing loudly. The girl didn't care, she looked expectantly only at Forkis, and he at her.

"Since you've already eaten, maybe you would go to the city and then report to me what is going on there?" Kiret asked achijes. "Just please, no dead bodies and fights."

The subordinates, disappointed that their promising entertainment had been interrupted, reluctantly started to carry out the order.

Before they left, however, they witnessed another incident.

"That's her! Childkiller!" Out of the kitchen room, came the blonde, picking up Velkee earlier, wanting to check if the guests didn't lack anything. In an instant, she turned from a nice, obliging employee into a furious panther. With her eyes filled with fire like a hellish cauldron, she began to march towards the newcomer. "We thought you were dead, bitch! You cracked your head open on these rocks!"

Velkee got up and grabbed her by the shoulders, otherwise she would have lunged at the object of her hatred with her fingernails.

The worker looked at the officers.

133

"Kill her!" She pointed at the girl with her finger. "Kill that beastly bitch!"

"Calm down!"

Forkis' baritone rolled through the room like the thunder of a rocket drive. Both young women shuddered the same. The dignitary got up and took a few lazy steps, looked at the frightened, silent worker from above, straight in the eye.

"It is I who will decide who deserves to live and who deserves to die here," he droned in a voice that congealed blood in the veins of the oderses. "Please go back to your tasks and don't make a scene. I want to rest here after a long journey in a metal can."

The blonde humbly retreated to the kitchen, she didn't return to serving the Kiritians.

"And you? Did you not receive the orders?" Forkis growled now at the achijes still grouped at the door. Then he sat down, and as if nothing had happened, he turned to the girl who was as moody as before:

"Where did the idea come from that any of us would kill you?" He leaned back in the chair and folded his hands over his belly when of the Kiritians, only he, Necron and Velkee remained in the room. "I suppose you'll agree that this is quite an unusual desideratum. What's your name?"

"Vanessa." She glanced at the officers.

134

Curious, Forkis understood the silent message without his telepathy, rose again.

"So, let's go upstairs, Vanessa, you will tell me everything. By the way, your courage is admirable."

Kiret and Velkee watched intrigued as the dignitary climbed the stairs, and the girl hesitantly followed him.

"I'm really sorry, gentlemen," she said to them, turning her head for a moment. Forkis was assigned the largest, most lavishly furnished room, with a huge balcony overlooking the astroplarn houses and a rocky valley, opalescing with pink and blue of minerals. One of the moons, peculiar, with black and gray stripes, was becoming full, flooding the area with eerie, intense light. The man stepped onto the balcony, spread his arms wide and rested them on the railing, for a moment he stared at the diminishing achijs on their way towards the Mirphak estate.

Suddenly he felt like laughing to his own thoughts.

"Incredible. If I ever lose my job, I think I'll start a killing-on-demand company. I shouldn't complain about the lack of customers. We can talk freely," he turned to Vanessa, who stopped uncertainly a bit behind him.

"I didn't believe your soldiers would even let me see you. It's a miracle. I saw that you were landing and headed for the inn, so I decided to give it a try."

135

"Sometimes I meet mediocre oderses, sometimes I don't. There is no rule for that. It depends on many factors, but usually on my mood. Why do you want me to kill you?" He turned to face her, resting his elbows on the green porphyry.

"Because only you ..." She bit her lip as she looked with shame at the tiny pebbles of the mosaic floor beside his armored boots, "can do it THIS way. You deal the gentlest death possible; some even say that it is unearthly pleasant. I'm afraid, but I am also curious to see how true it is ..."

"Look at me, Vanessa. Right in the eye."

As she looked up shyly, he allowed himself to telepathically brush her mind to finally confirm what he had read from the expression on her face earlier downstairs. Vanessa was totally fascinated by him, intimidated, she thought now about his look, stature and power, but in a naive, girlish way. Pure, having nothing to do with commercial lust or selfish planning. He charmed her, and she was a little angry with herself, because that was not what she had expected when she had come to the inn. Vanessa imagined what it would have been like to be in his strong arms, to feel the heat of his strong, drooly tongue against her skin, and just above, the warm breath of the mighty Kiritian. A delightful shiver ran through her.

Forkis managed not to smile. The girl visually liked him very much, the spontaneous modesty and this delightful embarrassment only added to her charm.

"So, will you answer the question that I asked you downstairs? Who told you that you can come to me and I will carry out the execution?"

"People say about you ... incredible things."

"Fine, but how could it have leaked out?" He wondered. He ignored nonsense said about him - even if part of it turned out to be true. Usually it even amused him, but he would have definitely preferred people to repeat it as rumors with a certain amount of uncertainty rather than coming to him with unusual requests. He did THIS no more than once every two months, always clandestinely, making sure there were no spy electronics, no rubber ears, or even one pair of eyes too many nearby. He couldn't foresee how achijes would have reacted to the news of their ruler's paraphilia, whether they would have condemned him and removed him from office ... or, on the contrary, his status as a cruel dignitary would have been strengthened more. Nevertheless, when any achij was unlucky enough to witness his 'methods of killing', Forkis sent him to a medical center and ordered to selectively clear his memory since Dr. Figam had developed such a procedure. Apparently, someone noticed something and released it into the universe, unless it was still a conspiracy theory that accidentally hit the spot.

"The oderses say all kinds of things about me. Kiritians, too. It would be easier just to kill yourself. Sorry," he reflected immediately. His old fanatical hatred of people, all without exception, had changed over time. Now he selected them according to his own standards. More and more often he was guided in his judgments by Onkalotian principles derived from Chulimal, on which the functionality of the Kiritian nation was also based. He grabbed the girl gently by the arm and suggested with a slight pressure that she sit down on a bamboo chair at a dessert table. As she did so, he positioned himself opposite her.

"Tell me what happened. Just don't try to lie to me."

To his surprise, Vanessa began to sob.

"Wiria in the room was right, I am a murderer," she confessed, staring at the edge of the table top, when she was already able to speak. "I killed my sister's newborn and threw the body into a trashcan. Out of hatred and jealousy! All Mirphak knows about it, but I'm afraid of lynching by the inhabitants, that's why I fled to the wilderness. There is a dilapidated house hidden among the rocks, which was left by the scientists terraforming Atla. I don't want to live, not with such a burden. I can't stand it ... I tried to kill myself, but I couldn't. I'm a coward. I don't even know if I deserve such a death," she looked at him with red and swollen eyes, "that you supposedly can put me to."

Forkis ran his hand over the face.

All the time she told, he probed her telepathically, analyzing every recalled memory. Everything seemed to be right. As she spoke, Vanessa saw through her mind's eyes traumatic events, real, not imaginary. Distinct and clear, as they had taken place only a week earlier. So she was telling the truth about what she had experienced. And this clarity, undisturbed by mind-jerking emotions, caught his attention. It was like watching a movie, detail by detail. Normally, in memories there should have appeared imperfections, some facts have always been forgotten, just like in case of a dream some time after waking up. And here nothing similar happened. Vanessa was shaky with the memories, yet she telepathically conveyed to him the perfect message.

Thinking about it, Forkis left the room for a moment and brought her a box of wet wipes. She nodded gratefully and took one, wiped her face with it.

"You understand now," she whispered. "And thank you for your precious time."

"Yeah," he replied slowly. "Can you tell me about the circumstances? Who is your sister by education?"

"A psychologist."

139

"And she wasn't trying to help you?"

"She hates me. She urged the mob to lynch." Forkis watched her carefully from under his partially closed lids as she finished wiping her face.

"Tell me about yourself," he demanded.

He found out that Vanessa had studied botany and astrobotany, and before the murder of the baby, like a third of the estate, she had worked in an astroplarn and knew her stuff. From the girl's recollection, he also established her address. Together with her sister Valerie and her partner Rytar, she lived in one of the houses there, sharing the rent; Vanessa occupied alone the top floor.

"All right, I'll end your suffering," ruled Forkis. "Quickly and efficiently."

She stared at him in horror, for now she understood, as he sat in front of her, great, powerful, terrifying, with a cold crystallized in his brown eyes, what she was really asking of him. She glanced over his broad, strong jaw, then down to where his belly was beneath the light biometal armor.

"Thank you," she whispered anyway.

Forkis walked over to Vanessa. He ran his gloved fingers over her cheek.

"You're pretty. It is a little pity to annihilate such beauty." He lifted her chin for a moment. "Do you mind if I spend the night with you before I settle the matter?"

"I'm all yours, lord ..." She really liked the Lord of the Immortals, no matter what she came there for.

"Call me just Forkis. And you don't have to agree to things you don't want, just because you consider yourself a sub-human."

She glanced at him in confusion as he used exactly the same term as she did thinking of herself.

She nodded.

He was no longer going to make Vanessa say aloud that she wanted to stay with him for the night. She would have had to admit openly that she was fascinated by him, and that was certainly embarrassing for such a hounded girl.

"If you like, go to the bathroom to freshen up," he suggested. When she got up and left, aware that the Kiritian was allowing her to preserve human dignity in the last moments of life, the dignitary leaned his back against the railing and connected via a communicator with Kiret.

"Nobody is to bother me until morning," he told him. Then he chose the number of Robert Milles who was with achijes in the city center. "Lieutenant, get me some information on Valerie Bondar," he ordered. "She's a sister of Vanessa, that girl from the inn. I'm

141

particularly interested in what her powers are. It's supposed to be in the morning on my PDA."

"Of course, sir," replied Milles. In the background one could hear dynamic music and amused voices.

When he went inside and closed the balcony door behind himself, Vanessa came out of the bathroom, barefoot, in her underwear and a thin T-shirt. She still looked at him with admiration, but also fear and resignation.

He approached her, barely reaching his chest. She closed her eyes as, shifting his thumb, he began to mark tracks on her face, jaw, and neck. He pulled her close and pressed his face into her still damp hair, he relished its fruity scent.

He stripped off the armor and went to wash himself.

When he returned wearing only pants, Vanessa was sitting expectantly on the bed. She looked like one of those unfortunate girls who had been kidnapped and forced into prostitution by pimps. But he couldn't expect other emotions from the person confident that she was about to die. At least she sincerely wanted to be close to him, she knew Forkis was going to use some of his tricks to make her de-stress a little.

The Kiritian verbally deactivated the light. Its source in the room was now the rays of a moon hanging low in the sky. He sat down on the bed next to Vanessa, slowly took off her T-shirt, and slipped off her bra. He touched the flawless skin between the small breasts with his tongue and pulled it towards the quivering girl's neck, then on the side of her head to the temple.

"You are sweet," he said figuratively and literally.

He bit her ear, licked her back, sucked on her fingers, making her moan, tremble, and breathe faster and louder. Then he pushed Vanessa gently down onto sheets and began to suck on her breasts, putting them whole in his mouth. He lowered his head and picked the tiny navel with his teeth.

He rested his arms on the girl's sides and looked at her with a thirsty gaze, keeping his face a few centimeters from hers. In Vanessa's eyes he saw not only the erotic fear of the barbarian partner - which accounted for several percent of the emotions she felt now - but also the primal terror of a victim pressed by the hunter.

That was exactly what Forkis reminded her of now - a big, hungry tiger, not a human being. Maybe that was because his hazel, marked by infravision in the twilight eyes looked disturbingly like cats', not to mention too long fangs for a standard human.

Satisfied, Forkis read her thoughts. If women like Vanessa had known how little they had been wrong in their associations ...

"So it's true what they said about you?" She asked softly.

"In this case, it is," he replied.

143

"Will it hurt?"

"Not even a little." He smiled predatorily. "I guarantee that you will be satisfied."

He continued to roam with his wet tongue on her body, the golden mouse's bone capsule wandered over the delicate skin near its owner's fleshy lips; Vanessa began to calm down. Forkis was sure that the artifact allowed him to retain the oncalonian substances and pheromones in the saliva from its former incarnation, because thanks to the tongue - and the right words and caresses - he managed to stupify women every time. More than once, thanks to this set, he made them feel really good before their death. Some convinced him that they had never felt better in their life. In any case, he hadn't checked the properties of his secretions in a laboratory.

"Don't worry about anything," he whispered into an ear of Vanessa, half asleep. "You will soon find yourself in a better place, warm and safe. Then it all will be over; all your problems will vanish."

Delighted by his stunts, she believed him and completely surrendered to him.

\*\*\*

It was a ripe night when Forkis woke up. After his belly stopped rumbling, he could hear muffled metallic sounds coming from the spaceport, single voices from the city, and a woman's groans from the upstairs room that Vandringen had taken. The owner of the facility apparently overcame this traditionalism or cut costs because he didn't deign to install soundproof walls. Or intentionally made it possible to eavesdrop on your neighbors, so that disturbed guests didn't make too much noise in their rooms.

Forkis glanced at Vanessa, she was fast asleep with her arm outstretched above her head. She looked even lovelier and innocent, adorned with a smile of peace. He removed his heavy arm from her waist and carefully sat down on the bed to reach for the PDA in an armor compartment. Lieutenant Milles fulfilled his task perfectly, because all the data on Valerie Bondar was waiting only for analysis on Forkis' personal assistant. Anyway, the task wasn't particularly laborious, it was enough to download personal data from the central database, and the Kiritians had access to all of them. The Bondar family, the only one in Mirphak, was legally registered.

Forkis was particularly interested in one piece of information, which he found quickly, as he had expected. In order to conduct therapy with patients, Valerie obtained the license to use a blue beam technique, which consisted in uploading false memories into a brain. In real terms, it was supposed to help convalescents deal with the unpleasant trauma.

145

"But people always have to turn a bread knife into a murder weapon," he muttered under his breath. He felt the girl change position behind him.

He put down his PDA, pressed his chest against Vanessa's back, and wrapped his arm around her again, slightly annoyed with the hunger that had begun to nag at him after the foul dinner. It is a miracle that with his weight bending the bed in such a way, he managed not to wake the girl up.

When he felt a small, warm body close to him, his mood improved. Soon he was overwhelmed by sleep again.

\*\*\*

The first thing Vanessa saw when she opened her eyes, because she couldn't quite see in the darkness, was a tight, warm, soft space around her. She woke up probably because she lacked air. She saw a pale, reddish light muffled by the thick layer of what she was in.

She panicked.

She wiggled her arms vigorously and threw off the quilt. Through the windows, were streaming the morning blue rays of a high-mass main sequence star, Atla's sun.

Panting, Vanessa sat upright in bed. She woke up Forkis, who was lying next to her.

"I'm ... alive." She looked at him questioningly.

"What were you thinking? That I would kill you just by word of mouth, without investigating the matter? Especially since your words were not credible."

"But you could have done it anyway ... Without a reason. You are usurpers."

"But maybe I was on a whim to take care of your question?"

He kept his face serious, so she couldn't guess if he was mocking her in retaliation for the unspoken comparison of the Kiritians to the soulless monsters for whom the life of oderses meant as much as sand under their shoes. She didn't know that he was flattered by comparing Forkis and the military nation to the oppressors; such concepts meant strength and might. And Forkis loved power that caused fear.

"You aren't a murderer, Vanessa," he announced. "I checked your sister. Do you know that, as a therapist, you are authorized to use the blue beam technology?"

She looked at him expectantly, understanding little.

"Your memories are false," he explained. "Nothing you thought was true happened. At least in case of your problem, because Valerie's child really died."

Vanessa shook her head, tears appeared at the corners of her eyes. Kiritians were characterized by truthfulness and honesty, because with their abilities they didn't have to conspire with anything, so she knew Forkis wouldn't have made empty promises.

"Why did she do this to me? And how do you know about all this?!"

"It doesn't matter now. Forkis didn't want to bring this sensitive, though gullible and silly girl down even more with guesses that in this case equated to the facts. "As promised, I will take you to a safe place. I meant my corvette, of course." He winked at her. It amused, but also amazed him that Vanessa seemed disappointed. "You're a botanist, and we happen to be colonizing a new planet soon. The help of people like you would be useful. You probably won't have life here, even after the matter is cleared up. For everything to be as it was, you would have to erase the recollections of all Mirphak. What do you think?"

"So, I would have to join your nation."

"No. You would be a contracted temporary worker. We would then help you find a new apartment, unless you wished to go to your distant family."

Vanessa got up, grabbed a guest robe from the back of the chair, and put it on. She went out onto the balcony, watched the blue star feeding the planet with heat for a moment, then sat down on the bamboo chair. She rested her head on her elbows. She sat still for a while, thinking.

"Please take me from Atla," she said resignedly to Forkis, not turning her head toward him, but hearing that he had come to the balcony entrance.

"Someone will escort you to the corvette soon and take care of you. You will live in an orlop. I still have a matter to settle here. I'll see you when we take off, in about three days."

\*\*\*

Valerie Bondar barricaded herself in the house when she realized the Kiritian soldiers had come for her. Sergeant Ivester, however, had over a century of experience in pacifying oderses. When the order to leave the building was unsuccessful, after the minute he gave Valerie to react, he ordered the achijes to smash the door down and go inside.

After more minutes, terrified Valerie and her partner Rytar were dragged into the central square filled with onlookers keeping a safe distance. The bright red, gaudy outfit of the woman among the gray, white and brown of the surroundings was immediately noticeable. There were tensions between the achijes and the mercenary army that gathered on the street, but this psychological clash was won by the Kiritians with stronger toys and a terrible reputation in space. Mercenaries guarding Mirphak were powerless and anxious. They only reacted to show their commanders and citizens that they were doing anything. They could solve any problem in this neighborhood, but no one knew how to deal with the Kiritians.

"You are suspected," Ivester was saying to Valerie, kneeling on her knees under the arm of one of the achijes, "of the murder and incitement to murder our man named Vanessa Bondar. The penalty after proving guilt is death with immediate execution."

Surprised, Valerie raised her head lowered so far, her face was white as a protective layer covering the nearby puffball houses.

"My sister? I didn't know she was related to the Kiritians!"

"I have nothing to do with that woman or what she did!" Rytar was animated immediately when he realized in how disastrous situation they were. It means ... he was found. "We had an argument and I was just about to move out!"

"Of course." At the gesture of the sergeant, the achijes picked up the detainees from the ground. He turned to the mercenaries:

"We're taking these two to Forkis, who will judge them. Valerie is probably the real killer of the newborn."

The sergeant shouldn't have disclosed the reason for the arrest, but he was given a free hand and said it to ease the situation. Now, when the murder of the innocent child was brought into play, the Immortals would automatically turn from usurpers into heroes who wanted to intervene in the uneasy matter and repair the consequences of the tragic mistake of the local community.

The residents and mercenaries scowled at Valerie being led away. Had it not been for the Kiritians, there would have probably been a lynching. Ivester looked at all of this with contempt - it only took a few sentences for the hatred of the mob to be transferred onto someone else. It had always puzzled him why people believed so blindly in the words of prestigious people (whether they were lying or telling the truth) without inquiring into the merits. But he had to admit that in this case it was also about tweaking the authority of the Immortals. They were hated, too, but their words were respected and believed - and it should have remained so forever.

The oderses followed the achijes to the Diamond Geyser inn on the edge of the estate. Forkis, waiting inside, ordered his subordinates to disperse the adventurous locals to their homes. He also dismissed the host Ramaphosa and all staff in the building so that they had full control of it until they departed from Atla. All cellules[12] inside were deactivated.

Valerie and Rytar were led into the inn, then forced to drop to their knees in front of Forkis sitting relaxed in a chair.

"I'd like you to tell me what really happened a week ago," he got straight to the point. "You probably know what this is about. I, in turn, will know if you try to lie to me. For telling the truth, maybe I'll moderate the sentence somehow. First you, Rytar." He stared at the intimidated man with a bored but penetrating gaze.

"Why would the Kiritians be interested in what is happening in Mirphak?" Valerie asked. Forkis eyed her up. In this red, loose uniform, she immediately reminded him of the character from the fairy tale told a day earlier by Kiret. She resembled her sister, except that she was a head shorter than her. "Perfect," he thought, unconsciously sliding his tongue from inside over his upper lip.

"I think my sergeant made it clear what you were arrested for. Vanessa works for me now, and I protect my people."

Rytar was never brave, so he yielded right away.

---

[12] A mini camera or vision cell phone, usually a fingernail-sized plate, that transmits vision (often with audio) to the receiver. It has a territorial, global and even interplanetary scope.

"Val and I didn't plan the pregnancy, but somehow it turned out that way," he began to talk without embarrassment, ignoring the look of his partner full of hatred, amazement and fear at the same time. When screaming reedily, she ordered the man to shut up, one of the achijes at Forkis' nod, hit her painfully in the back with his gun. "We decided that the baby was to be born. However, when it happened in our home, we got scared by the whole situation and the responsibility. On top of that, we were a bit drunk. Despite her profession, Val wasn't normal, she had killed before, but I didn't find out about it until she killed her own child. With a knife. Though I begged her to put it up for adoption. Under the cover of night, she dumped the body, knowing the cycle of sentry drones and mercenary patrols. Soon after, Vanessa returned from work. With a blue beam transfer, Val uploaded detailed, false memories into her brain - that she was the murderer. The investigation was unnecessary because Vanessa confessed to everything. The crowd wanted to tear her apart, of course, but stopped chasing her when she fled into the wilderness on the skulak. He knew that Vanessa would either die of hunger there or of a lynch here. After these events, Val and I thought that the matter was settled."

Disgust rose on Forkis' face as he listened to Rytar report the murder of the innocent child as if it had been about a broken vase. But at least he told the truth about everything. Perhaps he believed in a 'supposed' conspiracy theory that the ruler of Kiritian was a telepath, or perhaps he was just scared, pressed to the floor.

"It is enough for me. Get him up." Forkis waved his hand carelessly.

"What are you gonna do with me?" Rytar looked at him with eyes widened with fear. His muscles were stiff, which made him move like first-generation androids when he was being put on his feet. "I didn't kill that child!"

"You make me sick, oders. You smell like cowardice. Besides, you are completely demoralized. I think sending you to the Aristillus penal colony will be proportionate to your guilt."

The man moved sharply.

"Please, just not there!" Located on Earth's Moon, Aristillus was one of the three worst penal colonies ever created by mankind, in terms of both rigor and survival of prisoners and the reasons for their exile. "I'd rather die right away than there after a week in terrible torment."

"There you go, at least in this regard, you turned out to be a man. Since you have told me the truth, I will acquiesce to your plea."

Rytar froze with a 'what, the hell?!' expression; the dignitary knew perfectly well that the words escaped from his mouth thoughtlessly.

Forkis looked at Milles and made a short, telling movement of his head. The light-skinned blue-eyed lieutenant with fair hair nodded, took an energy pistol from the hiding place in a cuisse and shot Rytar dead on the spot, ensuring him a quick and painless death.

Valerie groaned as the body dropped onto the synthetic wood planks next to her.

Forkis' question didn't reach her, but she saw that he was staring at her wearily ... and with an unsettling gleam of satisfaction in his eyes, as if he had already made nasty plans regarding her.

"Now you," he said, rubbing the fingers of his right hand together. "Do you confirm that everything your partner told is true? That you killed your own child, used the help knowledge to arrange the lynching, and agreed, in your callousness, to sacrifice your sister to clear yourself of guilt?"

She bit her lip and shook her head.

"No. Rytar just wanted to drop off his guilt! I swear it!"

"You swear ..." Forkis smiled warmly. He walked over to her, crouched down, and rested his elbows on her thighs. She could barely withstand his cold gaze tearing dignity.

"I will ask again and for the last time: is what Rytar said true?"

This time she couldn't look away, as if both heads had been held together by an invisible metal structure. Memories of the near past began to flow freely through her mind, but Valerie thought her secret was safe, since the ruler of the Kiritian, in his foolishness, had ordered to kill the only witness of that event. Not counting Vanessa, of course, to whom we don't know what happened, although rumors circulated that she had showed up at Mirphak - Forkis didn't give details after all. If there was any truth to it, it's possible that it was she who arranged it all. Though fraternizing with the Kiritians was completely unlike that intimidated, perpetually frightened bunny.

Valerie didn't realize Forkis saw exactly what she saw. Apart from the events with the child and Vanessa, other criminal acts unexpectedly came to her mind.

Astonished at the woman's psychopathic tendencies, Forkis raised his eyebrows a bit when he saw Miki's dad in her memory. Valerie had always been annoyed by his son who made noise outside, and whom his father had allowed to do whatever he had wanted, so one day she had decided to finally solve the problem. Taking advantage of the absence of another neighbor, with the help of Rytar's hacking skills, she had secretly opened a remote-controlled gate and let two aggressive dogs out, which the owner had always meticulously secured on his property. When the tragedy had occurred, she had pretended to be one of the compassionate, jittery onlookers.

"That's not true," she said.

The dignitary rose, looking down at the woman as if she had been a larva eating crops.

"You're lying through your teeth. Great lady therapist who took the Hippocratic Oath. You've just signed your own death warrant. And you could have been granted the grace of a quick, dignified death." He glanced at Rytar's body.

"Do you ..." The woman had heard that Forkis had been familiar with telepathy. As a man of science, she didn't believe it, assuming that he was simply a master of questioning and deduction, and deification was a figment of oderses on a low mental level. Fear combined with a lack of knowledge had always resulted in inventing all kinds of nonsense. But now, looking into those judgmental hazel eyes in which she seemed to see her end, she believed that something might be there.

"Yes, I saw everything in your mind," he replied to the unasked question. He grabbed her arm, 'helped' her get up from her knees, and pushed her lightly towards the guest table, where he had eaten that nasty, low-calorie dinner lately. "You're not crazy - you are an ordinary freak, probably inspired by your own patients. A woman who chases the wolf out of other people's minds and takes him along a roundabout way in her dwelling. Damn Red Riding Hood. So, I will not treat you as insane. But the distorted old fairy tale could be put on the right track. Lieutenant," Forkis turned to

157

Milles. "Everyone gets out of here and leave me alone. Find yourself other accommodation. Report to me only when you get the machines ready for take-off. Until then, no visits, only the communicator."

"Of course, sir," Milles replied after a few seconds of silence. He wouldn't have left his dignitary without achijes, if he had had the slightest doubt that something endangered him. But he knew from practice that the order meant being on standby and deploy guards in the building so as not to disturb Forkis' privacy.

Valerie stood tense and pressed the seat against the edge of the table as the Kiritians left, taking the body with them.

Forkis went to her, bent over and put his hands on the table top on the sides of the girl who leaned back to be as far away from him as possible.

"And what was that for?" He said, holding his face a few inches from Valerie's expression congealed by anxiety.

"What are you gonna do with me?"

"You heard - I'll kill you." He pushed himself off and walked away. He looked for a moment at two crossed chains separating the kitchen from the main hall.

"And you had to send your people away? Who am I that the Immortals' dignitary himself wants to shoot me dead personally?"

158

"Don't flatter yourself. You don't deserve such a death."

"So what are you gonna do?" She could barely control her voice.

She didn't like the gaze he was looking at her with again - the hungry sight of a predator eyeing a prey up. All the more a smile that appeared in the place of lips pressed together in a grimace of indifference, lasciviously licked with tongue.

She was overwhelmed by uncontrolled, animalistic fear, because she didn't even think what the senseless escape would have given her. Forkis caught her before she could barely take three steps towards the door. He grabbed Valerie with an arm around the waist and threw her on the table with a thud.

"Undress yourself or I'll undress you."

Panting nervously, she stared at him with dilated, as if drug-induced pupils.

"Oh no ... You're not gonna abuse me, are you, you pervert?!"

"I didn't even think about it. Besides, I despise what you, in turn, have thought about."

Forkis moved closer to Valerie, who was lying flat on the table, and, leaning on his elbows, began to play with her blonde hair, winding it around his finger.

"All right. Then I will tell you now what will inevitably happen. First you will shout something about 'breaking the laws of physics',

159

maybe you will decide on the version that it is 'physically impossible'. Then one of two scenarios will come true: either you will scream and call me friendly a psychopath, or you will find it very pleasant and you will calmly come to terms with your fate. It is possible that one state will pass into the other. And so, damn it, it is literally every time ..."

"But what do you want to do?!"

It surprised her as he dragged his warm tongue down her nose.

"You already have one hint, the other is: what is an intended use of the piece of furniture on which you are lying?"

She turned her head, her look fell on silverware on the next table, specifically a knife. She understood.

"Oh no ... Are you out of mind, man?! Kill me normally!"

She tried to jump up, but Forkis forced her with the pressure of his hand to return to the previous position. Being directed by her gaze, he walked away a little and grabbed the knife. Valerie didn't make the third fruitless attempt to escape after her previous failures.

"And how do you kill normally?" On his return, Forkis assumed a questioning look on his face, then grew serious. The woman watched, on the verge of losing her senses, the movement of his hand as he made a contour with a knife on the table around her torso, sometimes sliding it harmlessly over her body.

"Unfortunately, you must be aware that you are dying, unlike the innocent child you killed cruelly and thrown away like waste into a litter basket. And the boy for whom you arranged death by being torn? What did he do to you except making noise? You don't even know how much I hate it when someone hurts innocent people who can't even protect themselves."

"Like you now me, you hypocrite?" She hissed, terrified that he had found out somehow about the crime that after all, she had managed to hide from the whole city! Who the hell was that monster?!

He ignored her.

"And no sentry drone will come to alert the forester." He ran the knife over the skin of her neck, which was taut as a burdened rope, without cutting it.

"What drone? What are you raving about?" She said when she didn't get a reply: "Please ... Not like that. Shoot me, smash my head, strangle me, whatever! I don't want," Valerie's voice turned into a sob, "you to tear my body apart. I'm afraid of this terrible pain and bloodshed ..."

"You went a bit too far with the subjective imagination, sweetie. There will be no blood." The utensil fell on the bench with a clang as the Kiritian tossed it behind him.

The girl was too scared to analyze his words. She watched as he pulled a small, unmarked bottle from the armor compartment and gulped down all its contents.

"It's a bone-dissolving agent," Forkis explained, "it works for days. Although I could have asked medics long ago to permanently modify my digestive enzymes and strengthen my stomach tissues, I prefer this method more. It is such a symbolic prelude to the pleasant ritual that awaits me."

Now she was really scared. Her heart was pounding as if it had been going to kill her before that freaky space warlord got to it.

"Why are you doing this to me?" She shook her head. "Why can't you settle it normally?"

"I gave you a choice, it was enough to tell the truth. Just it. Then you could have chosen how you wanted to die."

She watched cobwebs twitch under the ceiling from the warmth of the fireplace, trying to ignore Forkis' actions as, sighing lustfully, he caressed the side of her face with his tongue. She was shivering. Damn Kiritians who could do whatever they wanted in foreign territory! Spread their sick justice there!

"Apparently you can," she said, "clean a memory to zero. Change personality. This, too, is like death."

"But you know," he stroked her cheek with his fingers this time, "that you have to deserve it? Evolution seems to have developed

162

human reason and morality for some purpose. What would be the point of humanity and law if people lived in downfall? Did they do evil with the thought that medicine would easily help them to forget about the crimes they committed, correct them, and there would be no one left to punish?" He raised his eyebrows eloquently.

"But you don't have to eat me... This is sick."

"We're running out of supplies, anyway, it's hard to eat, with the lack of anabiotic sleep, that nasty food from the ship. Unfortunately, in addition, I found myself in an enclave of herbivores. I'm higher than you in the food chain, so everything adds up."

"You're crazy! Besides, cannibalism harms human health! Pathogenic prions, variant of Creutzfeldt-Jakob disease. Unless you belong to the group of transhumanists or modificants."

"The same literally every time," Forkis sighed in mock melancholy, shaking his head. "And you are right: anthropophagy harms human health." Smiling, he tapped her nose with his finger. "The problem is, I'm not really human."

Seeing that Valerie was unlikely to cooperate with him, he took her in his arms and, resisting with the force of a fly, carried her to the bathroom. There he stripped and washed her - he liked having clean food.

When he returned to the room, he placed the naked and wet girl on the dining table with her belly down.

"How are you going to eat me?" She stuttered out. Through the cocoon of fear, yet broke slight curiosity.

"Whole and alive. Nothing will hurt."

"It's impossible! You can't even swallow a whole orange!"

"Transmutation washings, sweetie. A kinetic skull like a snake's." She grimaced in disgust as Forkis pressed a finger under his ear deep between the skull and jaw. "I used to be a huge Onkalot. An object, probably created by an alien species, many times more powerful and wiser than the human race, turned me into a human. However, I have kept the best of my previous incarnation. Well, almost. That change regarding the strong digestive juices in my new body wasn't good idea, but everything else works fine. I don't understand myself how it actually works. As if I had additional food space at my disposal that I cannot feel. Or maybe it is exactly like that, some refraction of space?"

"So, you are not human ... And you admit it to me so openly?"

"In such circumstances, sometimes I have a necessity to make similar confessions. Because, you know - when the victims are dead, of course, they will share my secret with the universe."

Shedding the top of the armor, the Kiritian grabbed Valerie by the legs and pulled her gently to the edge of the table. He felt the woman's muscles tense as he slipped her feet into his mouth.

Valerie struggled and squealed.

"Fuck you, you freak!"

Forkis emptied his mouth, pressed the girl against the table with his forearm.

"A box of hypocrites," he said, amused. "Don't thrash like that, because you're just turning me on," he added sharply. "Then it will really hurt, if you force me to use strength."

"This loony madness is not about sick quenching of hunger or bringing justice to the city that you don't care about ... Onkalot."

He brought his face to her shoulder, rested his chin against it and whispered in the girl's ear:

"Bravo, miss psychologist. You know the history of colonization, right? I'm carrying a large empty container labeled 'revenge'. It will be filled with many sacrifices, just like the bellies of the ever-hungry Jun Kame gods who want hearts and blood. And I still accept an old tribal rule, although it doesn't apply among people, that women give birth to evil warriors. It doesn't mean, however, that I don't feel sorry for Vanessa, and the food is good here."

The brief reflection entered his head like with the blue beam transfer. For a moment he mentally stared at himself - the being he had become. He didn't even know what species he really belonged to. Over the decades, a hangman's syndrome had gotten worse in him, a vicious circle was functioning. Because of the group of Onkalots and the people who had hurt him and his loved ones, he basted all the kind scattered around the cosmos, wanting to cleanse it of the evil, of which Forkis had a peculiar definition. He did exactly the same thing that once had scared him.

Lolmet Kejnay, however, was right on a couple of points - for example, he loved what he was going to do with Valerie. The more the victim was scared and begged for mercy, the more it motivated him to act.

Having gotten roused from his meditations that might have spoiled the impending pleasure, he returned to the activity he had interrupted. The girl tried to break free, but Forkis effectively overpowered her with his left hand, helping himself with the meal with the other.

Valerie had never felt so panicked in her life, but as her squeezed legs sank deeper into the ex-Onkalot's digestive tract, she struggled less. Eventually she gave up. There was indeed something pleasant, even erotic, about this monstrous act, as her body was gradually engulfed in shrinking softness, soothing warmth, and a moist stickiness. Forkis' slowly moving tongue delightfully tickled the successive sections of her body. She succumbed to that strange ecstasy that only one man in space could offer her - or rather, a nonhuman.

***

Forkis, with his hand on the stomach, sat at the table where his victim had been lying less than an hour earlier. He felt an inner cat, which was still lurking somewhere deep in his mind, purring contentedly, well-fed. After such an amount of biomass and sixty thousand calories, the Kiritian would now fast for about two Terrenic weeks, and, as always in such cases, would avoid meals with the achijes, so as not to arouse suspicion. The most convenient thing for him was to lock himself in one of his apartments for this time and work remotely.

"Damn you, Kejnay," he said through clenched teeth. Like his victims, Forkis said certain things every time.

He got up, much heavier and thicker, to go to the upstairs room for a long, energy-consuming sleep.

***

167

He woke up before noon. After washing himself, he went downstairs to contemplate in an empty, spacious and quiet room. He lit a fire on logs thrown into the hearth. After telling Kiret that he was fine, he listened to his reports.

At one point he felt that he was going to back, as he himself called this physiological reflex. Sometimes it happened to him after a meal too coarse and large for a human body.

"Oh no..."

He fell to the ground on all fours, as he had once done in Quehnay after devouring Jenny, and bowed his head hard. After a few minutes of struggling with his own body, amid pursy gasping and muscle spasms, he released a partly digested fragment of what was left of Valerie. Being the solid bone, she rolled into the fireplace. Forkis watched as the fire physically added to the previous chemical process, blackening the molten bone. He got up, rinsed his mouth with a glass of bar water, poured the rest on the prize, then picked it up from the floor. He examined it for a moment, holding it in his right hand.

"To take it or not to take it - that is the question."

Ultimately, he decided to leave the bone in a visible place. The staff of the restaurant deserved moments of horror for serving terrible food.

***

Although all the cellulas were deactivated in the inn, monitoring was constantly active around the building, covering every cubic meter of the area. The property owner asked the mercenaries to monitor the area with drones. After achijes left, only the dignitary and Valerie remained there. Half an hour later, the girl began to alternately yell frantically, curse and sob, albeit for a short time.

In a nearby beer garden, frightened Ramaphosa didn't even want to imagine what was happening in his property right now. Killing Valerie was a certainty. And the Kiritians were famous for inflicting the worst kinds of death in all mankind. The Mirphan was helpless. Because what could he do? Beg mercenary commanders to react? They already shat their pants over the presence of the Immortals. Ask for help from the cradle, that is the Earth in the Old Zone, from where humanity had scattered across space? The earthly law didn't apply on other planets, moons or stations - the colonies-maintained autonomy. Anyway, the Earth wouldn't have helped militarily or politically, because the Kiritians had smashed the global government and its Army of the New Order before they had set off to sow terror in outer space. Get other planets to cooperate? Nobody wanted to mess with the Immortals, and the central power on Atla didn't exist yet, notabene, it would probably have proved powerless. Only the rebels remained, as a stable and still real counterbalance to the usurpers, but when a battle broke out between them, the parties left behind not two outside corpses, but two thousand. So, the best way was to be quiet, keep your head down and enforce the same laws as the Kiritians, then there was a chance they would leave a delinquent alone. Ramaphosa believed that someday there would be a stronger enemy that would annihilate the Immortals. For no power ruled forever.

Valerie's screams only became a memory; by the end of the day nothing happened. Nobody left or entered the inn; it looked empty from the outside. The eyes of all the inhabitants of Mirphak were focused on it, as if a reality show with the lord of usurpers had been taking place inside.

The second day was the same.

Oddly enough, the third also.

On the fourth, dressed in the light biometal armor, Forkis finally stepped outside to have it out with the achijes. They were due to leave the planet within an hour, having repaired their machines.

When a lowest-ranking Kiritian informed Ramaphosa that he could resume work, the man temporarily living with friends, with a beating heart, set off towards his property. There was a dense crowd around the Diamond Geyser, eager for news and gossip.

"What about Valerie Bondar?" The landlord asked anxiously Forkis, as they both entered and sat to the right of the door, away from the bar obscured by columns.

"Please don't worry. It's clean everywhere, there are hardly any traces." Forkis smiled worryingly at him.

"Did she ..."

"Yes, I got it done."

"And what happened to ... the body?"

Forkis picked up the white, empty vial and waved it.

"It dissolves hard tissue. The body was broken into atoms."

For a moment Ramaphosa was sure that he would lose his balance despite sitting in the chair and would fall over with it. The gruesome murder at his inn involving some acid! After all, customers wouldn't want to come there now! Despite finding the real multiple murderers of several Mirphak citizens, he felt sorry for the woman.

"By the way," Forkis handed him Valerie's red uniform, "the diversification would be useful for you because customers bring their own food." He smiled like a wolf, touching a corner of his lips with his tongue.

When he left, the landlord let the staff inside and instructed them to carefully inspect the property. He himself long checked the bathroom on the second floor, located next to the room occupied by Forkis, for any traces of the dissolved corpse under the shower bath. Ramaphosa, who felt sick as he mechanically tried to recreate in his mind the next stages of the bizarre execution, was sure the dignitary had killed Valerie there and had treated the body with acid. He hoped he hadn't done it in the reverse order!

Alarmed by Viria's scream, he ran to the first floor, which began to be checked after both floors were inspected.

Two stunned workers stood beside the chained entrance to the kitchen, staring at something. Viria was sitting at the far table, with her back to her friends, and her hand at her mouth, as if now it had been she who was about to vomit. The other workers were pale and scared, and avoided looking at the certain area of the floor.

Ramaphosa's eyes nearly popped out of their sockets when he saw the human skull on the ground, slightly melted with acid and its right eye socket blackened with fire.

He had made a mistake in his judgment that his business would go haywire.

After the departure of Kiritian, the Diamond Geiser began to host crowds, and in particular, Valerie Bondar's skull, conspicuously resting on a square plank attached to the wall, enjoyed special favors. Drunken customers placed two candles there, pentagrams were painted next to them. The landlord was surprised himself that he had agreed to this stupid idea to leave the skull in the building. However, the would-be bogy became kind of a local relic, and Valerie herself was considered a bizarre hybrid: on the one hand, a criminal aspiring to urban legends, and on the other, a martyr of the Immortals.

Looking at the freely feasting clientele, the man wondered who was a bigger monster - inhuman Kiritians or Mirphaks having fun at the scene of the tragedy, where its remnant observed them through her empty eye sockets.

# Crime and Punishment

## The Terrenic Year 2740

An air battle in the atmosphere of the planet KOI-4878.01 ended with a victory for the Kiritians. Their technology at the beginning of the century began to prevail over the rebellious one. The opposition gained its own from thefts, robberies and illegal transactions, rarely inventing anything itself. The Kiritians, on the other hand, had the genius named Maximus Figam, as well as the entire excellent research team, and plenty of achievements allowing to fund research and manufacture equipment. The rebels attacked them only out of despair, anger and helplessness, like a wounded fox chased by a hunter to a steep, rocky wall. Their losses were increasing, but they didn't give up, their aggression was inversely proportional to the firepower. Forkis, as a glorifier of courage, in a way respected them for their fearlessness and bravado.

He was standing on a hill near the ocean, next to his flag corvette, and he was watching the losses visible to the naked eye within several kilometers of land. There were, on average, nine rebel machines for one Kiritian machine shot down. The entire area was marked by columns of smoke from fires growing towards the sky like mighty collectors from an urbanized Morascrik.

The planet KOI-4878.01 orbiting in the Pisces Universe didn't have to be terraformed in terms of the atmosphere. Located one thousand and seventy light years from Earth, the globe had a mass factor of 0.99 of its mass, although a slightly larger radius - 1.04. The air was fit for direct breathing by humans, therefore Forkis allowed his achijes to walk on land without breathing apparatus. The planet was mainly occupied by an ocean full of oxygen-producing microorganisms, also large deposits of heavy elements and minerals were discovered on it and it was considered metallic. The crown jewel turned out to be painite deposits - it was a reason of the battle. Although billions of rocky planets circulated in the Milky Way, only on a small fraction of them have been found valuable raw materials in a usable form. The exploitation was mostly hampered by unfavorable space conditions, of which taming was possible, but was very time-consuming and costly. So it was more profitable to fight battles for metals and minerals on easily explorable globes, which, like KOI-4878.01, could be called the second Earth.

"Another source of painite will smash our enemies' market even more," Forkis thought as he stared at the yellow dwarf looking pale through the cloud layer. He hoped that soon the Kiritians would introduce their own currency in the colonies, and that they would proclaim an empire.

Looking thoughtfully at his achijes, he analyzed what he had created and how far he had come. He could no longer deny that after one hundred and seventy years of existence, the Kiritians had become a great family for him, he treated them like the Chiq'aq tribe. He believed that his approach might have been due to his having succeeded in creating the military nation based on Onkalotian customs. The attachment also did its job. Now he couldn't get rid of the achijes, as he had intended when Dr. Figam had created the first Immortals on Earth. However, he still felt an aversion to oderses. He enjoyed - like Jun Kame in relation to other tribes - bullying them, although his motives, unlike cannibals', were always justified. It was that particle from the other half of his blood, taken from the city of Chiq'aq.

"I wonder where this Yamaro is." The words of a nearby sergeant, talking to his colleagues, roused him from his meditations. "He should have contacted us long ago. I have a case for him."

"Maybe the guy wants to rest a bit and tune out?" The neighbor who was eating the apple replied. "After all, he's on vacation."

"Do you think the rebels did something to him?" Interjected the third. "I told him it was a stupid idea to fly alone in the current situation, since they don't like us everywhere."

"In the Capricorn Universe they like us," said the sergeant.

"Rather do business with us," laughed the one with the apple. He tossed the core away.

Forkis stopped listening to the conversation when he was informed via communicator that a full battle report had been prepared. He followed the pier into the open airlock and went down the corridor to the corvette's bridge. For the next minutes he listened to his officers. Lieutenant Milles was asked at one point to come to the instrument console[13].

---

[13] As Kiritians are immortal, military ranks are usually fixed, and everyone accepts their role. Promotion is rare, at least in times of nation-

177

"Excuse me for a minute, sir," he turned to Forkis. "Connection with Calcaris. Certainly, from my wife." He smiled.

As he listened to the rest of the report, Forkis glanced at Milles to immediately focus his full attention on him. The officers' words ceased to reach him, anyway they were slowly finishing. The dignitary ensconced in the commander's seat, the lieutenant, in turn, sat in front of the communications station, as if petrified. The people in the cockpit were busy working or talking to each other, and apart from Forkis, no one was interested in Milles getting up stiffly from his seat, turning mechanically and walking towards the bulkhead, as if he had been hit with a bullet in the breastbone and been about to fall on his face. He achieved kind of a mental void and the dignitary couldn't see his thoughts, but it wasn't necessary to use telepathy to understand that something very bad had happened.

He followed the officer into the corvette. Milles locked himself in his soundproof cabin, but Forkis had access to all rooms at any time of the board day, all he had to do was put his hand to the scanner.

The sight surprised him greatly. He had never seen naturally calm and composed Milles in such a state. The lieutenant sat

---

building. These rules don't apply during conflicts and wars, when it comes to the death of achijes.

huddled in the corner, with fists pressed to his eyebrows, sobbing like a little boy. Spasms shook his body.

"What's wrong, Lieutenant?" Forkis sat down on his bed.

Milles answered only after a minute:

"Lilly ... She's dead. She was pregnant ..."

"Are you sure? This is not a mistake?"

He shook his head.

"I'm sorry," Forkis said.

Only now was he able to receive the images which formed in Milles' mind with full clarity. These were scenes from his life which he had enjoyed with his girlfriend. Then he envisioned her hanging in the house on Calcaris he had bought for her barely a Terrenic month earlier. Lilly was an oders. Forkis decreed that the Immortals must have remained sterile, so that there was a biological meaning in this, but sometimes he gave the couple permission to beget an offspring in the traditional way. The Kiritian then received an injection restoring his temporary reproductive capacity for the duration of a successful intercourse. Milles was one of such people.

"Excuse me. I have to fly there." He got up and staggered. Forkis forced him to sit down in a chair at the table.

"Alone? Are you crazy, Milles? In your condition, and scarcely after we banished the rebels into space? I will fly there with you."

The lieutenant turned his astonished, tearful face to him.

"But sir! Who am I that you want to handle my private case?"

How often Forkis had heard this from the oderses and the Kiritians themselves.

"My achij, Milles." He started pacing the small room. "You are all very important to me."

The shy, taciturn by nature lieutenant felt a hint of warmth in his heart in the midst of icy despair. This was what their dignitary was like - he liked to get involved even in mundane matters and wasn't afraid or ashamed of anything. And when he did something, he turned out to be deadly effective, in the literal sense. Milles had never had the opportunity to find out about it for himself.

"Thank you ... although this situation is terribly embarrassing for me."

Forkis didn't want to stand at him and look down on him. They were now not a subordinate and a commander, but a person nervously broken and other providing help. So he took the other chair across from him, resting his arms on his thighs and lacing his fingers.

"Would you like to use psychological help? Get something calming, like alhedrimucosine? You know, medics can even selectively erase your memory."

"Thank you, sir, but no. I want to know and remember everything," Milles ground out, staring intently at the point on the dhurnsteel floor.

"Alright. The situation on KOI is stable, and the recently appointed Major Velkee Vandringen will take care of the painite deposits. I'll take an entire squadron, even a few battalions, and fly to Calcaris. Let them shit out of fear there."

Though he knew nothing of the circumstances, something for Forkis didn't add up in this suicide. Lasting Kiritian relationships with oderses were not very common, and he companied Lilly quite well. The woman had always been cheerful, loved life, never worried about anything. She had wanted to have a baby with Milles and suddenly she had been to kill herself when she had found out about the desired pregnancy?

It took over two Terrenic weeks to travel to the planet at hyperspace jumps.

Calcaris was one of the fourteen globes in the triple yellow dwarf system and was fully terraformed. It was inhabited by over two hundred million people, located in various, distant agglomerations, from large cities to villages. It was in one of them, picturesque, small and peaceful, that Lilly wanted to live after she moved away from her family. Milles was supposed to visit her between missions. When the girl settled there, everything seemed to be perfect, from the beautiful mountain nature to the mild climate and nice, hardworking inhabitants.

"We're far beyond the Roche border, so also the range of Calcaris scanners, turn on masking" said Forkis, sitting in his commander's armchair. He ordered to take the squadron of fighters, a cruiser, two battleships, two transporters and his corvette on the expedition.

"Will we be hiding, sir?" One of the officers turned to him, surprised.

"I just don't want the natives of the fourth part of the globe to get in our way. For now, we will land near the village of Dharsa Pass, unnoticed."

"The villagers will send a message from their tower for territorial defense."

"So, block their signals. They are to be completely cut off. Oh, one more thing. In the troposphere, launch an orb and target the Lilly Tedlock protein sequence with the nucloindector. She is legally registered in the central database."

"Yes, sir."

The squadron was no longer visible both by scanning and visually.

Kiret gave Forkis an eloquent look, but for the time being they had no chance to talk privately, pinned to armchairs, and in the room where several people were close together.

They broke through all layers of the atmosphere without any problems. A few kilometers above the surface, the squadron lost its speed. The released, masked orb went to the village of Dharsa Pass and began scanning, quickly located the hanged girl's body. Contrary to what Milles imagined after receiving information from the mayor Dönges, Lilly didn't commit suicide in her home, but on a tree far away from the Dharsa Pass. Forkis didn't want to inform now the lieutenant flying in the battleship about it, so that he wouldn't have another nervous breakdown.

Ships and warships emerged from their camouflage just before landing on the plain near the village, astonishing all terrified inhabitants. The Kiritians were lucky to find a lot of flat surface, for Dharsa Pass was located in a valley several kilometers long between two mountains. The view was truly fabulous: pink in the sky from the rising sun, a mass of greenery and flowers, arable fields on a soil brought in by transporters, blue mountains, a ribbon of a wide stream disappearing only beyond the horizon. It was hard to believe that such a tragedy could have happened there.

Once the Immortals had left the machines, Forkis signaled Kiret with a look to go to the side.

"We came here to scare villagers with toys like a lion with the claws a mouse or to explain the matter of suicide?" Necron asked offensively as they were both under the corvette's bow, out of earshot. "Why all this masquerade?"

Forkis looked at him severely.

"I know what I'm doing."

"The Calcaris Army will be here anyway, sooner or later."

The dignitary smiled unpleasantly.

"Well, what are they going to do to us? Even if only one of our fighter planes had flown onto Calcaris, they would be afraid to touch it. At most, they would send out procedural threats."

Kiret narrowed his eyes.

"You suspect something, don't you?"

"Come on, let's investigate the site of the so-called suicide." Forkis moved towards the rocks behind which, in an enclave of fertile soil, grew an unfortunate, mighty oak. The villagers closely watched the newcomers from afar, afraid to approach them.

The Kiritians found a depressing sight. The body hanging on a thick branch, exposed to the summer conditions and the stuffiness of the pass, was in a highly advanced state of decay. Lilly wore a celadon knee-length gown, still in a very good condition. An overturned stool was leaning against the tree trunk. As if to intensify the traumatic atmosphere, clouds as gray as rocky surroundings were starting to accumulate in the sky; a thunder boomed, echoing through the mountains. The stuffiness before the upcoming downpour was taking its toll, so the Kiritian armor automatically changed the endogenous conditions to such convenient for the wearers.

"They didn't even bother to take her off and bury," one of the achijes commented in disbelief.

"It's like they knew we're going to want to see Lilly," the other added, scanning the corpse and the surroundings with his equipment. After a while, he had the complete data. He turned to Forkis: "Everything points to suicide, sir. There are no signs of a struggle on the body, and no dangerous substances in it. Apart from the person who came to see the deceased, recent human biological traces were only beyond a radius of several meters. Probably the locals had come to watch, but someone had forbidden them to come closer.

With a serious expression, Forkis listened to the report, also to the monotonous creaking of branches, staring at the corpse swaying in the light wind.

185

"I found this in her dress pocket." The achij handed him a letter of synthetic paper.

"Dear Robert," the dignitary began to read in Anglo-American, pacing slowly back and forth. "I can't do that anymore. I didn't know how to tell you that I didn't want to be with you anymore, especially after you bought me such a beautiful house. My feeling for you was a momentary affect and faded long ago, only attachment is left. For the last few meetings, I only simulated that I was glad to see you. I was afraid. I've thought through everything - I don't want to be with you as a Kiritian. You are monsters, I was temporarily fascinated by your power and that of your military nation. I know you won't forgive me because you never do it. I don't want this baby either. There is only one way for me to let go of the anger you would probably give me. I'm sorry. Good luck on the further way of immortal life. I'm sorry that I hurt you. Your Lilly."

Forkis heard footsteps behind him, it was Milles. The lieutenant was speechless, shocked, pale and tense, staring at the corpse dangling on the branch like a nightmarish joke. His jaw began to twitch, he turned his head to the side, squeezed his eyes shut, and began to sob silently, flinching in a paroxysm of pain.

"Didn't I tell you, Milles, to wait on the battleship?" Forkis admonished him, but gently. He addressed the two achijes: "Take care of the lieutenant, get him aboard. Captain Biffter, take a dozen men and come with me to the village."

"Of course, sir," confirmed Kiret.

"And you three take down the poor woman."

The free march of the achijes, armed with the most modern weapons, wearing mid-class black ink-colored biometal armor with indigo elements, aroused widespread concern. Probably no one worked in the field anymore, the locals sat on the benches next to their houses, stood like monuments next to the streets or looked out the windows. Only a few children jumped up or fooled around some distance from the team, following it. The newcomers didn't cause fear also in dogs vigorously wagging their tails and barking, but none of them came closer than three steps. From what Forkis learned from the central network, Dharsa Pass numbered over 150 farmers, including children. This would add up because around the main square and a few streets there were several dozen chaotically arranged houses and a couple of public buildings, including the office of the village head named Dönges. It was a traditionalist village with a classic appearance unchanged for centuries, only a modern communication tower on the side, agricultural machinery and vehicles visually collided with the rest of the buildings.

Forkis wasn't surprised that the head Dönges didn't deign to meet him, but holed up in his office like a rat in a haystack. It is even possible that he sneaked away from Dharsa Pass.

He walked over to one of the houses, where a man was sitting on a porch chair and a boy was playing in the garden.

"Good morning," Forkis began, stopping at the fence. He noticed that the local tensed probably all his muscles. He got up and, with the difficulty resulting from fear, approached the fence. "We're here about Lilly Tedlock. We saw that she had committed suicide. How had it come about? Why didn't you take care of the body?"

Forkis read from his thoughts that the surprised man had expected an unproblematic visit of Milles himself, and not the armed team of Immortals, in addition the war machines settled near the village. He moved his mouth like a fool for a moment before he spoke even theatrically:

"Oh, gentlemen Kiritians, a terrible misfortune! She was such a good girl! Beautiful, calm, hardworking. Workers found her when they were going to crack stones for a road repair. She left a farewell letter."

"Yes." Forkis stared at him with a cold, piercing gaze, under which a man shrank like an omega wolf in front of an alpha. The boy ceased prancing, stopped a few meters beside the fence and began to stare at the stern newcomers with shameful curiosity. "There was a letter, but in the pocket of her dress. How do you know about it?"

The villager hesitated briefly, his eyes were wandering in different directions at the time, before he finally focused them on the Kiritian.

"One of the people searched the pockets, because in similar situations messages are sometimes left there. And indeed, there was a letter. After reading, it was put back in its place."

"Mhm." Forkis nodded. "What about the body? Why was it left on the branch?"

"It was certain that someone from the Kiritians would come, I mean from you. Though everyone objected to it - in the sense of leaving the corpse without burial, not your visit - Mr. Dönges told me not to touch anything so that you could inspect it. So that it didn't look like we're hiding something."

"I see." Forkis glanced indifferently at the child, curious if he would learn anything from the clear mind, but apart from admiring the splendor and the alien armor, the little boy thought of nothing else.

He had also used his psionic skill earlier on the local he had questioned, so he already knew everything. Telepathy was a really powerful tool conducive to achieving absolute power - no oders without brain dysfunction had secrets from Forkis. Any investigation could take a minute instead of weeks or months, especially since hardly anyone defended themselves against his skill, having classified that fact as rumors or conspiracy theories. Those who thought that something was up, tried not to mention too much in front of Forkis, but time was always against them - when the dignitary had an infinite amount of it. The peasant presented the classic dissonance characteristic of a liar: he imagined one and spoke the other. He was so stressed by the presence of the Kiritian dignitary himself in the tiny, forgotten Dharsa Pass that he confused the 'official' version of the event that the mayor of Dönges had told the residents to speak.

With that, Forkis could end Lilly Tedlock's case. In an investigation conducted using telepathy, one witness was enough to establish the correct course of the event, but the dignitary was curious about the version of the rest of the residents.

When he arrived with the Kiritians on the square with a well, surrounded by cottages, his attention was drawn to a so-called Jacob's pillar. There was a common practice among peasants from space colonies that a pillar was placed in the center of a village, and on it, was placed an object related to the region or the emotions of the inhabitants. The term comes from the name of one of the colonists who, in a newly established settlement, hung on a pole a fragment of a colonial ship's armor, damaged during landing. Apparently, life in this village was going exemplarily. The idea was liked, and on other planets people began to practice similarly, some believed that the totem brought good luck, others treated it only as a curiosity and variety in everyday life. Various things were hung, from the skull of a dangerous animal killed with a knife alone, through planetesimal that pierced someone's roof but didn't hit the tenants, to a valuable ruby or caldron found in the area, containing unused seeds from the first sowing. A pole never stood empty, because it was supposed to bring bad luck, but the one that rose in front of Forkis was just like that. The man noticed deep footprints in the sand, the distance between them was larger and larger - someone had jumped down and then started running. He accosted an old woman sitting by the well, looking at the Immortals with her oblique, stink eye. She said more or less the same as the man in front of the house, but Forkis was amused by her mental insults directed at the newcomers.

"Nice totem," he said at the end, with arms akimbo and looking up. "But there is no prize."

"There isn't any, they took it."

Forkis was surprised by what he saw in her mind when he made reference to the St. Jacobs' pole. He needed a few calms, deep breaths to prevent anger from blooming prematurely on his face.

As he left the square, the achij security guards followed him. Walking through the village and looking for his next 'victim', he kept a bitter smile on his face, receiving from everywhere mental messages of persons unaware that each word only made their situation worse:

"They know...

Kiritian scums!

Oh shit, so we are screwed!

I hope it won't occur to them to search in the fields...

We're dead!

And I told them to leave the girl alone.

Did they have to come here?

The tower doesn't work, they probably damaged it.

Goddamn bastards!

Go into the ground!

And what are you staring at, forbidden mug?!"

The third conversation, this time with a peasant cracking stones with a crusher, didn't bring anything new. He also eagerly said one thing and thought the other, mentally supported by his colleagues who nodded, listening to his account. Forkis obtained at least a full psychological cross-section of the inhabitants of the Dharsa Pass. He had dealt with similar conservative communities many times - that's why he worked out ways to handle them.

His attention was caught by a golden-haired girl dangling a stick in a puddle by a clay road leading to the fields. When he stopped beside her, telling the achijes to wait in the distance, she gave him a fleeting, dispassionate glance and resumed her play.

Forkis crouched down, clasped his hands between his knees. He smiled as the little girl thought: "Let that big mister go away!"

"Hi," he said gently. "It's so hot here. Will you get me something to drink?"

Without looking at him, the girl got up, ran home behind her back, and a minute later returned with a glass of water.

"Thank you." Forkis took the dish from her and took a sip, knowing from her head that she hadn't spit into the drink or had taken it from the toilet. This time the girl bravely looked him in the eye, although her face didn't express anything. "The most important thing in life is that you have someone to bring you a glass of water." Making another friendly smile, he brushed off the last drops and handed the item back to her. "What's your name?"

"Reya." She crouched down and started playing in the puddle again, this time placing a glass next to it and loading the mud inside with the stick.

"I see you're alone here. Are you parents at work?"

"I don't have parents. I'm with my aunt."

"Where is she?" Reya spun around, raised her arm and pointed with a finger at the village head's building, obscured by houses.

193

"Does she work there?" Forkis asked.

She nodded several times. He learned from her visualization that Reya and her caretaker, like Lilly, were not local. Her aunt lived in the other hemisphere of Calcaris, in a larger city, and for some financial embezzlement she was sent to Dharsa Pass to pay the penalty there. Naturally, the girl didn't present the events in a mature and clear manner, Forkis himself came to such conclusions.

"Good girl. You know what, maybe you can help me. Have you heard about Lilly?"

The little one nodded, she had already loaded a third of the glass with mud. Now she thought about nothing at all, she answered questions mechanically. The man thought that if she kept these qualities for a long time, she would be a great achij in the future. He was amazed at the fact that, unlike adults, children's minds were calm, empty, and silent, with no chaotic thoughts flitting through them like fragments of a broken asteroid through space.

"Reya, please look at me." She looked up at him from the swamp. Forkis got rid of his warm smile and asked seriously, "You know what happened here?"

She nodded.

"Would you like to talk about it?" She denied it.

"I'm afraid of people from the countryside," he received.

Not wanting to tell her what he had picked up telepathically and to scare the child with his knowledge, he opted for the classic further steps.

"With me, you don't have to be afraid of absolutely anything," he said temptingly and convincingly. "There is no man in the universe who can defeat me, and those with whom I relate are safe. Come on, show me what you're afraid to tell me about."

His posture, armament and authority, plus the guarantee of safety made Reya quickly take to him, in addition she trusted him. When he got up, she gave him her hand and began to drag Forkis towards a pepper field, where the residents were again trying to do their routine tasks.

People working at plants with equipment or physically straightened up like grazing antelopes in the savannah that noticed a jaguar. Some of them, like anxious animals, began to slink away, the rest stood and watched with concern the Kiritian walking among the bushes of yellow pepper. They looked at each other meaningfully. Forkis didn't give his achijes order, so they waited in an extended line next to the field and intrigued, watched their dignitary.

Reya stopped, indicated with her finger a point on a rise above which, in the clearance of thick clouds, two of the planet's five very tiny moons flashed pink and red. Forkis walked briskly in that direction, on the way he found among the bushes a helmet from an armor of Yamar - a civilian Kiritian worker who had recently gone missing, returning from rest. In contrast to the achij combat armor, where it was necessary to quickly put on or remove the strobilus headgear, civilians often wore traditional helmets. The Kiritian picked it up, cleansed it of the earth with his glove. He didn't need Reya's company any more to know in detail what had happened in Dharsa Pass - the frightened people around unconsciously added complementary elements to Forkis' puzzle.

On the hill, he found a fragment of recently disturbed ground. With the nucloindector, which was a part of the scanner of multifunctional bracer, he examined tens of cubic meters under the soil - and discovered the macabre contents. It turned out that it wasn't the only such surprise in the area.

When he turned towards the village, there was no one left in the field except Reya, staring at him, standing where he had left her. Blueness flashed in the sky, and a thunderbolt sounded almost right after over the fields. Forkis didn't pay attention to the fact that at one point he picked a pepper from a bush, and ate it almost entirely. Its spicy taste made him feel thirsty again.

"Kiret." After he finished munching, he didn't bother to speak formally via the communicator. He walked back in a sweeping step. "We're pacifying this hole. Take all the children to the transporter, by force if they resist. Gather the adults under arms in the square. Leave alone only the village head's building and the house where the girl was playing nearby.

Biffter responded grimly only after a while:

"Yes, sir." He didn't ask questions, knowing Forkis had found a good enough reason to give such a monstrous order.

"Go home," he growled to Reya as he passed by. He didn't need to repeat it. Streaming her skirt, she overtook Forkis and hurried to her aunt's hut, where she slammed the door shut.

Kiret called for more help from the landing site, Lieutenant Milles also agreed to take part in the pacification.

The moment Forkis opened the door to Dönges' three-story headquarters, he could hear screams, pleas, crying, scuffling sounds, even gunshots. A fire broke out as well - probably some achij thoughtlessly used a flamethrower, which, however, didn't matter anyway - from which the houses located close to each other managed to take fire. "At least the fire won't break in here," he thought as he stared at the stone walls of the building.

In the hall, he saw a woman with the stereotypical appearance of a clerk: obese, middle-aged, with curly short hair and glasses that normally poor oderses wore, having little chance of repairing their eyesight or replacing their eyeballs.

197

"I want to see the bastard village head," Forkis greeted, standing by her desk.

The woman glanced at him fearlessly, just like her niece had before. And like the girl's, her mind also wasn't blemished by thoughts about the secret tragedies of Dharsa Pass. Forkis already knew that both of them had nothing to do with these events, the aunt who hadn't known what to do with Reya had been sent here forcibly and stuck in the armpit of the planet.

"Do you have the appointment?" If it was supposed to be a joke of the former city clerk, she did it perfectly. A hint of a smile appeared on the Kiritian's lips. She immediately understood the gesture when Forkis' hand touched the hiding place in the cuisse with a X17A4 pistol using self-renewing light ammunition. She nodded gravely toward the two-way door on his right.

The man leaned over the top.

"Please leave the village as soon as possible and take Reya from here. It will be very unpleasant here soon."

Locked within the walls of the office, the woman didn't know exactly what was going on outside, she read everything in Forkis' menacingly narrowed eyes and got really scared. She was perfectly aware of the Kiritian methods of dealing with colonists who had upset them with something. Forkis was famous for murdering and spreading panic in space, the woman knew that, for some reason unknown to her, she was granted the enormous honor of receiving the warning. She didn't multiply the difficulties.

"We don't have any vehicle to fly or drive from here. We were brought here by a transporter, and in it I was to return after two years, when my penalty of restricted liberty passed."

"You were wrongly accused." She lifted her incredulous, deep blue eyes to look at Forkis. Her demonstrative, practiced calm of the clerk collapsed. "Despite this, you accepted your punishment with humility, even came to the conclusion that staying in the remote province, in the small town, would help you and your niece to rest from the hustle and bustle of the city.

"How do you know that?"

"I have my ways. Forkis connected with his subordinate. "Captain Biffter, take to the transporter also Reya and ..."

"Charlotte Kris," the clerk helped.

"Charlotte Kris, her aunt. They both have my immunity. The woman will leave the office right away."

A wooden, ornate door to Mayor Forkis' office was open; when he pushed it with his hand, it opened slightly, creaking. Behind the desk sat a thin, middle-aged man of a kind who wasn't tainted by manual labor, although formally belonged to such a community. Instead, he preferred to engage in agitation and indoctrination, in which he was quite effective, because he was able to persuade most of the villages to commit specific acts and then lie. He turned pale and got moody at the sight of the mighty Immortal, recognizing him as the leader of the Kiritian rabble. However, he panicked the most at the sight of the helmet that the newcomer was holding with his left hand.

Forkis approached his desk and set Yamar's headgear on the top with a snap. Words turned out to be redundant, the formalities of greeting and polishing would have sounded as pitiful as the poor Kiritian civilian had ended up.

The dignitary looked around at the slightly hunting-style room, which to the Immortal dealing with plastic, metal and masterfully worked stone (many Kiritian buildings were modeled on the millennia-long pyramids of ancient Onkalots) seemed ancient. Four chrome sconces glowed faintly on the walls, keeping the room lined with sandalwood in twilight. The decor was quite specific, because the walls were decorated with dangling handcuffs next to the heads and skulls of wild animals - but not only. Forkis hissed under his breath and almost tilted his head to one side when he saw the head of an Onkalot among the trophies. The poor sod had false eyes attached, but the expression of his muzzle as well as his muscles stiffened for ages showed that he had been wincing in pain and fear of being killed. He had been preserved in such a state. Of unusual objects, the dignitary noticed mini blades stuck in the walls, which Dönges threw for fun at the deeply carved animal skulls, as well as at the forehead of a specimen of jaguar-man.

Pressing the desk top with his fingers, Dönges rose slowly, with fear on his face, as if the office, had entered one of the great animals whose dead relatives adorned the walls. Forkis looked into his eyes with no less wild eyes, heralding misfortune. It flew through the mayor head whether he should have reached for a weapon in a desk drawer.

He had already started to move his hand when one of the frightened, sweaty, and out of breath villagers burst into the office.

"In the street they are murd..." that was how much he managed to shout as Forkis outthrusted his pistol from the hiding place, extended his arm, and took out the target with shots to the head and torso, and he did it all, still staring frostily as a reptile in Dönges' eyes. The body, with the face preserved in a silent scream, fell to the floor with a thud.

The murder completely deprived the mayor of the self-assurance; logical thinking was suppressed by panic. Despite the gruesome display of the Kiritian's skills, he lunged toward the side door.

Forkis ran up and grabbed the man before he could make it to the exit. He dragged him back to the previous spot and pressed him against the wall. He glanced towards the window, among the smoke and fire one could see scenes as if from the war - lifting of crying children getting away, mothers rejected onto a pavement, men stunned with the blows of butts and fists, people brutally forced to march.

The Kiritian's gaze fell on the steel handcuffs dangling from the hooks. They had to be used in real terms to put a human into them, maybe erotic games, because their spacing perfectly suited the uncomfortable enslavement. Forkis chained Dönges in them, spreading his arms wide.

The local nearly fainted in fear when the torturer then reached for the cleaver, yanking it from the horned modificant's skull. Forkis leaned down and brought his face close to that of the man being held, who would have most likely blended in with the wall.

"Be patient, Dönges, this will be over soon. I think you know what I'm here for. You have something to tell me?"

"Children..." coughed up the mayor. "What the hell are you doing?! Leave them alone! Get out of our place!"

"We will take them with us and incorporate them into the nation." Forkis tossed a cleaver, twiddling it and grabbing the handle. "Those that will not be suitable will go to the orphanage or to cousins once removed or guardians."

"You have no right, self-proclaimed, to do what you like on Calcaris. This is not your world." The village head couldn't take his eyes off the blade which cast pale reflections in the dim glow of the wall lamps.

"But will be. Soon most of the colonized worlds will be under our auspices. Only the run-up remained, which is weakening the rebels. Anyway, we already have a technological advantage over them." He clenched his fingers on the sides of his lower jaw and lifted his head. "So, Dönges, will you honorably tell what happened here?"

When he withdrew his hand, the mayor's head dropped; panting Dönges stared at the floor. The dignitary crouched down.

"Too bad, so I'll be telling. Our man Yamaro was flying near the planet when two rebel squadrons shot him down. They didn't bother to check if he survived, they probably thought that the damaged transporter would burn in the atmosphere. However, Yamaro managed to land very hard, he was badly injured. You found and killed him only because he was a Kiritian, you buried the transporter fragments in the field, the body as well. You placed the helmet on the pillar as a trophy that wasn't due to you," Forkis spoke more and more aggressively. "When you noticed that we were landing, this guy here," he pointed to the corpse, "you ordered to get rid of the helmet. So, the peasant threw it deep into the field, certain that we wouldn't be walking in the bushes. Lilly Tedlock was also a victim of xenophobia. When it turned out that she went out with the Kiritian, you harassed and teased her, thinking that she would end this binational relationship or leave the village. The girl bravely endured insults, naively believing that she would assimilate, that you needed time to accept her choice. But it didn't

203

happen. You repaid her with hatred for her love and forbearance, you explained all your misfortunes with the presence of Lilly. Eventually, you dragged her out of the house, spat on her, whipped her with the sticks, hurled spoiled food at her like at a supposed medieval witch. After the way of the cross, you hung her on the tree, regardless of the fact that she was pregnant. You came up with the story about breaking up with Milles, wrote the pathetic note, cleaned the crime scene thoroughly, leaving only traces of the person who allegedly found the correspondence in her pocket - here I have to congratulate you as peasants - so that everything pointed to a nervous breakdown and ultimately suicide. You knew it would be a while before we arrived with the Alcubierre propulsion after hearing of Lilly's death. That is why you left the body on the tree, in heat and humidity, so that it would start decomposing faster, which would have masked the traces of torture. However, the dark secrets of Dharsa Pass don't end here. Many of the bodies of people who had stories as sad as Lilly and Yamaro, rest under the roots of your plants. This is a frigging hotbed of crime." Forkis grabbed Dönges by the hair and raised his arm so that the mayor looked at his face congealed in a mask of anger. "Have I missed something?"

"How do you know all this?" He croaked. "Our plan was perfect. Certainly no one blurted out ..."

"You didn't take into account a little detail thanks to which I achieved it all." The dignitary waved his hand with the cleaver towards the window. "I'm a telepath. The villagers confessed silently to me, one after the other, although they didn't know it."

"President Calcaris protects us. He'll send an entire army here as soon as he finds out."

Dönges flinched, his pulse quickened as Forkis lifted the blade and made a cut along the mayor's right cheek. Droplets of blood flowed from the wound.

"Even at such a moment you don't regret the crimes committed, you are not at all sorry." The dignitary shook his head, smiling sadly. He pulled the blood off his face with a finger, parted his mouth and smeared it on his tongue, relishing the fear that was building in the man. "You're thinking how to get out of this shit. Do I recognize now ARh+? I like this group the most. Me and mosquitoes too."

He got up and began to pace the room slowly, examining the various items. Uncertain of his next move, the victim was losing his mind.

"You have terrible heat here, the mountains protect you from the wind," said Forkis, "not to mention spicy peppers. I don't see anything to drink in the office, not even an alcohol cabinet. Quite unheard of for a village head."

Returning, he crouched down and ran slowly the cleaver blade over the throat of the terrified victim. From the neck cut almost half, spurted blood at high pressure.

Having thrown the ax away with a clatter, Forkis held the shivering body by the shoulders and lapped the hot liquid like a nutritious, mineralized rock spill.

After drinking a few liters, he clung to the late Dönges' neck to suck out the remnants of the sweet gore. Its quality was much worse than that of blood which he often obtained from women, but at least it satisfied his thirst sufficiently, and it also pardoned his hunger with its density and richness in nutrients.

Forkis walked over to the desk. Wiping his face with a few synthetic-fiber documents scooped up from there, he stared indifferently at the pale corpse hanging in handcuffs.

As he left the building, smoke from rapidly spreading fires was just overwhelming the hall.

Outside, he was found quickly by Kiret who looked anxiously at the bloodied front of his armor.

"It's not mine," said the dignitary. Broody, Necron didn't have to ask about the rest, he had dealt with Forkis for over two hundred years and knew his habits well, or so he thought. Also this time the dignitary first locked himself with the victim, then took out his insatiable frustration on him, killing the leader of the next community that had gotten into his black books - Kiret was sure he had shot dead the unfortunate or killed him in some other classic way.

"Did you do everything I ordered?" Forkis asked.

"Yes, sir. The children are in the transporters, including Charlotte Kris with Reya. All the rest, we gathered in the square."

As they walked around several burning houses, Forkis was amazed at how, in the twenty-eighth century, they could use flammable materials in construction, and not have fire drones or other machines close at hand to extinguish a fire immediately upon detection. On the other hand, he had respect for keeping tradition and the ability to cope with life at such a low level - as long as it didn't go hand in hand with the stupidity resulting from the fear of change.

They stopped next to the well and the St. Jacob's pole. A dozen or so Kiritians stood there with weapons in their hands, guarding the compact group of adult peasants, cursing, silent, weeping.

"Line them up," Forkis casually ordered, waving his hand. It thundered more and more overhead, the air was no longer so thick and muggy, but there was still no rain. The immortals, not without brutal interference with the reluctant ones, quickly formed from the locals a line as such. Forkis stood several steps in front of him, clasped his hands behind his back.

"Now," he began to speak loudly, in a formal tone, "each of you is to think intensely about the events of Yamaro and Lilly Tedlock. I want to see your role in them. Anyone who tries to suppress memories or think hard about something else, will die immediately."

With a movement of his hand, he signaled his achijes to part into an extended line before the locals, he himself approached the right wing of the row and began walking slowly along it.

"You, two steps ahead," looking at the next frightened faces, he ordered someone to step forward from time to time.

After he walked along the row of villagers, seventeen people stood at the front, wondering if their fate was in their favor or the other way round - they should have started praying to the gods for forgiveness. Forkis looked at Yamaro's helmet, which he had taken from Dönges' office.

"Kill the rest," he said at Kiret's ear, having approached him. The deputy dignitary didn't hide his distress. He signaled to Lieutenant Milles, and he, in turn, to the firing squad.

There was an energetic volley.

After a few seconds, only seventeen selected people remained alive, who for moral reasons didn't get along with Dönges, which caused them a lot of unpleasantness.

"Go away!" Forkis shouted at them.

"Sir, what are we to do now? Where should we go?!" One of the brave ones began tearfully asking, trembling as if Dharsa Pass had been attacked by frost.

A curtain of downpour fell from thick mouse clouds, as if the rain had also received a signal from the heavens to attack. The curdled blood on Forkis' armor-soaked water again, began to run down the biometal, marking it with paths of red.

"I don't care. You don't have your own brains or what? Dönges fluffed them up so badly? We've done our job here, we'll turn on the tower soon, you can go and complain. The fields are intact."

"And children?"

"They will live, but not here. Go away!"

The downpour, powerful as in the tropics of Chulimal, quickly dealt with the fires. Puddles began to form in the square, as well as in every street.

Forkis told his people to go back to the machines. He himself being washed by streams of water, stood in front of the pillar and stared at it for a long time with his thoughtful gaze. As the pillar had cavities for climbing, the dignitary, despite his one hundred and several dozen kilograms in armor, managed to get to the top and place Yamaro's helmet there.

Splashing the water from the puddles, Kiret approached his commander who was already on the ground. For a moment, they looked at the top of the pillar in silence.

"I don't know," Necron began to say, what had lain on his heart for a long time, "what happened to you in a past that no Kiritian would like to belabor, respecting the privacy of their lord, but it was certainly something monstrous. Whatever it was, you cannot continue your crusade like this and take revenge on all mankind."

"I spared a dozen people and children, this time not all of them died."

"Well, congratulations, there is some progress," said Kiret ironically. "So far we have achieved only successes. I admit that it is incomprehensible to me why this is happening. Five million people in the nation ..."

"And the best technology," Forkis chimed in, "constantly being developed by Dr. Figam's team, plus my telepathy and the mass of nonsense about me that is a spring that winds up fear. The size of a nation is not key, quality matters. Hernando Cortés defeated the Aztecs, the empire from the Pacific to the Gulf of Mexico, with ten cannons."

"And a lot of Indian allies."

"Onkalots, in turn, were defeated by some drones and ships." Kiret only understood the comparison of Onkalots to Indians. Like

210

the other Kiritians, he couldn't have known that there was something far more serious behind this than Forkis' love for humanoid jaguars. It is thanks to this that he called the Immortal soldiers achijes, and on the planet Morascrik he built the indestructible pyramids.

"However, our successes won't last forever if we don't change something," he said. "We will lose in the end, and those who defeat us, will surely have no mercy. We must finally ease our policy, stabilize ourselves. Enough of these conquests already, we have a lot, Forkis. All that remains is to tame the rebels. Think it over well."

Forkis stared at the helmet on the top of the pole for a while, in the silent company of his friend, but loud one of the incessant downpour.

\*\*\*

After unblocking communications, the surviving villagers informed a polis, where the president was in office with the Commander-in-Chief of the Calcaris Army, about the events in Dharsa Pass.

Contrary to what Forkis thought, that the Kiritians would get away with the massacre as usual, they were attacked from the air by the planet's air force. However, it was done in an act of desperation to prevent people's trust in the government from being wrecked. The cruiser itself and the two Immortals' battleships, however, had almost the same firepower as the enemy. The dignitary additionally brought part of his fleet closest to space, and within two local days a battle took place on the planet.

Losses amounted to over a thousand machines to seventeen in favor of the Kiritians.

Forkis was open to the requests and suggestions of his achijes, he was able to listen and consider other points of view. He believed that Kiret was right - whatever had happened to him in the past, he couldn't live forever only for infantile vengeance which couldn't satisfy him anyway, just as devouring women as another material symptom of a vendetta that had dragged on for two hundred and twenty-nine years. Just as he wasn't saturated with all the blood sucked from Dönges. Peace appeared at the time of digestion and the later period of his body's reluctance to human tissues. But the hunger finally came back.

Decades later, their new home, the planet Morascrik, the same one Kiret had once told him about in the Diamond Geiser, was already terraformed and fully ready for settlement. After moving the nation's core to the capital, K'otz'ib'aja, Forkis complied with Necron's request and changed his space policy from aggressive to more passive. The Kiritians introduced a currency known as the uinal, also the official Kiritian language for all conquered colonies.

Forkis proclaimed himself the First Galactic Dignitary, and his nation became an empire.

# Aytar

**Selected rights from the credo of the collectivity of Adil Ibn Yusuf al-Aswani, mentor of the city of Sibuna of the planet Calvary**

It is the duty of a member of the collectivity to obey all the laws of the credo. They also apply after voluntary leaving the guild or exile. Exemption from compliance with them occurs only after death.

Taking any stimulants or substances that change the biological program of the body's activities, especially those affecting sanity and physical fitness, is forbidden. The exception is the administration of a drug in the event of a threat to life or health repair.

The penalty for the murder of another member of the collectivity, of any rank, is death. The guilty person has the right to honor suicide within two Calvary weeks of committing the prohibited act. After this time, the execution takes place. There is no point in running away or hiding, even in another world.

## The Terrenic Year 2848

The transaction on the planet Calvary between the gangsters and the Kiritans took place in a pleasant atmosphere. Forkis bought all the boring weapons and acquired the project exclusively for his nation. The ammunition of this handgun had sensitive nanoprocessors that exploded effectively when they found themselves inside an enemy body or machine. Hegemons such as the Kiritians didn't need new weapons, as no one threatened them now (sometimes the rebels tried to rock the boat), but each time it resulted in heavy losses for them. Nevertheless, the First Galactic Dignitary knew that, according to the rules of co-evolution, nothing was motionless in space. If they rested on their laurels, the opposition would eventually give them an explosive surprise. The innovative weapon, created in the laboratories of wealthy gangsters, he intended to pass on to Dr. Maximus Figam. He would improve it so that their armies, with their technological advantage, would have peace for many years.

Terraformed Calvary was practically entirely inhabited by every underclass, from agile street urchins who wanted to steal trinkets from passers-by, to fences and pimps, who had an influence in several worlds. The planet was hovering near the Kiritian cosmic matrix, but the latter didn't mind the criminals' base outside their homes, although they could have killed them all in a few Terrenic days. Instead, small deals and transactions were sometimes made. Life was nice for Calvary inhabitants, so they didn't attack the Immortals, even though many didn't tolerate them. All animosities were kept to oneself. Therefore, Forkis was free to wander the streets of the planet, with only his own armor and achij team as protection.

He had nothing important to do anytime soon, so he gave up the ride in the transporter and decided to walk through the richest district of the planet, where the most eminent gangsters had their residences. Behind the team, a line of delighted kids grew quickly. Kiret, now as the Second Galactic Dignitary, even entered into conversation with them.

The Immortals' ship was stationed on a spaceport behind a small tropical plant sanctuary; after leaving the city, they had to cover a few more kilometers. The evening sky turned on the shades of deep pink, orange and indigo. The air was more oxygen-laden than on Morascrik, gravity was slightly different from that of their main planet, and the local yellow dwarf still burned fairly hard. achij armor, however, provided their organisms with optimal conditions.

They were walking on a road alongside a gusty river that rushed towards a waterfall. Kiret was talking to Forkis, tossing his dhurnstcel knife with a shaft that was a demon's head.

The emperor looked at a detail different from the surroundings and noticed a girl on a high stone bridge. The sight of the body balancing on the edge of the abyss left no doubt as to her intent, especially as the foaming water, tens of meters below, crashed against the protruding monoliths.

Forkis through the centuries of reign as the Immortal led to the extermination of three billion oderses. He had probably seen all kinds of death by now, and none impressed him. Suicides occurred even among achijes who had undergone a meticulous selection, checking whether they qualified for being injected with Dr. Figam's super virus and living in immortality for the nation's eternal glory. Yet many didn't stand the test of time and attempted against their own lives, unable to bear for instance the thought that those they loved had been long gone. Now, however, at the sight of the anonymous girl, wanting to take her own life, he felt as if he had been pierced by an energy bullet.

He had experienced something similar with Pek and a few other humanoid jaguars in his former life, but he hadn't expected it to happen to him with the human woman whose facial details he could see perfectly thanks to his Onkalotian eyesight. He had to admit that there was only one thing in the splendor of power which he lacked - a proper, solid relationship. He tried building them with a few Kiritian girls, but it never worked. With concealed envy, he looked at his achijes, even those of low rank, who had wives and girlfriends. As for an oders, he approached women only for vendetta or amusement, and many didn't live long after such an encounter, anyway. He x-rayed each of them telepathically and when it turned out that they were women who wanted his death or wanted to harm the nation in any other way, he killed them or gave them to achijes to execute them. Sometimes he locked himself in his apartment with some and announced that he would be unavailable for several days. At that time, Kiret took over his duties. Afterward, Forkis left alone. Nobody managed to establish what happened with the courtesans. The accepted version was that he tired them out sexually to death and then dissolved the bodies in the bathroom. Once it happened that Biffter disturbed the third day of his isolation with an urgent matter and came out of an encounter with a face the color of bones, for he had already acquired pallor as a result of kiritianization. Forkis traditionally ordered medics to erase his traumatic memories.

Now he felt an incomprehensible, irresistible urge to help this girl.

He gently brushed her mind telepathically - and was surprised to find a barrier. Only Kiret could close himself off to his telepathy, but probably because they worked a long time together and privately practiced blocking Forkis' abilities, though Dr. Figam theorized that the cause might have been Biffter's death before the kiritianization and brain changes before he was revived by the super virus.

"Sir?"

He didn't react to Kiret's question. He walked hurriedly towards the bridge. The deputy followed him.

"Don't do it, girl! Stop!" Forkis didn't expect an ambush, having scanned the area with a bracer bioctovisor and for someone else's electronics signal. Despite the armor, he efficiently climbed the rocks to get to the bridge, taking a short cut. The imperial manners were not Forkis's forte, who had an inclination for wildness and the simplest solutions.

He was afraid that he wouldn't make it, especially since, like the last, pensive idiot, he had stared at the stranger, almost within the power of the White Lady.

When he got there, the girl didn't pay attention to him at all. She stood still above the precipice like a bridge carving, staring at the furiously rippling water.

At last she deigned to turn her head towards him.

They stared at each other for a moment as if it had been a staring contest, until Forkis let out a sigh of delight. He hadn't seen such beauty in a long time. Cool, aloof, beyond examination with telepathy. Instead of seeing the expected sadness on her face, grudge against the whole cosmos and resignation pushing her to the final deed, he saw a dispassionate mask like that of an older generation android. The marble beauty of the girl was emphasized by icy, blue eyes, belonging more to a person who is confident in their clearheadedness, rather than nervous one. The void visible in them was associated with outer space. Her shoulder-length hair was dyed the color of the irises. She could boast of a pale complexion like Forkis'. Her age was difficult to determine because of her girly build and very short stature. On the face of it, she might have been about a hundred and sixty centimeters tall and might as well have been fifteen or thirty-some years old. Even more so, if she was genetically altered, but a poor, worn uniform didn't indicate the owner's wealth.

Forkis easily took her off the railing and put on an expanded clay, for which she gave passive permission. He tried to penetrate her mind again, but with the previous result. The girl was thinking about nothing - an incredible skill for a human, especially when you stood before the First Galactic Dignitary and had tried to kill yourself a moment earlier. Forkis considered she might have some sort of mental illness.

"Interesting ... What's your name?" He asked, holding her forearms. He ignored the puzzled stares of his men who had just reached the bridge and wondered why the emperor would have cared about the girl. Well, pretty - they had to admit.

"Zira," she replied. Her voice was just as melodic and beautiful. "Zira Aytar."

"Are you a child?" He must have known that immediately.

"No, an adult for a long time."

"Good," Forkis replied with imperceptible relief. "Do you know who I am?"

"Forkis, the emperor of the Zodiac Universum, First Galactic Dignitary," she replied calmly.

"And it doesn't make even the slightest impression on you? You are not afraid?"

"Believe me, I would love to feel fear," she replied enigmatically, looking down at the river again.

\*\*\*

Forkis took Aytar to K'otz'ibaja, to which she agreed. After the research, it turned out that she was neither an android nor under the influence of drugs, but fully sane and healthy, unless the disease was considered to be her bizarre anhedonia with a non-depressant cause. Even with the equipment in the infirmary, it was impossible to read anything from her mind, because she still didn't think about anything, and didn't want to talk about herself. However, Forkis x-rayed her using traditional methods of an intelligence sent to Calvary.

It turned out that she was not just anyone. She belonged to the best, and at the same time the most radical, indoctrinated guild of thieves and assassins on the planet. She developed perfection in both professions. Fast, agile and deadly introvert - that's how she was described. She was an orphan. She had grown up in slum streets where she had had to fight for survival. This might explain partly her self-isolation. Forkis would have thought several times if he wanted to bring someone like that to the capital if it hadn't been for the fact that Zira had all the physical characteristics (maybe except short stature) and the psychological ones of a good Kiritian. Also, the body was of an age suitable for kiritianization, so that she wasn't killed by a cytokine storm caused by a systemic infection of a super virus that reprogrammed every cell in the body. If she could have been talked into getting infected and encephalon correction, she would have been a great achij. Why mentor Adil had kicked such a valuable member from the guild couldn't be established. It was a collectivity affair, and its secrets didn't come out.

Although Kiritian medicine could easily stabilize Zira, she didn't agree to the neurological intervention. She fanatically adhered to the credo of the former guild and still dissociated herself from all medical substances. On the one hand, achijes admired her faithfulness to her principles, on the other hand, they didn't understand her standards of conduct. But at least Zira worked on getting her emotions back. Forkis, who liked her more and more as the weeks passed, was eager to help her. However, another obstacle appeared - it turned out that Aytar was an asexual virgin (how she could be celibate among criminals - he had no idea) and she announced that she wanted to keep her condition. The emperor respected this, though it worried him that she didn't intend to be fully devoted to him. He hoped her thinking would change over time. However, she satisfied all his needs and fantasies

223

that didn't require a classical intercourse. He, too, gave a lot in return, although he could see, without telepathy, that she simulated the pleasure so as not to discredit his ego, or she simply didn't want to upset him.

It wasn't entirely true.

Zira felt something for the first time in a long time. But only when Forkis licked her body (he could do amazing things with his tongue), and especially when he took her hands and feet in his mouth and could suck for long minutes. He had an astonishingly large spacing of his jaws, which never caught her eye. In everyday life he looked ordinary, just like any human being, his inhuman quality was only noticed when he took something large in his mouth. She sighed and groaned seriously as he played with her like this, sometimes inflicting pain with his teeth. Classic, hackneyed bedroom tricks didn't arouse any emotions in her. She sensed that it was rather not normal when pressure in her lower abdomen and blissful fear made her imagine she was about to be devoured. She didn't tell Forkis this out of shame, even though it might have been the solution to her emotional blockade problem.

So, she had to try something different, since secret suicide attempts and sleeping with the First Dignitary himself were of no avail.

\*\*\*

The imperial building in which Forkis had his residence was inhabited by a total of about a hundred achijes, ranging from council members to officers. There were also sentries from the city guard of batab[14] Rudiard Gareth's command. They served more officially than to protect the authorities. Among the Kiritians, everyone had all their needs met, no one was anyone's enemy, so the military nation operated without rigorous supervision or monitoring.

Aytar had an apartment near the Forkis mansion. She could move around most of the building, but was constantly supervised by someone. With time, it turned out that she didn't pose a threat to anyone, anyway, as an oders, she had no right to carry a weapon. The emperor even gave her dermatoglyphic access to his bedroom so that she could visit him freely.

Forkis went to bed early that evening. He was tired after the day spent telepathically infiltrating several hundred recruits. However, he didn't send Aytar away when she came to visit him in his bedroom, clad in a blue slip. He was lying on the bed in his pants, his head was resting on his intertwined arms. The bloody glow of

---

[14] A Mayan term for a village guardian. Here in the sense of the commander of the city guard.

the giant Betelgeuse, disappearing behind the cones of inactive volcanoes, continued to penetrate through the obscured portholes of the ceiling. The smiling girl in its glow looked like a dualistic goddess of water and fire, which Forkis liked very much. He extended his arm and beckoned his fingers invitingly. She straddled his belly.

Forkis placed his hands on her shoulder blades and was about to bring her closer to himself when he saw a military knife in her right hand.

He recognized it. It was Kiret's knife, the one with the demon's head.

He cursed Zira's mental barrier, but more his stupidity. The girl's smile turned into a grimace of hate. Even at such a critical moment, the man recognized that it wasn't natural.

Aytar screamed and stabbed him.

Forkis squeezed her right wrist with the agility of an attacking cobra so hard that she dropped the tool on the bed. He twisted, trapping her under his own weight. She wasn't amazed or surprised, as usual she looked as cool as medical center refrigerators. Only a faint expression of disappointment could be recognized on her face.

"Shit, are you serious?"

There had been many unsuccessful attacks on Forkis, in a way it was starting to irritate and amuse him. He was not afraid for his life, even if Kiritian immortality meant only freedom from disease and aging. This time, however, death came very close. A quick stab in the right place - and that's it. But it was his fault that he had succumbed to the appearances of the petite body and the weeks of Aytar's gentleness.

But was it really about his death?

He took the knife, turned and threw it a few meters at the wooden sculpture of a human skull. The blade bit into the center of the frontal bone.

Into the room, burst Kiret in armor and with the X17A4 pistol, almost crashing into the automatic door.

"Fork! Are you all right?!"

The emperor sat on the edge of the bed, also forcing Aytar to do so, pulling her arm.

"As you can see. Can you explain to me what you are doing here?" Biffter ran a glove over his bald head.

"Let me guess, cellula," Forkis replied for him, looking at him askance. "You watched us, you pervert."

"It's not like that, I swear. You trust your achijes, so do I, but not this oder viper." Necron nodded his barrel and chin towards

Aytar. "There was something I didn't like about her from the beginning. And it's good you got the bug."

"I got over it without your help." Forkis didn't want to dwell on the subject, because he would have sunk himself. Just in the bedroom were all the people of the capital resistant to his telepathy. Kiret would have never hurt him, but Aytar naively trusted him. The thoughts of any other, Forkis would have picked up on the front door of the mansion, his mind was awake in this matter even during sleep. "Take off the cellula, Necron, and no more such pranks." He stood up with the girl who didn't resist. "Who's on duty today in the west wing?"

"Corporal Victor Shane."

"How many people?"

"I think four."

"Then tell batab Gareth to send Victor and his entire team to the planet Aj. To the hemisphere where there is winter. And let them think of some stupid tasks for them, just for a month."

"Of course."

"And how do you explain that?" Forkis pointed to the knife embedded in the skull.

Necron, who had just removed the cellula from the dhurnsteel cornice, began to feel his waist in amazement. When he had seen earlier on his PDA that the emperor had been in danger, he hadn't had time to look closely at the murder weapon of the assassin.

"My knife! I had it on me all the time, sometimes I left it in my apartment. But no one had access to it and was allowed to go inside!"

Forkis looked at Aytar with ostentatious contempt, though he suffered.

"Can you explain why you did it? How did you get Necron's knife?"

The girl looked him in the eye and was silent, showing her standard mask of indifference.

"Do you realize that by this act you signed your own death warrant?"

"I was hoping it would work this time," she whispered, glancing to the side. The men waited silently for a moment, but she said nothing more.

"Take her away." Forkis brought her hand closer to Kiret. "You know what to do."

Necron looked at his gun.

"Should I execute her right now?"

"Let the achijes throw her in the jail under the building. The emperor turned to Zira without merriment: "Congratulations, you will be the first inmate there in ten years. You spoil our statistics. I'll give you all night and all day to reflect. Perhaps the death that will come at dusk tomorrow will finally make you speak.

Zira said nothing, only smiled mysteriously, astonishing Forkis. Keeping her under arms, Kiret left the bedroom. He forgot all about his knife.

Forkis only now got rid of his appearances of indifference. He walked over to the bed and fell heavily on the bed with his back. He covered his face with his hands and, sighing loudly, ran them through his thick hair.

What had just happened made no sense. Aytar's act was a combination of perfectionism with the worst amateurishness, and only the first option suited this girl. Forkis knew Wiktor and knew that both he and his people were exemplary in their duties, so if they didn't see the intruder at Kiret's or at the emperor's residence, she must have been better than them. Nevertheless, he decided to punish the entire team on principle. Aytar outsmarted so many achijes in the building and, unnoticed, took the knife with which she got to the First Galactic Dignitary. On the other hand, she screamed and showed the murder weapon before she struck. In addition, she aimed at the shoulder, not the heart or the throat, which only now Forkis realized when, after cooling down a little, he recreated the entire scene in his mind. Did she miss on purpose? Did she want to be caught and punished? She had lived in K'otz'ib'aja long enough to know that an oders' attempt on the life of any achij, from private to emperor, ended in execution. So what drove her to such an act, if not a desire to die, as then on the bridge?

He lay for a long time, unable to sleep. He stared at the illuminated aquarium with Turritopsis nutricula jellyfish, whose physiognomic properties were the basis for Dr. Figam's creation of the super virus.

***

In the morning it was reported to him that Aytar hadn't said even a word all night. During the day, she was also silent, didn't take any meals. Hiding sadness, Forkis also went hungry all day, which made him growling at anyone who had any matter for him.

At first, he wanted achijes to end Aytar's question quickly, but despair and a desire to know the truth led him to the underground stairs a quarter of an hour before the appointed time of execution. Four guards were just leading the girl outside, with her hands chained behind her back, under the bloody rays of setting

Betelgeuse, hanging over Morascrik like an announcement of the apocalypse.

"I take her over, you have to uncuff her," he said to the guards, surprised that the emperor himself was dealing with the minor prisoner. After all, as an autocrat, he could do what he wanted, so they returned Aytar to him without asking. "Get back to your duties."

"Yes, sir." The master sergeant saluted. He had enough self-preservation instinct not to inform the emperor that walking alone with Calvary's best assassin was not a good idea, especially after yesterday's incident. He didn't worry about Forkis, however, knowing that this time, fully alert, he would take control of the situation.

Holding Zira by the forearm, Forkis walked a bit of the floor, took the elevator to the upper one, and then walked down the corridors to his residence. With unbending indifference, he ignored the curious glances of the passing achijes and dignitaries. He only exchanged serious and meaningful glances with Kiret as the latter went to do his tasks. Necron put sympathetically a hand on his shoulder, then walked forward with a stern expression.

The mansion door closed behind them. Forkis walked from Aytar through the hall, office, atrium and directed her into the bedroom.

"Go wash and change your clothes, you smell like the basement," he ordered. He tossed the girl clean clothes, which he hadn't yet removed from the room.

When she returned a quarter of an hour later, she found Forkis sitting at the table. There were two glasses, a jug of water and several types of alcohol on the top. The twilight in the composition with glowing faint blue lamps directing the light upwards created a sleepy, soothing atmosphere. In other circumstances, it could certainly be called romantic.

"Sit down, Aytar." Forkis indicated the chair opposite. He poured himself a full glass of vodka and swallowed it in one gulp without grimacing. "It will be useful to you too."

He smiled half-arsed when the girl fell on the chair and didn't even flinch. It just so happened that they had never drunk alcohol before.

"I thought you were used to such things on Calvary."

"The collectivity's credo forbids taking drugs."

"Does it have something to do with the fact that you didn't want medical attention?"

She didn't answer. She decided to take a few sips of water.

"Aytar ... Let's put all cards on the table now. Unfortunately, you will not leave my residence alive. I will have to execute you. Sorry."

He slid the X17A4 out of his cuisse and set it gently next to the liquors. He sighed, extended his arms and covered Zira's hands on the table with his.

"If Kiret hadn't burst in here like a storm, and after a few minutes the whole building hadn't known about it, I could still save you. To pass over in silence everything that happened here. It is a terribly difficult decision for me," he said regretfully, "but I would lose my authority in the eyes of the nation if I forgave you for the attempt on my life, even though I'm the Law myself. Favoring would make no sense, since I have killed every other torturer, regardless of status and circumstances."

"I see. I agree on everything." She stared at the aquarium.

"So can we allow ourselves a little honesty in your last hours? Please ... I still love you, Aytar. I don't understand your behavior and what led to your loss of emotions. You didn't want to kill me, did you?"

"No," she admitted.

"So, what is it about? Tell me at last." After a moment, when it had no effect, he added, "I could have already long ago captured and telepathically or medically probed anyone in the Adil collectivity, even he himself, and he would have squeaked everything about you. But I didn't do it. Love is not about pulling secrets from your partner's past by force. I wish you would tell me everything voluntarily. I just want to hear about you, guilds are of no interest to me, unless the obstacle is the credo still binding you."

They looked into each other's eyes. Forkis brushed her mind - and for the first time he could read Zira's thoughts. To his amazement, she opened up to him; he hadn't expected success out of habit.

"Alright then. It wasn't about the credo all this time. It doesn't forbid telling about your dilemmas and weaknesses, although these become weapons in the hands of enemies when they are revealed."

"Aytar ... I'm not your enemy."

"I'm really sorry, but I was hoping to finally change, being with you. It, however, didn't happen. For the time being, she chose not to mention those sensations in his bed which had the effect. She didn't think hard about it. "I hid everything, I didn't confess anything, because I was trained this way. I was taught not to think, not to feel and not to suffer, to be empty like almost all outer space. Moreover, I have my own strict rules that I follow. If you think that something traumatic happened to me, you will be disappointed. Yes, sometimes it was very difficult, but no one raped me, tortured me, abused me in any way.

Forkis probed her and knew she was telling the truth.

"So that I could survive and not go crazy in this brutal world, I was trained for years to be like an android. I liked it very much in my early youth, I thought that lack of emotions meant being better. I suppressed my grief towards the victims I robbed, and I happened to do so even with starving families with many children, when I took from them valuable, generational souvenirs that they were not going to sell. I had no sympathy for innocent people dying because of my worst intrigues. Adil praised it, said he was proud of me, and the only thing he really enjoyed was the fact that he had the low-maintenance and easy-to-use machine. I realized this when I got older. Everything went too far over the years. I crossed the line; I couldn't come back. I felt literally nothing, no human emotion. I became insensitive to everything. My mind told me to do something about it. On my own, I started looking for extreme solutions, but even the most sophisticated situations in which I risked my life didn't help. I tried suicides too, but I didn't have the courage to reach for the last option. And then I did it ..."

"What?" Forkis encouraged her as she fell silent.

"I killed someone from the guild. It had nothing to do with my problem, Al-cyone and I just hadn't liked each other for a long time. There was an argument. I drew my gun; I was faster than him. I must die for this. This is the sacred law of the collectivity. Since you took me away, the guild no longer has power over me.

My time for honorable suicide is over, and Adil's henchmen have no way to pursue me. Everyone is afraid of Kiritians. Maybe they think you killed me. So, I was given a lot of time. Before the death, however, I wanted to be human again, to feel emotions like in the times before Adil had recruited me. All their explosion. Even if it was to last only for a moment. This was my only wish. Unfortunately, our long-lasting romance had no effect, which is why I attacked you. I thought I would feel something when I raised my hand against the emperor himself, the most powerful man that had ever existed. Unfortunately, that failed as well, but at least I won't have to kill myself - you'll do it for me. After what I did to you, I don't deserve an honorable death anymore."

Dazed, Forkis didn't know what to say. He ran a hand over his face. He stood up, took Aytar by the wrists, and sat down again, placing her with her legs apart on his lap, facing him.

"Girl ... Why didn't you tell me? You needed help! You needed a doctor! Figam can really work wonders ..."

"It's not in my nature to complain, I always coped by myself. This is no pitiful pride, but my essence. And you know what the credo says about substances that change the functioning of the body and mind ..."

"Credo, shmedo," he interrupted, indignant. "It's your past! It no longer applies to you. Adil has no power here."

237

"You're wrong. Only death can free me from the law of the guild. I knew what I signed up for, voluntarily joining its ranks. There must be a penalty for the crime, and I sincerely want death. Anyway, in a sense, I'm already dead."

Astonished, Kiritian thought he was about to go mad, but didn't dwell on the subject. Not even his entire army could have done anything about Aytar's fanatical devotion to the principles of the collectivity. He madly admired her for her respect for the law, honor, and lack of wangling, but the credo was at the same time the main source of their problems.

"As for sleeping matters ..." she whispered, seeing that the man wouldn't say anything else. "As you remember, I'm asexual, Forkis. I don't know if I became like that due to the reasons I mentioned. I can do that a little ... but not entirely. It disgusts me. You really please your partners, but you came across the wrong person. The problem is in me, not in you," she added, just in case.

"I know my value." He managed to smile at the bad joke.

He didn't stop her as she reached for the gun and began examining it. She didn't endanger him now or ever, moreover, the weapon was coded for the use by the owner. He knew Aytar's thoughts, she told only the truth - as befits a Kiritian, although she was an oders.

He took the gun from her and set it on the table with a crash, not taking his hand off it.

"Your confession changes things. I won't kill you. Since you've lived for a while in K'otz'ibaya, breaking the collectivity law, anyway, with those ridiculous two weeks of suicide time, you can live for decades to come. It was the only argument he could still use to fight for Zira."

She snorted.

"You haven't realized what I was trying to convey to you? I had already made my final decision the moment I stole Kiret's knife. I can't be fixed anymore. I don't want to live anymore. And I dragged out my well-deserved punishment too long, anyway. I just want to feel the rapture that may arise just before death itself. Do you want to take it from me? Do it my way, against my will? Either way, you've done nothing else with the oderses over the past centuries."

"You surely won't feel anything when I shoot you in the head. It will take a moment."

He rested his forehead against the girl's. He took a long, deep breath, inhaling her sweet scent. Against Aytar's fanaticism and her washed brain, he was unfortunately helpless. He would have achieved his goal by forcibly taking her to the infirmary, ordering Figam to rummage about in the girl's cerebrum to artificially correct her behavior and erase her memory. However, he couldn't treat Zira like any other oders, what she had just pointed out to him.

After the confession, Aytar understood how different their realities were, how distinct needs they had were. He would have liked to absorb her world into his own, but the significant differences made it impossible. For him, as an immortal Kiritian, the life of achijes was the greatest value that could be squandered at best in extreme cases, such as fighting a stronger enemy when there was no other choice but to die on the battlefield. Life had to be maintained at all costs. He didn't understand the ignorant approach of the oderses in this matter. Though their lives were short, up to a maximum of one hundred and fifty years, they still treated their end as banal. Twenty, thirty, seventy - what's the difference? Since they didn't respect it, he, too, had had no qualms about killing them in the past. Zira hit the nail on the head here.

It was disturbing to think that he was ready to apply the same rule in her case as well.

"You assassins and thieves and those idiot rules of yours," he said after a minute of silence. "I don't understand your values. But I know from research that you are sane, however messed up it all looks like. So let's recap. You say you want death ... And only death could set you free from the credo. But before you die, you would like to feel strong emotions again. Did I understand your words and thoughts well?"

"Yes," Aytar also replied after a short silence.

"Let's go to bed then."

"Forkis, we already did it many times ..."

"You didn't understand me. Let's go so normally, make love. You claim to be asexual and you loathe these things. So why not try to go in this direction?"

"I can't."

"So, you are afraid and you feel something?" The Kiritian said accusingly.

"I didn't say that, I just don't want to have sex with you. It doesn't turn me on."

"How do you know if you're a virgin?"

"You don't understand anything, because you are common," she clapped back coldly. "You talk like those hotshots who say that the best way to deal with depression is a hard training, work that absorbs your thoughts, or 'going out to people'. It doesn't work like that, man."

Instead of getting angry and wasting time bantering, Forkis smiled slyly, wanting to move on to pleasure.

241

"Let's find out. Of course, I'm not forcing you to do anything, but that could be the solution. Then we'll talk about dying," he added playfully, still thinking that it wouldn't come to that. "So, will you try something new?"

She ran her hand over her ear.

"All right. But it won't work, I'm saying at once. I'm doing it because of you."

They undressed and got onto the bed. Aytar had seen Forkis naked many times before, but his manhood touched at most her buttocks or thighs as they slept huddled together.

He placed her on her back, and he positioned himself above her on all fours. With delight that had lasted for weeks, he again admired her small, beautiful and at the same time strong figure, the cascade of blue hair scattered on the sheets, similar to the neck frill of a charming tropical bird. It seemed inconceivable that this seemingly innocent woman was so deadly and didn't require a great deal of physical strength to kill someone. Aytar's cleverness and speed usually did the trick.

He was afraid that he might have been exaggerating, given the combination of the huge difference in size and the fact that his partner was a virgin - it would have meant too much pain for her. He looked seriously at her face, Aytar nodded. Her face simply expressed no emotion, and her mind was calm as well.

He leaned; their lips touched. Forkis descended lower and lower, kissing Zira and, like a cat, rubbing his face against her lean but muscular body. With the primal gleam in his eyes, he dragged his tongue across her smooth skin, sucked on the fingers of her hands, and he felt that the girl reacted with shudders and almost inaudible sighs only to this kind of unusual caress. He failed to probe her thoughts because she meticulously masked her feelings. He frowned. Their eyes met. Did he catch a hint of shame in Aytar's eyes, even of fear?

He tried to be gentle, as always with virgins, when he took a stab at the intercourse. He really believed that they would get some effect, but Aytar's face was only contorted with reluctance and a slight pain. Finally, she moved away sharply, as if the Immortal's body had turned into hot metal. Forkis achieved virtually nothing, amazed and embarrassed as ever.

"It didn't work," he gasped, sitting on the edge of the piece of furniture.

"I warned it was pointless," said Zira, pressing the covers against her. "It's not that, Forkis, I told you. I don't want to do this anymore, now I know it."

They dressed in silence and sat down at the table. One wasn't looking at the other. Forkis also experienced something new that he absolutely didn't like - for the first time in his life, he didn't satisfy a woman.

Sipping alcohol, he carefully analyzed every second of their bed failure. A detail haunted him.

Something dawned on him on the periphery of his mind. He bit his lip and stared blankly at the reflection of light on a red wine bottle. A current of anxiety rolled over the Kiritian's insides as the thought crystallized.

"There is a way," he broke the neurotic deadness, "but I didn't even plan on telling you about it at all ... It's something that's not for women like you. It's a form of revenge. Anger. Ecstasy. Monstrous delight. Just like you, I was taught something terrible once ... which I really like. It's ten times better than the roughest sex."

He got up and started pacing the bedroom. Aytar had never seen so many different emotions on his face before. She would have liked to feel them too.

"I can't," he muttered a few minutes later, debating with himself.

She saw the peculiar expression in his gaze again, as if that of a hungry animal, and she understood. A thrill of gentle delight and fear of the unknown ran through her as she recreated in her head the moment Forkis sucked her hand, caressing it with his sticky tongue.

244

In the end, she rejected that shame so carefully masked still in the bed. She got up and, with a firm resolve to go off the deep end, walked over to the Kiritian, took his hand.

"So, the rumors about you are true. This could be the solution. Let's do it. I want such an end."

He gave the girl an incredulous look, shook his head.

"Aytar, what's wrong with you?"

He really didn't understand it. How many women already wanted him to do this, even though they knew it would end in their deaths? Admittedly, the mildest possible, preceded by unimaginable ecstasy and often orgasm, in safety, warmth and softness, but it was still death.

He sighed as she put her thumb in his mouth and began rubbing his gum. Then she put in more fingers. She shifted them onto his tongue, grabbed it. Forkis gently bit her hand. As she pulled it out, she looked down at the string of thick saliva that was stretched between her fingers.

"She's crazy," he thought.

"The first time I felt something in a long time was when you did this to me in bed during the first closeness, after arriving in Morascrik. I was ashamed of my sensations, so I didn't tell you anything. I thought I would find a different solution. In the cell, however, I wished I had told you the truth, no matter how messed

245

up it was. But there will be no better time for confession than now, and besides, you yourself came out with this embarrassing initiative, saving me the trouble. I want it. To feel the fullness of life, sometimes you have to bring yourself to the brink of death."

He knew exactly what Aytar was talking about, so they continued talking, using periphrases, afraid to call a spade a spade.

"It won't be the edge, but the end. No turning back."

"Do it for me, Forkis." She stroked his face. "Let this be your highest act of love for me."

"Are you sure?" He asked softly. "What a crazy situation!"

"Of course. In a sense, this is the only way we can unite forever since I can't give you anything more."

It was indeed the first time he saw her so agitated. To the hidden despair, he also saw in her eloquent eyes that she wouldn't change her decision. "You stubborn, indoctrinated girl with the washed brain ... And those goddamn rules of yours. Anyone else would just break with the past and start their life anew, and not want to lose it." He sighed deeply. "Alright then." He lifted the bracer, selected Kiret's number on the communicator and connected to him. "Necron, replace me for three days, I'll be indispensable."

"Yes, sir," replied the dignitary after a moment of silence. There must have been an achij around as he said officially, "Do you need

246

anything, sir?" The obvious content of the question was the desire to assign bodyguards nearby, so that the last situation with Zira didn't happen again.

"No. Over and out."

Kiret didn't ask for details, he knew that the emperor was fine and just wanted to spend with Aytar her last moments.

They hung up.

Forkis gently grabbed the girl's sweatshirt, she raised her hands to help him take it off. Then, as if with religious anointing, he slipped off her pants, T-shirt, underwear and shoes. She stood completely naked in front of him and clung to his armored body, almost drowning in his embrace. After brief caresses and kisses, the man bent down hard and ran his tongue from the tip of her tiny nose to the top of her head.

"I will do it out of love for you. I've never done this before." In his eyes she saw only regret and pain, feelings practically absent in Forkis' life. "It has always been my tool of hate. A sense of unnamed power much greater than the imperial one."

Now Aytar helped him get rid of the armor and part of his uniform, this time they acted slowly, as if it had been a prelude to a solemn ritual. With only his pants left, a detail such as the removal of the belt turned out to be crucial in the episode that awaited both of them. They thought the same thing when it hit the floor.

Zira went to the bed and lay down. Forkis sat on his calves in front of her legs, then leaned over her, resting his hands next to the girl's shoulders.

"I haven't eaten anything since this morning because of you. I don't know if it's good or bad in the current situation."

"I'll fix everything in a minute."

"Not so fast."

She began to stroke his broad, strong jaw with her hands. She ran a fingertip over Forkis' teeth, stopping for longer at the slippery fang. She tucked strands of his short black hair behind his right ear.

"It's amazing that you can do it. You are big, but you look quite ordinary. I have a feeling that you are more than a modificant, if you are it at all. And it's not hard to guess that you want to keep this secret only to yourself."

"You're right about everything. You're generally smart for a slum girl."

"I hung out with various criminals, and believe me, most aren't idiots. So let the subject of your origin be nipped in the bud. I honestly don't want to know it."

"Nevertheless, I can assure you that it won't be cannibalism." She felt better when he dispelled her fears, probing Aytar's thoughts.

She lowered her arms and lay limp on the bed. Smiling, she looked at him longingly, determined and ready, but not terrified. Surprisingly, she really wanted something like this, but unfortunately bombs away. Forkis wouldn't defeat Aytar with arguments. Even if he had given up on the oddity, he could see in her gaze that she would have eventually found the courage to kill herself. Honorary, not wanting help, on her own terms. He regretted that everything had turned out this way and she didn't want to join the nation.

He leaned down and began to gently nibble her ear, enfolding Zira's face with the warmth of his breath. As she enjoyed ASMR[15], he licked her closed eyes and cheeks, then slowly moved to the scar that marred her neck. He nibbled the nipples of the small breasts with his teeth, his tongue circled around them. He sucked them all into his mouth. Aytar only groaned as he bit her belly and navel, arousing in her something stronger than just tickling. He went down on his feet. The girl rubbed her side with her hand, wiping away the spiderweb of saliva that Forkis left in every penetrated place on her body.

---

[15] Autonomous sensors meridian response. Pleasant, relaxing tingling sensation caused by sensory stimuli.

"It's rather necessary, you'll get in sooner," he replied embarrassed.

"Okay, I like it," she said honestly, feeling the heat in her lower abdomen as if a hot water bottle had been placed there. She sighed with pleasure as he slipped her feet into his mouth. She felt the hardness of his teeth against her skin, and the strong, warm, moist tongue moving, sliding successively between her fingers.

He turned onto his back, dragging Aytar with him. He lowered her a little and placed her head on his belly. She cuddled up to him, Forkis stroked her blue hair. They lay so for a moment, he once again feasting his eyes on the sight of her tiny body, she - for the first time, with a slight anxiety, listening to the hissing, throbbing and rumbling in his gut. The girl's heart beat faster. She calmed down as she felt the soothing warmth of his mouth on her hand.

The man's tongue, now sliding down her back, buttocks and backs of her legs, acted like lemon balm gel mixed with an opiate. "Like a drug," she had to say to herself in her mind.

"You still want this?" He wanted to make sure. He was ready to quit, as long as he didn't act against Aytar's will. He quietly hoped it would end there.

"Yes," she replied, excited by the strange foreplay. "It works."

And hope faded.

"Ready?"

"I've never been more. Thank you, Forkis."

"I hope you're not claustrophobic. I love you, Aytar."

His jaws parted as he pushed her head into his mouth. He paused for a moment, letting Zira get used to the first station inside his body.

She felt the already familiar fleshy, warm tongue under one cheek, and under the other - a hard palate for contrast. She stared at his strong molars, being swept with the heated air from his esophagus.

After a while, she began to slide deeper. All she could think about was how such a thing was even possible. How Forkis would breathe during maybe an hour and a half of the ... consumption. What about collarbones and chest bones? As her face was in his stretchy throat, she stopped seeing anything. From now on, she only felt and heard. The rubbing of her body against moist, soft tissues. Smacking, as if jelly had been squeezed with a hand. The rumbling of his mighty heart. The sound of blood. The skeletal muscles spasm. Fortunately, she was still able to breathe, but with resistance. Before that, she hadn't taken it into account - the lack of air could shorten her experience.

And finally, after all these years, she began to feel the emotions again. Strong as never before! They seemed unreal, alien, as if blown from another plane of existence.

251

Excitement.

Ecstasy.

Horror.

Bliss.

Somnolence.

Languor.

Well, also a little claustrophobia.

All at once!

She finally succeeded, albeit in the strangest way in the whole cosmos.

Forkis pressed his arms firmly against her sides, but not enough to shatter Aytar's bones. Although she was going to die in the finale, he didn't want to damage her, treating her with respect and dignity. He didn't even scratch the absorbed body with a tooth.

After a few minutes of squeezing, Aytar finally gained some dark, pepsin-like space - the head squeezed through the stomach. A moment later, Zira was already rubbing her back against the slippery, folded wall that lay comfortably under the rest of the body, sliding down his smooth esophagus. She still had air that got inside with her.

Tired Forkis just gritted his teeth, definitely trapping Aytar in his body. Until now, he used his hands to support the work of the throat and esophagus stretched to the limit. The previously inoperable peristalsis finally functioned, drawing the lesser mass and volume down. Forkis managed to swallow the last contents with great difficulty, but succeeded.

The cardiac orifice closed.

Aytar found herself completely inside his enlarged belly, compressed, placed in the fetal position.

Afterwards, the tired emperor got motionless on his bed. He was breathing heavily as the windpipe and lungs finally ceased to be compressed.

Aytar had enough room to run her hand covered with the mucus over the undulating interior of his mobile stomach. She was breathing harder and harder, but she still could do it. The digestive acids treated earlier with high proof alcohol caressed her naked body more than prickled it.

She listened with delight to the powerful beating of his heart and the work of the organs surrounding her.

The oders' and Kiritian's hands met, separated by the tissues.

"Aytar ... And how are you there?" Forkis' baritone sounded like a bass coming from all sides at once. It was both amazing and terrifying for the girl, it was like the speech of a demon.

"Very good," she replied. "I feel so ... safe. I feel warm and pleasant. Better than my mother's house."

He didn't know if it was a joke.

"But you don't know your mother," he replied in a similar tone. "Oh, the collapsed star, I don't know how to comment it ..."

"And how are you?"

"It's almost like an orgasm, especially when you are moving," he continued this bizarre conversation. "It's best not to say anything, you will keep the air for longer. Here you are."

He choked on it and swallowed. Aytar smiled faintly.

"It's not necessary, it's okay. It's so cozy I'm getting sleepy." "You are rather running out of oxygen," Forkis thought. The situation was abnormal. In such moments, one person should save another, and here it was just the opposite.

They stopped to talk. The emperor turned from his side onto the back, they found their hands again and held them as close as possible.

Staring at the ceiling, he closed his eyes. He was physically perfect, but something strange was happening to his mind. He didn't want to lose Aytar, at the same time he was anxious to fulfill her last wish.

And to think he had been normal once. Meeting Lolmet Kejnay, and Jun Kame in general, became the first link in the butterfly effect. But at least over the centuries he had evolved to eat only demoralized women, taking full advantage of the unique properties of his body.

Aytar wasn't depraved. She adhered to chivalrous principles, preferred to die than to be doomed to someone's grace and help. Although she did kill for the guild, no one arranged orders for the innocent. And she did it all with her true being locked inside her mind. Forkis didn't think killing was a bad thing, especially when it was about a threat or 'nursing cuts' in a spoiled society.

And all mankind was spoiled.

Except for the Kiritians.

And Aytar, in which humanity had been destroyed.

He favored her because he loved her ...

He made a mistake.

He shouldn't have succumbed to her.

He couldn't lose her.

The feeling as if he had been falling down the stairs in his sleep effectively dispelled his thoughts.

Concerned, he opened his eyes.

He stroked his big belly.

"Aytar?"

She didn't answer. During the brief observation as he changed positions, he neither noticed nor felt any movement.

"What did I ..." He fell back on the pillow, squeezing his forehead with his hand. Drops of sweat appeared on his temples.

As if this trauma wasn't enough, Kiret entered the bedroom, staring at the PDA screen.

"Fork, forgive me for bothering you, but the matter is urgent. I can't make a long-term decision myself. At the border with the Scorpio Universum, a rebel reconnaissance has flown up ..."

He looked away from the screen and was speechless, his eyes widened. The dropped PDA slammed against the metal floor. Although Kiret had already lived three hundred and sixty-five years, and most of that time had to do with Forkis and his sometimes-strange actions, he had never experienced anything like this before. Not counting the forgotten situations, of course, when the medics had erased his neurotic episode from his memory.

"Fork, what the fuck did you do?!" He could usually control himself at their private meetings, but that was beyond human comprehension. He hadn't even thought that someone in the hall might have heard him roar. He grabbed his head. "How did you do that?! There is Aytar there, am I right? Did you dismember her?!"

"Necron, get a grip." Forkis sat on the edge of the bed. "Breathe, man. You have to help me."

Kiret walked over to the chair, fell heavily on it, leaned over and laced his fingers over the back of his head.

"Do you see any blood here?" Continued the emperor. "I didn't dismember anybody; I swallowed the girl whole."

Hearing this, Necron leaned back and banged his head against the hard headrest. Unknowingly, he began to rotate a Christian cross on a silver chain.

"Fuck, I think I will go mad." He didn't recognize himself. He had usually radiated calm and melancholy, had never sworn. But caring now about refinement was the last thing he needed.

"KIRET!" Forkis thundered. "Help me get her out. I want her alive. There is little time. No more questions!"

"Throw paper into fire, then wish it wasn't burning. Anyway, I don't want to know what happened here."

Necron pulled himself together. He walked over to Forkis, who got up. Despite the fact he had gained forty pounds, he moved smoothly, though sluggishly, as if he had worn heavy armor and gear. If one had insisted, they might have thought that he had grown a beer belly.

"I don't care what you think. Help me get her out right now," he ordered.

"How long has she been inside?" The words barely passed through Kiret's throat.

"More than a quarter of an hour. I think I dropped off for a while. I woke up a minute before you came in, she already didn't move then."

"So bombs away."

"She may still be alive," said Forkis. "I drank high proof alcohol; it slows down the digestion of human proteins."

Necron got faint.

"I'm calling the medics."

"Before they prepare the equipment, another quarter of an hour will pass. Every second counts now."

"What are you suggesting?"

"Help me get her out."

"Me? How? Can't you make yourself vomit? I'll go for some agent ... Do you have salt here somewhere?"

"Kiret, there's no time for that!"

"Then put your hand down your throat."

"It doesn't work for me. Otherwise, I wouldn't be able to swallow so much content at all because I would be puking every time."

"I'll take care of it right away. Get on all fours. Back in the day, when I was still an oders, this is how I made my son vomit when he swallowed a small element. It always worked."

Forkis obeyed. Necron stood behind him, leaned over, and wrapped his arms around the non-convex part of his stomach, at the height of his wings of ilium. Putting pressure, he pushed with his hands towards the esophagus, wanting to move the stomach contents in that direction.

Then batab Gareth entered the room with another case. He saw the emperor in pants only, with his big belly, on all fours, and his deputy in light armor standing and pressing against Forkis' loins. His eyes widened and he stayed that way.

"Onto the chair, Gareth!" Forkis didn't even bother to use the official tone. "You sit there, you don't move, and you pretend you're not here! Did you read the order on the PDA that nobody should disturb me?!"

The commander of the city guard obeyed like an automaton.

"Nothing. She's too big," Kiret said resignedly. "In addition, she's lying in a bad position. The back covers the cardiac orifice. So, what's now?"

Gareth nearly got palpitations as he watched the ruler of eighteen of the twenty-nine colonized planets roll on the floor and change position in various ways by moving his belly with his hands.

"I can't move Zira. Necron, put your hand in my stomach, try to turn her. Or grab her by anything and pull."

"Fuck, I can't believe it ..."

"Just do it!" Forkis urged him. "There is a bathroom near, so you will wash."

"I don't know if my paw will get in."

"Seriously?"

Not believing what he was doing, Kiret removed the glove and armor elements of his hand, leaving it in the sleeve of his uniform. After a brief moment of thought, he shed all the armor of his torso and took off his shirt, staying only in his pants, just like Forkis.

The emperor was on all fours, with his neck parallel to the ground. He held his breath.

Looking at the legs of the chair on which pale Gareth was trying to encompass reality, grimacing Necron slipped a hand into Forkis' mouth. With a squawk, he began to press his hand into the esophagus, and soon he broke through the cardiac orifice, where he encountered resistance.

After two minutes of digging around the stomach, Kiret pull out his arm.

"I can't ... She's stuck," he said, brushing mucus, searing digestive juices and saliva off his hand. "I'm sorry, Fork. Too much time has passed."

The emperor's gaze fell on Necron's knife, still embedded in the wooden skull.

"Perform a C-section on me."

Kiret gave him a firm, shocked look.

"Forget it. It will be a serious, painful operation, you must be connected to the apparatus ..."

"Necron, did I mention we don't have time? Just do it! I can bear it. Did I get hurt only a few times?"

"She's dead anyway."

"If I can tell you something, sir," Garcth managed to say. He continued as they looked at him. "I was out in the field for my new squad's exercises, I came about it - I needed your telepathic skills, sir. I always carry molecular glue, because there are accidents, I still have it on me. I also intended to kiritianize three recruits, but one of them wimped out of getting infected. So, I also have the plunger of super virus." The man slid off his backpack.

"Great," Forkis said. "Kiret, you cut, and Gareth will then pour glue."

"It is too much for me ..."

"It's an order, dignitary!" Worried about the passing time, Forkis could hardly keep emotions in check. "You have several hundred years of experience, you helped wounded soldiers. You even delivered like this."

"But for God's sake, no one told me to cut an emperor without any medicaments, apparatus, and on a floor! If I screw up, I'll be charged with murder."

"You won't, because you do it on my own responsibility, on my behalf. Gareth is a witness. Do it, otherwise you will end up as a corporal. Or I'll even kick you out of the nation!" Forkis allowed himself a strong emphasis. Gareth and Necron had to undergo the deletion of memory, anyway.

The command pronounced in this form immediately convinced Kiret. He knew that the emperor wouldn't throw him out or degrade him, but only acted in affect, still believing that he would save the girl.

Necron grabbed his knife and yanked it from the forehead of the skull, then poured vodka over the blade from the bottle on the table. He took the first aid kit from a recess in the wall. Giving Forkis a painkiller injection to his side with a plunger, he tried to ignore the fact that an agent to dissolve bones had rolled out of the tilted medical kit.

"I can help," Gareth offered. Forkis liked the fact that he didn't ask questions.

"You'll be insuring Kiret. Do whatever he requests."

As Necron set the strongest light in the room, they were flooded with halogen white. Gareth spread the blanket on the floor and Forkis lay down on it with a fierce face. He reached for Kiret's shirt that lay closest to him, rolled it up and tucked it between his teeth.

The men who arrived weren't wearing nose and mouth covers. The Kiritians were able to cure any infection in a moment, should one break into the body being operated.

Kiret knelt beside his emperor. He pressed the fingers of his left hand next to his convex belly, checking the arrangement of the girl's organs and body. He looked for the best place to make a cut. When he made up his mind, he looked into Forkis' eyes. The latter nodded firmly. Although Necron didn't have to, he sprayed out of habit his hands and the patient's skin with the disinfectant, just as he had automatically poured alcohol on the blade. Many battles fought on land, especially when he had still served in the New Order Army on Earth, resulted in a field experience. He had dealt with human guts many times; nevertheless, he was afraid of damaging something. The pressure and responsibility were immense.

As he began making a slow but firm cut, Forkis gritted his teeth on his shirt. The painkiller was already working, but it only partially relieved the pain. The stronger one wasn't given to personal first aid kits.

Blood began to trickle down onto the blanket.

Gareth was helping to keep the belly in its proper position, while also checking the emperor's pulse.

After the first cut, Kiret made a right, deep one. He cut the stomach muscular layer. He expanded the tissues. The acrid smell of stomach juices wafted through the room.

Forkis didn't even groan, his blood pressure decreased due to the draining blood, but the persistent desperation kept him from passing out.

Gareth was shocked to see in the stomach Aytar, crammed like a fetus in the mother's womb, glistening with digestive juices. He had never seen anything like this, he felt sick.

Necron was shocked no less, but he kept working, quickly and efficiently. He carefully pulled out wet Aytar and moved her to the quilt beside Forkis. The first acid-scorched spots were visible on her skin.

Forkis watched it all, panting heavily. He rested his hands on his elbows and kept them stiff, as if he had been benching. Shifting the open muscles into a physiological position, Gareth poured molecular glue over the gash on the stomach and side. The blood stopped flowing immediately. The stem cell modificant slime became similar to the host's proteins and immediately began the repair process.

"You must lie down now, sir, for at least three hours," said Gareth.

"How is she?" Forkis asked.

Kiret, examining the girl, shook his head with a sigh and a grave expression.

"She's dead. I'm sorry. And how are you feeling? You have to be brought to the medical center."

Forkis ignored his deputy's inquiry. He felt an almost physical pang of despair.

"Inject her the super virus." It was the only sane thing that could still be done.

"It probably won't work."

"Do you remember your case? In London, at the headquarters of the global government, I shot you in the head in front of the crowd to demonstrate my power to them. I injected you with the super virus and you came to life. Necrogens were boosted, they regenerated your wound together with foreign biological materials."

"But that was seconds after I was killed."

"Do you always have to multiply problems, pessimist?" Kiret complied with Forkis' request. In fact, they had nothing to lose. He took the plunger from the batab and injected the girl with the super virus in the same way as in the case of the emperor and painkiller.

Gareth sat down at the table, took a long sip of vodka. Bloody Kiret dropped to the floor and rested his back against the bed, not even bothering to wash. Worried, Forkis extended his hand and grabbed Aytar's dead hand. He stroked the girl's cheek.

They could only wait.

For a quarter of an hour no one moved, only a few sentences were spoken between the Kiritians.

And then something started happening - Aytar twitched as if she had gotten a shock. She took a deep breath of a would-be drowned man on the surface, arched her back, her glassy eyes looked as if they had been covered with endosperm.

Made from a combination of the most dangerous human viruses, also artificially made, the super virus rapidly multiplied in her body. It infected and changed every cell in the body, which

266

resulted in immortality. Like the primitive organism Turritopsis nutricula, also the advanced evolutionary Aytar's body from now on, every few years, would return to the state from the time of the kiritianization. Her biological age would forever remain close to that of a 30-year-old woman.

"I can't believe it ... And yet it worked," whispered Kiret, chuckling goofily in a fit of relief.

"The same thing happened as to you. Aytar's situation was even worse." Gareth immediately approached the girl, crouched next to her.

Forkis ignored the men's remarks about his condition and also knelt beside Zira, knowing that his sealed wounds wouldn't open again. He touched her, then hugged.

"She's unconscious," he announced with great relief and a smile.

"The worst is yet to come," Kiret joined the company. "We can't give her anything because it would disrupt the infection of the super virus. The body has to deal with it on its own, i.e. lose the fight against the pathogen."

Minutes passed and the unconditioned reflex didn't repeat itself, Aytar didn't regain consciousness, but she was breathing calmly. The infection seemed to be mild in her case.

Gareth went to wash himself. Kiret returned to his previous seat and leaned against the bed. Forkis was washing himself and Aytar with rags soaked in the agent from the first aid kit.

"If the girl survives," Kiret asked, waving his hand, "how will you explain that to the achijes? Your authority will be crushed when it turns out that you have pardoned your own would-be killer, and besides introduced Aytar into the nation. They will stop being afraid of you and they will make the girl's life hell."

"She didn't want to kill me. She tried to restore homeostasis to the mind, searching for extreme emotions. She was pointing a knife at my shoulder. She did unblock herself - I was able to probe her telepathically afterwards. Let's say it was BDSM." Forkis smiled crookedly. "The problem of the assassination attempt is therefore obsolete. And this we will tell the Kiritians, that there was a misunderstanding because of the disease of Aytar, which remained silent and refused to receive medical attention. She was going to heal herself on her own terms. Moreover, she was limited by the collectivity's credo, which had just expired."

Necron looked at his emperor's belly as it was regaining its normal size.

"You can, Fork, have fun in the bedroom. No way in hell I want to know how you broke the laws of physics."

\*\*\*

An hour later the emperor was feeling well. There was not even a trace left of wounds that had disappeared surprisingly quickly. He put a bathrobe on unconscious Aytar, wrapped her in a blanket, picked her up and, accompanied by the men, they left his residence. They headed towards the medical center. The information about Zira's innocence was made public, so the achijes observing Forkis saw only that he wanted to help his injured girlfriend. He didn't in any way lie to the nation, who invented the scenario for itself - that the emperor had shot Aytar, which admitted at the same time that she was innocent, allowing Forkis to do a telepathic probe. It was impossible to disprove it and see the wounds, because the blanket covered the body.

At the medical center, Kiret and Gareth's memories of the last few hours were deleted.

Placed on the couch, Zira began to suffer the infection more drastically. She screamed in her sleep, thrashed, terrified and unaware of anything, she opened her eyes covered with endosperm many times, as if she had been struggling with enormous pain and a terrible nightmare at the same time; the super virus infection could have produced thousands of symptoms. All they could do was tie her with straps to the couch so that she didn't hurt herself.

At the suggestion of the medic, Forkis left the office; there was nothing else he could do apart from worrying and looking.

The condition of the girl remained unchanged for two hours.

Finally, exhausted, kiritianized Aytar opened her eyes consciously. It was over. Physically, the super virus didn't change her.

The medic unhooked the safeguards and examined her.

"Can I go in?" Forkis asked as Aytar was left alone, still resting on the couch. During this time, she managed to think through a few things.

"Come in. You acted against my will, making me a Kiritian woman and taking me out of the way I took ..." she said as he walked.

"We have the serum. The disease of immortality can be reversed, but only in a few years," he replied, sitting down next to the girl. "Earlier, your body might not be able to withstand it, it has to adapt to the new biological program. I, in turn, had to make such a decision so that you didn't die. I decided for you, let's say it was the law of the stronger. And I was terrified when you were inside. It's a miracle that you were brought back to life. You died, so you are now completely free of the affairs of the collectivity."

"Thank you." She was polite but strangely distant. In a completely different way than before. Forkis used his telepathy.

"I can read you, I can see your thoughts flow," he pointed out.

"I'm afraid of the future and at the same time I'm happy for an undefined reason. I'm so relieved. Probably because the case is solved. So it worked. You unlocked me. It's good to experience emotions again after all these years." She smiled kindly, but without feeling. "I remember the events until I passed out from lack of air. What happened next?"

Forkis described the desperate but at the same time comic struggle to save her. "If it's traumatic for you," he said when he finished, "I'll erase your memories like Kiret and Gareth's."

"No, I want to remember everything. It was an amazing experience." She took Forkis by a hand. The grip wasn't like that of a woman holding her man, just a friendly grateful clasp. "I'd love to experience it again. I won't tell anyone what happened between us. Or anything I heard in your bedroom."

"I know. From today on, you won't be able to hide anything from me. However, we need to talk seriously about our future. If you don't want to now, we can put it off for another day."

"Now's a good time." Aytar took a short pause, collecting her thoughts. "Tell me honestly ... What would you expect in our relationship? You do care about normal intercourse, right?"

"Apart from many more important things, such as honesty, closeness and mutual support, which we wouldn't have problems

271

with - yes. In time, I would like something more, although it has been good until now. I would adapt to your needs so as not to hurt you, but I would feel unfulfilled."

"I won't be able to give it to you, Forkis. As I said, I'm asexual. You saw for yourself what happened. And I'm so sorry, but I don't love you. I was selfish. Everything we went through together I did to restore my humanity. I didn't feel anything, so I didn't know if I had any affection for you either. You healed me, but you lost me at the same time," she added in a whisper, looking at her hands.

"I see." He withdrew his hand. "My decision to make you a Kiritian woman didn't result to be hasty, though I have killed two birds with one stone. You are brave, faithful to your ideals, honorable, you don't break the rules, even far from the place where they apply. These are the qualities of a good Kiritian, and very rare ones. In terms of health and psychology, you are also fit to be immortal, and this happens with one person in several hundred. I just ask you one thing: no more fanaticism related to any credo that could destroy your entire life. You are now starting your career in the nation, Private Ziro Aytar." He smiled and saluted playfully.

"If I ever fail enough to be condemned to death, you can eat me," she said with amusement. "And this time without cesarean sections or inducing vomiting."

"I have a feeling that this will be our private, sick joke. You're pretty short. How about making you taller? For example, one meter eighty? So that the prospect of finding yourself in my belly doesn't tempt you anymore. But seriously, your height is much lower than that of other achijes."

"I'm thirty years old. My skeleton has long stopped growing."

"For the Immortals' medicine, almost nothing is impossible." Forkis winked at her.

\*\*\*

He hid from Aytar how disappointed he was, and he was sorry. As the emperor, he mastered the public control of emotions to perfection, so no achij could read anything from his official face. Forkis had it all: the highest power among the human race, wealth, charisma, immortality, look, perhaps not beautiful, but dignified and austere. Despite this, he couldn't find anyone, unlike for example Corporal Victor Shane, whom he had seen with his wife more than once - two happy and fulfilled Kiritians. Though Forkis believed that a man's fate was in their own hands, he sometimes seriously considered whether space had punished him for his totalitarian rule and the great deception in which he still lived.

Aytar began to avoid him.

When they dealt with each other militarily or officially, she behaved towards him like any other achij. A couple of times he caught her hiding behind a coign or column when he was around, certain he couldn't see it. She wanted to forget about their affair? Maybe she was afraid of something? Was she ashamed she had hurt him? In certain circumstances, telepathy shouldn't have been used.

This time Forkis did her way.

It was comforting, at least, that Zira reacted coldly to every male attempt to establish a closer acquaintance with her. She had her rules and others respected it, especially since on missions, she turned out to be a perfect achij.

Forkis sometimes walked alone onto the rocky peaks of extinct volcanoes near the capital. Today he went there too; as a favorite of all Kiritians, he needed no protection on his own planet.

His thoughts were interrupted by Kiret, who sat down next to him on the terraced stone slope. Together they watched the sunset of the great Betelgeuse. Two of Morascrik's three moons were even visible.

"I have a nice new girlfriend for you," Necron announced, opening the backpack he had brought. He pulled out a bottle and goblets. "Her name is Radioactive Supernova, vodka out of this galaxy. The entire human tribe worships her by rooting in soil with the nose.

Forkis laughed sincerely.

At least the friends never left.

# Guru

### The Terrenic Year 2936

"Do you know how many attacks have already been carried out against him?" The slightly frustrated man with an icy, mafia-like look sighed. He said it in a tone as if he had been trying to suggest something to a child who had come up with a brilliant idea. Unfortunately, brilliant only for them.

"Of course, I analyzed them all carefully," the woman informed without boastfulness, smiling with nonchalance inadequate to the upcoming event. She changed the position of her legs and was now resting her right one on the left one. "That's why I know perfectly well what mistakes were made by my predecessors. I intend to beware of them earnestly."

The other man, with a silver chain around his neck with a pendant representing a mountain, didn't seem to hear her words.

"And I think I don't have to say," he replied, "that they all ended in a flop? The bully is still breathing.

A group of three sat in one of the rooms of the underground facility in the far north of Proxima Centauri e, where a small circle of the red dwarf was barely breaking through fast-moving clouds. Even amid the metal walls, admittedly close to the main gate, the whistle of the wind could be heard in the icy wasteland. Centuries earlier, it had been believed that giant flares from Proxima Centauri e, unconnected by gravity to the stars Alpha Centauri A and Alpha Centauri B, would annihilate all life on the orbiting planets. It turned out, however, that the measurements were incorrect due to the primitive apparatus, and besides the star's activity itself had decreased over the centuries. Proxima e was therefore not only unsuitable for colonization, but also ultraviolet

277

and millimeter waves didn't affect the health of the new inhabitants, against which moreover the centers of civilization were protected by appropriate safeguards.

The woman assumed a less pleasant expression, resting her arms firmly on the amethyst table top, at which the conspirators were debating.

"I've prepared for this for many years. I've analyzed, collected information, created scenarios, and the longest, I've waited for a convenient moment. Now is the perfect opportunity related to the activities of the Procibro company, and I don't want it to be wasted. It is not known when the next one will appear."

The man with the chain cleared his throat and clasped his hands.

"So, let's summarize. With the support of third parties and his brother, Lord Tisamo," he looked at the mafia boss dealing with smuggling of unregistered technologies in the Old Zone, "he will bring dignitaries here, having made them interested in the high-quality innovative goods, which they will definitely not find in Calvary ..."

"Military technology preferably," the woman said.

"They have it all," Tisamo commented softly.

"We've been through this before. The transaction cannot be successful, the Infected must be irritated, because this increases the chance that they will work their failure off in our city. They always do it; it is part of their behavior pattern. It absolutely has to happen. Your only job, Lord, is to get them here from Morascrik, then through Procibro to show the desired goods that they will reject. But nothing will happen if something interests them. Once they leave the company's gates, I will take care of the rest." The woman smiled like a kitten given a mouse to play with.

"It's good that at least I won't have to do anything," said the man with the chain, "I'll only rent you out the facility and send the remaining handful of workers in the Percent Lab on vacation. But I wouldn't want any faux pas anyway, because we'll be dead. The pissed-off First Dignitary is ready to do the reverse terraforming, and despite the fact that Proxima e is mostly abandoned and aging colonies."

"Don't worry, Casijo," the woman emphasized sharply. "I have a deal with highly trained mercenaries, ex-herders and prison overseers who know the job also from the other side, and who can keep their mouths shut. A few will suffice, and they'll encompass everything, plus your walking robots, once guarding political prisoners. We will involve a maximum of fifty people in the project, not more. Of these, a few, including us, must know the whole plan, but under no circumstances can find themselves near the First, because he would surely find out everything. The rest will be eliminated when they are no longer needed. Every of them will have to be incinerated afterwards so that the Infected can't read

279

anything in their dead brains. So we have to choose people who are sufficiently well-versed not to mess up their simple tasks, but also insignificant ones. I repeat: fifty people maximum. Fewer people can't handle it, and with more people always something is screwed up. Someone might rat. This is one of the main reasons why all assassination attempts failed - too many people always mean a mess in the ranks of the conspirators.

"Then use only androids, Laureta, and that's it," suggested Lord Tisamo, with his arms clasped.

"The Infected will prefer living objects." Casijo smirked. "Am I right, Laureta?"

The woman got up.

"We don't need androids, apart from the trouper Sefiroth, of course. It is enough that there will be combat robots in the Percent Lab. You will give me the access codes for them at the right time, Casijo. The Proxima e Archontat[16] won't find out what will happen in their former prison facility, and it is now a private complex anyway. However, if they want to assign someone to us just then, I will be able to stabilize the situation."

[16] The form of power exercised by nine high officials, where one is dominant, mainly performing a representative function.

"That's obvious." Casijo grinned. "You are not stupid, otherwise I wouldn't have given the Percent Lab under the auspices of yours and your mercenaries."

Laureta smiled pityingly at him.

"Thank you for this meeting. At least you don't have your tail between your legs like the rest of those capitulators biting the dust. It will take another month, local time, to prepare. We will be constantly in touch. So, to the death of Forkis, gentlemen."

Having gotten up briskly, the three of them clinked their glasses of alcohol. After the sips that sealed the collaboration, the conspirators laughed.

Minutes later, Casijo led his companions down a metal corridor to the exit what was watched by Sefiroth leaning against the wall. The android, grimacing, looked at the back of Laureta walking away, who would soon take over temporary power in the facility.

\*\*\*

Forkis sat on his diorite throne in an audience chamber that had been once a grotto, near the Utza'm Achij Cave. He had just finished giving tips regarding the restoration of a power plant in the capital to a group of architects whom he preferred to meet traditionally. The First Galactic Dignitary appreciated face-to-face conversation; he could infiltrate an interlocutor immediately if necessary. In the case of the more senior Kiritians, this practically didn't happen.

Free from his duties that evening, he allowed himself a moment to relax as he nonchalantly sat down on the throne. He drank well-chilled vodka from a glass in small sips, contemplating black stone columns and small-flame artificial fire generators when his PDA communicator rang.

"What's up?" He asked Kiret which was somewhere out of the way in the communications center building, which he recognized in the image on the display.

"Interesting matter, Fork. A man from the technology company Procibro from Proxima Centauri e, a certain Vicente Cortez, just turned to our sales representative and offered the products. By the way, do all these names have to start with "PRO'?"

Forkis put the vessel down, got up, and started pacing the dark, cool room.

"Unbelievable. We rarely have contact with this planet. Let me guess: the company is in decline, another dare-devil overcomes fear and dares to contact us, seeing no other financial possibilities, but knows that the Immortals pay a lot?"

"Not exactly. It is a small, new company - but with employees with many years of experience because they have moved away from the competition - which immediately contacted us about innovative products. I must admit that it is impossible to set the bar higher for the start. Vicente Cortez is said to be some kind of inventor."

"And of course, you checked this company, Kiret?"

"Surely. Nothing arouses suspicion. I even have a list of proposed products. For encouragement, only photos and a laconic description of the intended use. It's military technology. I have to admit that the guy knows his stuff - he transferred the message to us via a direct channel from Proxima e, without amplifying the signal or changing intermediaries like satellites. Clean transmission without surveillance."

Forkis immediately felt curiosity about what the oderses, and from the Old Zone, which also included the Earth - a depopulated shelter set aside, could offer to the Kiritians.

"Send me everything to the kapripod."

"Of course. You already have it, Fork."

"And what exactly does this guy expect?" The dignitary began projecting sequentially high-resolution holographic materials over a desk located to the side of the chamber.

"He wants to come to Morascrik and meet us."

283

"Well, a moron or someone very desperate. By flying here, he will have to wade through the Capricorn Universum, and the gangsters will beat him there."

"I ordered to convey in the center to let Cortez know that we'll contact him once we've made our decision."

"Okay. I'll go over everything I have here and call you after that."

Having returned for his glass, Forkis started moving and analyzing new inventions. The ideas were rather average. Many things Cortez found innovative, the Kiritians had long had on the equipment, which they didn't share with the Universum. The oderses saw their equipment in action, especially the rebels in battle, but failed to establish the specifications of a given weapon. They would have to break into the achij databases or get their machine, which, with the Immortals' current technological advantage, seemed impossible.

Several things, however, caught the attention of the Galactic First Dignitary. It immediately occurred to him that if Dr. Maximus Figam had improved them, the Immortals would have expanded their assortment with a new collection. Normally Forkis would have ordered the contractor to fly over to him, giving him a bodyguard (unless he had his own) to stand in front of his throne, but this time he decided that he would go to Proxima e. The situation with the rebels had stabilized some time earlier, the

Kiritians were now at war with no one, and Forkis lacked the adventures which he had gotten used to over the centuries. That is why, among other things, he came up with the regular 'wild parties' called harroweeng for his subordinates in Utza'm Ahiy Cave, so that they could go crazy a little. A flight to the Old Zone would certainly not turn out to be an exciting trip, but it would always be a long trip to a foreign place.

After dark, when the sky was marked by a rusty backwater of set Betelgeuse, Forkis headed to the communications center. He found Kiret working there.

"Tell this Vicenty Cortez we'll come see his toys. You heard right, I will go to Proxima e," he added, seeing the surprised face of Necron. "It has been a long time since I visited those regions of space. There will be two birds killed with one stone. Tell Captain Milles to prepare four squadrons. I don't expect an attack by the rebels, but a bogy, as always, will be perfect, not only against the opposition." Forkis enjoyed the oderses' fear of the Kiritan fleet, which he never said directly, though it was an open secret. In terms of the presentation of strength, he didn't even try to pretend to be the mental heights of the three on the Kardashov Scale, to which the Immortals were approaching. "Also, contact the Kiritian military embassy on Proxima Centauri e, so that before our arrival, they send masked spy orbs to ... What is this city's name?"

Kiret looked at the capripod screen.

"Provelkava Grihorsk," he pronounced slowly that tongue-breaker.

"Of course, 'pro' had to be in the name," the emperor thought with amusement. It was about identity and planetary affiliation, about which the once xenophobic Proximans were crazy, but it was not a coincidence that it was an abbreviation of professionalism, which was an open message to Earthlings even during the colonization of space: "We are strong, we are autonomous, we don't need you or your worldviews."

"Get those at the embassy to check the security status," Forkis ordered. "Then we'll also use our own orbs."

"Of course," Necron replied without enthusiasm.

***

Forkis ordered Kiret to stay in the capital K'otz'ib'aja as a deputy, anyway, the Second Galactic Dignitary was reluctant, for personal reasons, to go near Earth. The emperor selected officers, including Milles, which took their achijes, then the Kiritians set out in five squadrons from Morascrik toward the Old Zone.

The journey for about five hundred and forty light-years was without incident, especially since they traveled almost the entire route in hyperspace jumps. Letting them into the atmosphere of Proxima e also went smoothly. F-314 hybrid fighters belonging to the air defense - autonomous or manned - covered with smooth armor with barely visible, hexagonal patterns, didn't even twitch. The planet's archont, the supreme official of the group of nine, had no choice but to accept the visit of the most powerful visitors in the Zodiac Universum.

Proxima Centauri e, the fifth globe orbiting in the Proxima Centauri system, was the first exoplanet of the solar system to be colonized by earthlings. Originally uninhabitable, it had undergone full, intense terraforming. Its gravity was seven percent lesser than that of Earth. Once bustling with social life, it had become depopulated over the centuries, mainly due to further migrations. Derelict colonies and industrial facilities gradually began to age, inspiring urban legends and horror stories, especially about ghost towns.

The Kiritians landed on the outskirts of the still thriving Provelkava Grihorsk colony, full of towering buildings and colorful lights, devoid of naturally growing vegetation. After refusing the numerous taxi drivers offering a ride, causing a general sensation, the Immortals clad in mid-class armor with covered faces approached the metal high building, which was the seat of the Procibro Company. Forkis and a few achijes accompanying him were awaited by Vicente Cortez's deputy, a young, short, black-haired man. He was surprised and scared - he hadn't been told that the First Galactic Dignitary, who slid open his helmet out of sight of the locals, would come to see the merchandise himself. Nonetheless, that gave the dealer a boost, as he thought the Kiritians had recognized Procibro as a significant, valuable contractor. The emperor smiled indulgently as he walked over and examined his thoughts telepathically.

"Doris Kagawa, Mr. Vicente Cortez's first deputy," the employee introduced himself with a deep bow, then blurted out in one exhalation: "It is a great honor for us to see the First Galactic Dignitary and his achijes in our humble abode."

Forkis nodded at him.

"Is Mr. Cortez who talked to us home?" He looked into the bowels of the great building, which, behind the soundproofing and security cover, was no different from a workshop. He spotted people or androids at work, maybe a mixed team. A little boy, led by his mother by the hand, approached the edge of the entrance gate.

"Good morning," the woman greeted Forkis, not knowing who was standing in front of her, especially since all the achijes had the same, unmarked armor. She turned to the child: "You see, Alejandro, what cool soldiers have come to visit us?"

The two soon headed for Cortez's house, built at a safe distance from the hall.

"I'm terribly sorry," Kagawa replied with sincere regret and shame, drawing Forkis' attention again, "but Mr. Cortez had to leave on a very urgent matter, he didn't say what. However, I assure you that I'm a worthy deputy. I will arrange everything just as if you were talking to the owner himself, sir!" He added eagerly and bowed again. "Please follow me."

This 'urgent matter' seemed at least strange to Forkis: someone made the appointment, brought the Immortals from afar, and then boldly didn't deign to take care of them personally. The oderses were simply afraid to do like that. Whether they were liked or hated, virtually everyone respected them, except for the rebels. They were afraid to be late to a meeting even a minute. Thanks to his telepathy, Forkis learned that, according to the information provided, Kagawa knew nothing about the mysterious disappearance of his boss. He had only gotten a message in the morning onto a holonot that he had been supposed to replace him. The knowledge about the trip also coincided with the thoughts of Vicente's wife. Doris seemed fine, appearance and demeanor indicated that he had descended from the terrestrial Far East, where honor had been cherished for generations.

The hall, which the dignitary ordered achijes to guard, did indeed turn out to be an ordinary city workshop, with the highest safety standards. The workers, a minority of which were people, dealt with their work diligently; in their minds, Forkis found no interesting tidbits. Accessible only to selected personnel, the underground hid technological laboratories. Even though the guests were Immortals themselves, Kagawa could only let them into the yellow zone, where the items had already been prepared. After a few hours of viewing and presentations, Forkis decided to purchase a spy orb engine, operating according to the perpetual motion principle, and, to the surprise of achijes and Kagawa himself, a bio-ionic inhibitor. It was a small device that made its host invisible to oders military and civilian scanners, masking at the same time other living organisms within a radius of several meters. In practice, this meant that a person with the device integrated with an armor or a weapon could walk through an electronically guarded facility and be visible only to human eyes. The Kiritians, as hegemons and dominators, invested in offensive technology, especially aviation, but Forkis simply liked this tiny device.

"... such a long way to get some shit," he heard when he was leaving the hall. The two achijes talking freely, immediately flinched, overstretched and froze with their weapon pressed to their chests, as if they had been on an honor guard duty on a national holiday.

"I've heard it," Forkis replied with a serene smile. He was in a good mood. "Corporals Rasmus Darkoris and Viktor Shane ... How about a day stay in the colony?"

"We're really sorry, sir!" Rasmus, who had previously commented on the expedition, replied vigorously, thinking that the words of the First Dignitary meant some filthy tasks in the penal colony.

"There's nothing to be sorry for, it was a private conversation after all. I'm glad that my achijes have their own opinions. So that also you get something out of this trip, take the guys and relax a bit in the city. Under the same condition as always - try to avoid fatalities. This is not a trick. One should always have fun after their duties. But first check the entire region with the orbs in the masking mode. To be safe in Provelkava Grihorsk, we only need mediocre armor, but forethought is a virtue."

"Yes, sir," Shane replied faster. "We'll take care of everything."

After boarding the corvette, Forkis went to the wardroom to quench his thirst. He found Captain Milles at the bar and joined him. Seated at a large table, a cheerful group of lower-ranking achijes was listening to the narrator:

"... so, we are flying this cruise ship in the Proxima Centauri planetary system. The twenty-sixth century was a time when the Kiritians were no longer liked, but no one was particularly afraid of us or attacked us back then. Nevertheless, during this trip, a Proximian ship, hung in orbit, accosted us and gave us an earful that we had violated the spatial zone of the planet. We answered it, so what? And we were going to continue exploring the Old Zone, as planned. The captain of the ship told us to get lost, our pilot said no, because this wasn't yet the Proxima e military space. So they moved their ass and began to ostentatiously fly towards us, they set a collision course straight to starboard. The other oderses' ships from orbit did nothing, their officers stared, waiting to see what would happen next. We do nothing either, we keep going, our pilot ignored the others." The achij grinned. "And now the best! The Proxima e ship hit our starboard - and they got fucked up!"

The audience burst out laughing simultaneously; Milles and Forkis also started to giggle softly.

"They exploded?" One of the achijes at the table asked.

"That's weird, but no. Their nose broke, followed by the hull. More than half of the board was depressurized. The crew wore combat suits, so they only pulled the covers over their heads before being thrown into space. We on this cruise ship almost started to pee ourselves laughing as they spun on their own axis, waving their arms and legs! Someone from us got in touch with the commander of the Proximians cleared out into space and somehow managed to ask seriously if the others needed help. They say no, because their friends were about to come and catch them."

Another dose of thunderous laughter.

"And then these general network entries: 'So, you are saying your ship lost to the cruise liner?' 'Yes, but with Kiritian one!"

When cheered up, Forkis and Milles went to the bridge, they found another achijes indulging in entertainment combined with work. Rasmus Darkoris and Viktor Shane were so engrossed in what was going on on the holographic monitor with the audio transmission that they didn't hear the door being opened slightly or the footsteps.

"Check this out," said Rasmus enthusiastically.

Forkis and the captain approached the instrument panel noiselessly and noticed that the corporals, bent over, were watching a cellula image of one of the masked Kiritian orbs flying over the evening city streets. A combat and spy ball hung in the air near the city drone patrolling Provelkava Grihorsk, then rushed forward, hitting the technologically inferior cousin. The drone turned and swayed as it tried to level the flight. A drunk observing it from below, widened his eyes, not sure if he had witnessed something real and unusual, or alcohol made him confused, and that's why he saw the drone hit by the air.

Forkis folded his arms over his chest.

"Yhym."

The junior non-commissioned officers looked at each other and got confused.

"Is the city safe?" Asked the dignitary.

"Yes, sir," Viktor immediately announced. "The orbs have found nothing that threatens us."

"Then go out, take your friends from the galley. I'll leave thirty percent of the squadrons in service."

"Thank you, sir," said Viktor.

"Perhaps you would like to rest a bit?" Having sat in the commander's seat, the emperor gently turned to Captain Milles. Since the tragedy in the village of Dharsa Pass, where Lilly Tedlock had been killed, the officer had avoided some kind of entertainment.

"Someone has to protect you, sir," he replied with a smile.

"Everyone's aware that if they point the barrel of a pistol in my direction, I'll pay back with the battleship's cannons." Forkis looked at a bioronic inhibitor, 2 free units of which, Kagawa gave him before he decided to buy the rest exclusively, along with the design. It turned out that the flexible device fitted perfectly in the niche in the bracer intended for this type of interchangeable inserts. The dignitary rose. "Scan me with the thermoindector, Captain."

Milles detached his gun from his belt and started a heat scan for living organisms.

"There are positive readings, sir, but weak, with the 'ghost effect'."

"It's better than I expected anyway. Ibek is partially blocking our instruments; I'm sure that when confronted with the scanners of the oderses, it won't be detected at all, and neither will its user. Doris Kagawa assured me about it anyway." Forkis peered through a puronax cover of the bridge. At the entrance to one of the streets he saw a few laughing achijes, talking to equally cheerful prostitutes. From this distance, he could even see that the girls were well-groomed, looking healthy and wearing expensive clothes - Provelkava Grihorsk was famous for one of the most prestigious brothels in the Old Zone. "Shane and Darkoris gave me an idea. What do you say, Captain, to test ibek on the oderses' equipment?"

"You mean you want to go out, sir?"

"We'll go together, Major Ivester will replace me on the corvette."

Forkis had read from the officer's mind earlier that he would like to take a longer walk, so the answer came as no surprise:

"With you always, sir."

***

A miniflot itself stationed nearby, as a visual factor, was enough to make Forkis feel at ease. In addition, the emperor's safety was protected by achijes scattered across Provelkava Grihorsk, his middle-class armor, and the fatal reputation of the 'mortal differently'. With their helmet covers lowered, he and Milles looked like another subordinates who had been granted leave for the night. Doris Kagawa and the rest of the Procibro employees were not to spread the word about the identity of the business partner. All these precautions were dictated by reason and the position, but not by fear. Forkis simply didn't want oderses to stare at him, threaten him, run away, or beg for something on their knees; he intended to test Cortez's invention in peace.

In the evening the district hummed with a pluralistic life, which was associated with a chaotic flow of thoughts, so Forkis completely gave up telepathy for a while. Lots of vehicles flew around, conversations, music and laughter could be heard from everywhere. Among androids, robots, cyborgs, modificants and ordinary people, he even spotted two lycans leaning against the wall and freely discussing, which surprised him a bit. These fanatical sectarians and transhumanists hardly ever came to Proxima e. These two seemed wealthy, maybe they were an escort of someone from their priority circle, because they didn't look like tatterdemalions with funny metal teeth, but uniformed werewolves in the stereotypical, classic version: with claws, fur, tail, head and mouth. However, it was impossible to determine which sect they belonged to by their attire.

"Milles, that city drone that is approaching, behind us. Tap into it," Forkis said to his neighbor as the lycans were far behind.

The captain obeyed seamlessly, using Kiritian technological superiority. After a moment, he had a preview from the flying ranger's cellula on his PDA. He smiled broadly.

"You'll see for yourself, sir." He showed Forkis the small screen. "The drone is moving slowly over us, but the machine and possibly the operator can only see me."

"The drone shouldn't see you either, Captain, since ibek's range is supposed to be several meters. Okay, now check out this powdered mineral store." Forkis gestured to another test object.

Milles also this time easily and unnoticed tapped into another cellulas at which they stopped. Again, he only saw himself on the PDA.

"Doctor Maksimus Figam could have done something like this for us a long time ago. Oh, you plum the depths, sir, as you started to invest in the defense." The captain brought himself to joke, which Forkis summed up with a short chuckle and a shake of his head.

They moved on.

Along the way, two achijes went past them, who were ordered not to salute or otherwise demonstrate that they were dealing with the highest Kiritian authority. The four exchanged a few words with each other. They were Corporal Victor Shane's senior privates which were in a hurry to use the best local attraction.

"Another ones," Forkis commented with amusement. "Everyone's going to the Paradise."

"This brothel has a great reputation. It would be a pity not to use it."

"Is this some kind of hint, Captain?"

"I was only commenting on the achijes' behavior."

"Mhm ..." Forkis muttered loudly and eloquently.

"Your captain is right," a tempting woman standing nearby, with her imperfections medically removed, accosted in an alluring, velvety voice. Forkis looked at her from head with cascades of blond pods, to toe, obscured by a thin, flowing tunic. He entered her thoughts and saw that somehow; she had mistaken Milles for his commander. Perhaps this was due to the stereotype functioning in some colonies that low people exercised higher power, as if it had been to compensate for the physical qualities that nature had allocated for them.

Apparently, the girl was unfamiliar with matters beyond her competence, including the fact that adding an adult height was not a problem, at least among Kiritians. It had happened so for example with Zira Aytar, who was now one hundred and eighty centimeters tall.

The blonde approached them without making any encouraging gestures, her angelic appearance alone was enough for a good, lively advertisement. Forkis also learned that she wasn't a prostitute, but a local student whose job was merely to bring customers to the Paradise.

"To fly to Provelkava Grihorsk," she said as she walked around men, "and not to visit its most famous place of entertainment, is an unforgivable sin. Whether the gentlemen are bachelors or not, there is something for everyone. Whether a faithful moralist or an exile from hell." She paused in front of Milles.

"Exactly," added the second beauty with voluminous curves and red hair. Unlike her friend, she indulged herself, for she began to run a finger along Forkis' breastplate and gaze hungrily at the shield of his face. "We guarantee that you will forget about all your problems in a natural way - without any medications and stimulants, which, however, we have in abundance. All types, from all planets. Kiritians like you, however, don't seem to have any worries because you are a powerhouse. Having dealt with achijes many times, she easily folded Forkis' strobilus helmet on the nape of his neck. Though trained to her role as an unshakable lure for men whose sole task was to leave hundreds of uinals in the Paradise, she sighed at his stern, menacing, almost barbaric beauty, suiting his very tall, powerfully built figure. Forkis checked the girl's mind as well, and was amused by the thought that 'he looks just like Forkis, but it definitely isn't him'.

299

Both girls, wondering how to get another money machines, were harmless, and their minds, simple and transparent. They were just doing their job. Forkis sensed no trick. He looked at the captain, who also folded his helmet. Though Milles had been kiritianized at thirty-one, and he would keep the young body forever, his eyes had seen many things, so he wasn't impressed by this kind of encouragement. So he didn't feel the excitement of young achijes, he sent Forkis a mute reply souped-up with a shrug: 'Why not?'

"All right." Forkis took the red girl's hands away from his neck and closed them in his grip for a moment. "Let's see what you have to offer there."

The blonde beamed.

"I'm glad you let yourself be convinced! I cordially invite you, please follow me."

While the redhead went on the further hunt, the student led Kiritian to the Paradise.

The entertainment center, stylized as an ancient Greek building, was truly impressive. From the outside, it resembled a gigantic museum, several government buildings in size; the mouth of the great portico bared the columns' teeth, and the role of the tongue was played by a ramp replacing the stairs. On the sides there was real fire in bowls.

300

In the center of the atrium, watched by android guards, was a pond with an islet overgrown with tropical vegetation. Colorful birds, especially dozens of parrot varieties clung to it. Above the water's surface, protruded the head and neck of a plesiosaurus. In the hall, where hundreds of customers and employees were staying, wandered various animals, from several-meter-long herbivorous dinosaurs to the most fanciful varieties of domestic cats, usually with additions from other species in the form of wings or horns. Forkis checked them out of curiosity with the bioctovisor and found that all of them, apparently real, were in fact a holographic material projection or robots. It made sense, since the facility was visited by people suffering from various phobias or allergies (although probably rarely, because getting rid of an allergy medically was much cheaper than the costs of Paradise attractions).

Passing swimming pools, conservatories, and arcades, where they noticed their achijes sometimes, the blonde led Forkis and Milles upstairs to an orange-lit procuress' office, then began to walk back to a gate station.

At the sight of Forkis, the procuress'[17] eyes who could be between fifty and a hundred years old, sparkled like a child's at the sight of a dream toy gift. She just didn't hit herself with her fists.

---

[17] For oderses living up to 150 years of age, the age of 100 is

"I can't believe Forkis himself has visited our fabulous abode!" The woman was genuinely surprised and overjoyed at the presence of such a guest. "So much for the incognito excursion," the emperor thought. "If I had only noticed it sooner ... I would have gone out in person to greet you gentlemen. Forgive my oversight, gentlemen, but you all look the same! Call me Lura."

"My friend and I would like to have a good time," said Forkis. "But we don't know what would be the most appropriate. Why don't you choose something for us, Lura?"

"Of course, sweetheart! Rely on my extensive experience. I guarantee that you will be extremely satisfied, possibly even the most in your long lifetimes! Well, let's see what we have here ..."

Lura began to appraise both men with her professional eye, a bit like horses at a competition. It turned out to be nice in its naturalism, because at the time, suitable play partners were usually chosen by machines and algorithms.

"Oh yes, I guess this choice will be appropriate. Mirella, Doni, come here. But quickly, please!"

"How much will it cost us?" Milles asked.

"For the two of you, the first visit is free!"

---

considered average.

Two prostitutes entered the room a minute after being summoned via the intercom. Milles treated this off-schedule springboard with indulgent interest, but was stunned when he saw his assigned Doni, a girl similar to Lilly almost like two peas in a pod. His first impulse was to refuse and leave, but his curiosity prevailed - he wanted to find out to what extent Doni would turn out to be psychologically close to his killed girlfriend. Maybe the meeting wouldn't end with the unpleasant memories and picking scabs?

Forkis, on the other hand, got his complete opposite. The girl was young, petite, not bad, but also scared, which he immediately recognized from her eyes and her body language masked with practiced gestures. Mirella tried to hide her reluctance to do this work under a false smile and mock openness, but the tricks were useless when, at the sight of the Kiritian emperor, she got overwhelmed by fear. At least this one knew who she was dealing with, as opposed to her pretty but stupider friends. Mirella's false start didn't bode well. Forkis assumed that someone had gotten her the job in the Paradise because he recognized right away that the girl qualified for the type of people that were kind, even intelligent, but muted by a social phobia, perhaps a trauma from the past, which prevented her from getting out of the bog in which she was stuck. Such people worked in low, undemanding positions, where they could count on peace and relative psychological comfort, but not on attentiveness and decent earnings.

The girls were dressed in white peploses with gold trim and matching sandals, their hair was adorned with colored ribbons and braided into buns, some of which ran in locks by the ears.

Milles and Doni had already chatted in the next room, sitting at an alcohol cabinet with drinks in their hands.

Having sent a message to his people, enabling the security location, Forkis took the initiative to make Mira feel comfortable in his presence.

"Hi. Nice to meet you. I'm Forkis." Smiling heartily after saying the friendly words, he extended the open hand to her.

"Great, stupid cow has spaced out," he caught in the procuress' mind, who winced a little, certain the First Galactic Dignitary couldn't see her, which he just did for a moment out of the corner of his eye.

"Come on, square! What are you doing?"

"A special offer for the ruler of the Kiritians," the woman said kindly.

Looking him appraisingly in the eye, shyly like a virgin, Mira felt more confident; his openness and gentleness gave her spirit. He looked now, not like the emperor, about which there were stories related to harm and death, but like any lower-ranking achij. She smiled more appropriately for her trade, took the Kiritian's hand and began to lead him toward the exit.

"Mira. Something to drink?" she suggested.

"Maybe later. What is this special offer?"

"You'll see for yourself in a moment. Let me take care of everything." After a few minutes, she led him to the central room in the middle of the corridor, as if to a place of honor at a long table. The ornate, detailed hall with a huge pool and a fountain in the center looked like prepared for a party for at least fifty people. And privileged ones. The lights came from a fluorescent liquid suspended in transparent tubes stretching from floor to ceiling. The somewhat kitschy stone throne with a pillow and a headboard covered with heavy material, which differed from the style of the hall, spoiled the quite well overall effect. The Kiritian scanned it with the thermoindector from the bracer, and except for himself and Mira, found no one else alive, but he tracked down a slightly warm, dormant android.

"That's in case the customers mess up," the girl explained as she pulled back the curtain in a niche where the artificial guard was located.

"So I'll probably be given a hammering because I'm going to make a lot of trouble today," he replied with a smile.

Chuckling, Mira led him to the throne, set him with his face toward her, and, submitting to her efforts, she pushed Forkis so that he sat down like a proud king, resting his arms on the armrests. She, in turn, having slid her peplos to the ground and staying nude, straddled his thighs, resting her shins on the wide seat. The throne turned out to be stone only visually, being in fact heated plastic. Whether it was convenient - Forkis couldn't determine yet, because he was still in armor and was following Mira, curious what more she would come up with.

"Maybe you would like to talk a little first, confide in, tell something about yourself. I humbly listen to everything." She tried to slip a grape from the platter into his mouth, but Forkis gripped her wrist firmly. With two fingers of his other hand, he took the fruit and put it between the girl's lips. After she bit and swallowed it, he handed her a few more. They didn't seem to be poisoned, judging from Mirella's reaction, but what did sacrificing a not-so-respected prostitute matter if someone decided to get rid of the ruler of the Kiritian?

It is possible that he began to carry this caution to excess, but the adventure with Aytar had sensitized him that overconfidence and ignorance could easily lead to the downfall of a ruler.

Mira was acting kind of natural, but Forkis still felt her uneasiness with the onkalot part of his personality, in fact, also with the human part of his personality, trained for centuries to interpret non-verbal cues. In the girl's mind there was one big burning confusion. It terrified her that she had been thrown without help - apart from the android - into such a deep end, that

306

she wouldn't do well, that she would anger with something the emperor famous for his cruelty, which in the best case would end up with her being fired.

"Don't worry," he said soothingly, stroking the back of her head. "I'll be your support."

She looked at him in surprise.

He brought her head to his with his hand and began to kiss the delicate, fruity-tasting lips with his large lips.

Mira clung to his armor, pressing her hands to the sides of the Kiritian's head, then ran her finger along his chin. Forkis found an activator that lowered the headrest to a level, turning the throne into a bed. He used it. He placed Mira underneath him so that he didn't hurt her with the biometal and dhurnsteel, then began to wander with his tongue and mouth over all her body with tattooed flowers and butterflies, not wanting to take off his armor for now.

Unexpectedly, he felt a strong desire to sleep, as if he had been shot with an anesthetic, which couldn't have happened because his body was secured. Nor had he eaten or drunk anything in the Paradise. The air? Mira kept her full vitality and was genuinely concerned about his changing state.

Before Forkis could connect with Milles, he lost the strength in his legs and arms, and consciousness at the same time, and fell on the girl with his weight of one hundred and several dozen kilograms.

***

He woke up with his head aching, throbbing, his ears were buzzing. When he raised it instinctively, he felt like he was going to pass out again; the cloud of physiological blue fireflies blurred the already murky field of vision even more, so he returned to his previous position, with his face pressed against the hard, flat surface. Forkis tried to rely on hearing, but also this organoleptic form of gathering information proved to be unreliable. Except for the occasional sounds, very soft and muffled by the thick surface, he was surrounded by silence like a stomach muscular layer surrounds a meal.

He did better a few minutes later on the second attempt to raise his head and torso; his eyesight also improved considerably. He looked around with the sore neck. He was in a rectangular, smooth metal room with a few white lamps directing the light upwards blended into the walls at the top. In the distance of a longer spit there was a solid locked door. He was sitting on his calves, and his arms raised behind his back were held by chains with hoops around his wrists. The length of the harness allowed him to lie completely on the floor and to take a few steps, but on the condition that his arms were taut and directed towards the wall. Forkis recognized an alloy, of which were made all surroundings except the lamps. Exagon, a metal tougher than steel of oderses, but pitifully brittle compared to the Kiritian dhurnsteel. Nevertheless, it proved to be a good building block of a prison room - because it was obvious that he was in such.

All his equipment and clothes were taken from him, except for the dark gray uniform pants and the pendant on the chain that was probably considered a harmless sentimental ornament. Forkis must have been dragged along the ground because he felt his back sore from bruises and cuts. Some of it bloomed also on his arms and face.

He got up, walked towards the door, and jerked the chains that got taut with a rattle, but as he expected, he achieved nothing more. Powerful buckles, capable of holding even a bear, were electronically locked and didn't deign to fail.

"Show yourself!" He demanded loudly, leaning against the taut chains.

Nobody said a word.

The man sat cross-legged against the wall, placed his sore, numb hands on his legs.

However, he had gotten caught, though he had no idea what had happened. The situation hardly looked like one of the extravagant games for the Paradise's clients looking for a more thrilling experience. It was possible that Forkis wasn't even in the entertainment center anymore, especially since the surroundings clearly resembled a large laboratory cell, a physical testing room, or some empty warehouse, and wasn't associated with the aforementioned 'special offer'. Before Dr. Figam had created the super virus that ensured immortality as a side effect, he had worked in an underground complex with similar cells for keeping large lab animals.

"Who are you? Show up!"

The torturer remained silent, Forkis considered the possibility that the complex might have been abandoned, though he doubted it.

For the next hours, nothing changed, the irritated prisoner only changed his position.

When he dropped off, staring earlier at a ventilation grille under the ceiling and analyzing his situation, he got surprised by the screech of the door being unlocked. The wing slid into a recess, creating a clearance that was filled by two walking robots. Forkis recognized them immediately by their bulky, crude appearance and the markings on the hull prefixed with pro. So he was still on Proxima e, which seemed obvious. These were military robots operating in the open ground, but someone intelligent differently decided to use them to work in the tight - as Forkis assumed -

complex. They might have been effective in terms of arm and leg strength, but also that depended on the size of the corridor. If they had opened fire, it would have rather ended up with the strain or even collapse of the load-bearing walls, not to mention less, but still dangerous, damage.

When one of the colossi entered the room, having barely fit in the passage, the hoops holding the prisoner opened. Forkis was captured with a pincer forceps of robotic limbs around his neck and forced to leave the room with his bent silhouette. The other robot stood motionless in the corridor, keeping the weapon attached to its arm ready to fire.

The Kiritian entered the short corridor of the exagon, lit in the same way as his place and decorated as minimalist; a dozen or so meters to the left it was connected with a perpendicular passage. Leaning, Forkis noticed that in 'its' small branch there were a total of four cells, most likely twin ones, judging by the appearance of the armored, but already slightly dilapidated door. It didn't look like a prison of the first novelty, here and there you could see blight and rust, under the ceiling lingered old cobwebs. It was still too little information for Forkis to be able to pinpoint his location. There were many aging colonies and outposts on Proxima e, he might as well have been in some basement of industrial Provelkava Grihorsk.

The robot didn't take him far, only to the bathroom to the right of the cell, equipped with a primitive toilet in the floor, a shower and a dryer. It went inside with Forkis.

Deducing that he was in no danger of death, the Kiritian used everything he had available, among others he drank water and washed his wounds, after which he was dragged to his place in the previous way. The robot threw him forcefully on the floor, so strongly that Forkis did a limp somersault, then it put his wrists in the hoops of the chains, which proved to be a painful activity because the machine had no fingers. Immediately after that, the door slammed hollowly. The Kiritian listened to the heavy footsteps of the receding colossi, feeling the weakening vibrations of the ground.

"And how do you like our hotel conditions?" Sounded a relaxed female voice, coming from the ventilation grate in the ceiling. Since the person holding him hadn't yet deigned to reveal themselves personally, probably out of cowardice, Forkis didn't rule out that the sound could be altered electronically, making recognition difficult.

"They're rather poor. Two out of ten, and that two is for the pretty good mobile equipment and burglar protection, but it is unlikely to stop Kiritians."

The voice chuckled.

"For one specific, however, they are enough, and no other Infected is likely to come here. Unless, once, to find only your chained skeleton, Forkis, when the arrangers of this macabre ornament will be long gone. So, you are not interested in the explanations?" The woman asked sweetly after a long stubborn silence of the detainee.

"What difference does it make if I ask or not, if you say as much as you see fit or nothing? I suppose it's not a continuation of attractions in the Paradise ..."

"It wasn't hard to guess," the supervisor's tone showed that she was playing with him all the time and was in no rush.

"Well, now it remains for me to wonder," Forkis also began to be ironic, he smiled, "if it is another political coup or maybe a personal matter. Are you a human?"

The interlocutor ignored the first question.

"'There is only one android in this place and I'm not it."

"So, enlighten me at last what you want."

"Are you kidding me, Mister emperor? You are here to die."

Forkis waved his hands as much as he could, jingling the metal and skinning his left wrist.

"And I assume you're preparing something showy for me."

"That's right," the voice grew colder. Forkis imagined the woman's eyes narrowing simultaneously. "But first, I want to discover all your secrets, separate nonsense from facts. That you are a telepath, I have known for some time."

"Alright, enough of this bullshit," the Kiritian said firmly. "Tell me what happened, because you are probably eager to laugh at my indolence and to humiliate me more."

"I have been planning to catch you and kill you for a long time, the preparations have taken me many years and a lot of analyzes. But as you can see, the hard work has paid off - I'm the first to capture the First Galactic Dignitary!"

Forkis felt tempted to cut her off and childishly tell her not to shit herself.

"I involved a small number of partners in the action so that the plan didn't fail. One of them told Cortez to bring you to Proxima e, but as Vicente already knew too much and you could read everything in his head if you met, he was pulled away from the business. Doris Kagawa got a message from his boss to replace him on the deal. However, the plan didn't go as we expected, because Kagawa was supposed to be rude, and you were to get upset and go out in that state to work it off according to your custom. You ended up going there, albeit unplanned. The bitches you met along the way also didn't know they were dragged into my plan, and neither did Lura. The other people from the Paradise who took care of the preparations, on no account could come into contact with you. This telepathy of yours is a goddamn mighty obstacle."

"Mira?"

"She was just doing her job, too, following a learned pattern for distinguished guests. In the chamber next to the bowl of grapes there were relaxing salts mixed with aphrodisiacs. She dipped her hands in them before touching you and rubbing your face. The anesthetic added, made of Boranevich's snake's fangs worked as well as ever. Mira, whom you kissed, also dozed off not long after you."

"Boranevich's snake ..." Forkis smiled incredulously. He was sincerely impressed. "It puts the victim to sleep before eating it. Who would have thought? And how did you deal with my achijes?"

"You've gotten into the swing of it." The stranger also smiled.

"I don't deny it. An attention-grabbing story. And as you can see, I was very busy before." He jerked the chain at his left hand.

A holographic projection was displayed under the ceiling - an editing of preview from several cellulas located in the Paradise. Forkis was seen walking across the second floor at night, down the steps, through the atrium toward the exit. He waved his hand at the few achijes greeting him he encountered. He got into a discussion with a few of them and dismissed them. He left the facility, crossed the gate and disappeared somewhere in the eastern part of the city.

"A look-alike," Forkis said immediately.

"Yes, android excluded from the throne room, where the regulations prohibit watching customers with cellulas.

"And how did you break the security of my armor? Signals, locators?"

"The armor was taken with you. What the monitoring captured was a dummy without Kiritian electronics. We had to make a dozen or so versions of your armor because we didn't know which one you would arrive in. The android hidden inside said the achijes with your voice that they shouldn't have escorted you to the corvette. It was the second time when my plan could fail, because such an order seemed illogical, but the subordinates, although surprised, obeyed, sure of their security in the city. Android was hanging around Provelkava Grihorsk to rock the boat the most among drones and other monitoring devices. Finally, where they were not, he dumped the armor in the swamp and returned to the city."

"That still doesn't explain how the Kiritians failed to pick up signals from my armor."

The holograph displayed another image, this time a spatial map of the city along with a huge network of natural tunnels in this part of the planet.

"Few of the inhabitants know about them, and that handful aware of their existence, don't care about them, because they have no significance for the city. The tunnels are located deep below the ground surface, this is enough to interfere with electronic signals, and the feet of the layers above them are highly mineralized. The Paradise is linked by passages to one of the natural corridors that only ... certain people know about."

"Probably the ones with something to hide and bigger fish. Standard."

"I think the rest doesn't need to be said."

"So, I understand we're not in Provelkava Grihorsk," Forkis said. "You probably wouldn't have risked imprisoning me right under achijes' noses."

"We are in the second hemisphere of the planet, in a very unpleasant place for humans. Your beloved soldiers are currently scouring the entire city. By the time they find out about the tunnels and then conclude that the entire planet has to be scoured, it will be too late for you, my dear."

"So, what other attractions await me? I've already met robots, not very social and gentle characters. In addition, they get into the toilet."

"I've heard interesting things about you. As I said, I'd like to check them all one by one. Since we already have telepathy checked, let's go straight to the most interesting issue. It will take a while, but I'm patient. And unlike you, I have time. Don't fail me, Forkis."

"I understand that you don't deign to introduce yourself either?"

"You can never be too careful. I will think about it in the last moments of your life, and you probably know this trick very well. Meanwhile, bye bye," she added ironically at the end.

The political matter of kidnapping and imprisonment was out of the question, Forkis was sure of it, because everything had been organized in a too little way, though cleverly. Personal one neither - of people to whom the Kiritian confided before his death to satisfy their curiosity, no one survived.

So there remained either fanaticism or revenge for a loved one.

\*\*\*

"You are completely crazy, Laureta!" Mirella wanted to pour out her anger on her friend from school years, but her outburst ended in screams lined with tears that had already been streaming down her face for several minutes. "Why did you get me into this?

Because of you, I'm a dead man! What have you done?! This is FORKIS, do you get it at all?!"

The two women were in a large control room, from where Laureta - a slender guru with boldly red lips and a thick of fire-colored hair - could manage the robots and other components of the former Procent Lab, as well as giving orders to a small group of current staff. An older generation android, with a white mohawk and orange eyes, which had been working in the facility for over two hundred years, sat at the next table, watching the interlocutors, but wasn't interested in the discussion in any other way.

"Shut up at last," Laureta snapped. She jumped up from her chair. "I can't listen to your moaning anymore; my head is buzzing! You didn't have a job - bad. I got you the job in the brothel - bad. I got you out of the brothel - bad too! Get a grip, because I don't know what you mean anymore!"

"Certainly not to participate in the kidnapping of the Kiritian emperor!"

Laureta was fed up with Mira. What made her take the girl with her, since their friendship had faded away much earlier? How could she have ever been friends with this loser totally helpless in life who, without her, would have probably dealt with begging in the streets? They both had started on the same level, with the same opportunities, but Laureta had gained power over a large social group when the trusting, sensitive and kind Mira, a disgusting

319

model of virtue, had still been idle, waiting for miracles and a prince charming.

"Okay, let's not argue anymore, Mira. In any case, you did quite well. I thought you were going to wash out." Laureta sat more comfortably in front of the control panel and looked at the preview from one of the three cellulas with a vision of Forkis' seclusion room. Not having much room for maneuver, the man sat on the floor and stared at his hand, moving his fingers. "You know that if I had left you in the Paradise, you'd be the first person they would take care of. You should be grateful to me for picking you up from the tunnel in the transporter to the far north. You are safe here, we had no tail or any spy."

"I'm trapped now and so is he." The prostitute nodded at Forkis. "I won't have any more life anywhere."

"We will wait out the storm and leave here as winners incognito. No one will ever know how Forkis died and who killed him. Now get ready to have fun."

Lauret smiled cruelly, which scared Mira as if the other girl's bestial plans had been meant for her.

"Sefirot, take care of the girl as agreed."

Mira, terrified for a traumatic moment, was sure that it was about her, but the android, over which Casijo had given Laurent full power, obediently stood up and headed for the exit.

***

Hours after ablution with a ready-to-fire heavy cannon, the cell door cracked open again, this time briefly, and the young girl was pushed inside. She gave Forkis a fleeting, worried look, then turned to the door and got onto hitting it thoughtlessly with her open palms. She ceased this senseless activity when, tired and sweaty, she realized that she would have rather not been locked up there just to be released a moment later. After catching her breath, she started to walk nervously around the room, each time avoiding Forkis, maybe not giving a wide berth due to the size of the seclusion room, but she tried to stay out of his reach. Finally, resigned, she slid to the floor near the door, hiding her face between her hands wrapped around her knees. In her confusion and delicacy, she reminded Forkis very much of Mira, and also Vanessa Bondar from Mirphak - the kind of good girls of the 'twist the knife in the wound' type whom, for some reason, fate in the form of wayward people constantly basted.

About the one here, who was fifteen years old, Forkis learned telepathically only that she had been kidnapped from a poor neighborhood, being injected in the neck. The girl didn't know who was the culprit, because everything had happened in a flash and out of her sight. She woke up in the cell opposite, completely not understanding her situation.

Forkis also didn't know why the girl was thrown into his cell.

She kept silent, lost in her sorrow, avoiding looking at her fellow prisoner; Forkis almost reciprocated, watching her sporadically. Anyway, what were they supposed to talk about? To even cheer someone up, one has to be sure of the future, and not deceptively claim that everything will be fine, targeting the possibilities of probability.

"And what do you think, Forkis, of your new companion in distress?" Laureta asked from the control room. She kept her legs on the control panel and feasted on her lunch. Doesn't she seem sweet to you?"

"And you will keep adding more and more companionate people?" The Kiritian stared at the cellula tiny like a fingernail that was distinguished by blackness against the silver of the room, as if a beetle had dozed off in the corner under the ceiling. That's why he had noticed it earlier.

"Relax, she'll be the only one. Please, Forkis, show your commitment at the highest level. I hope for a good spectacle. And as I said, we have time and I'm patient."

The voice gave no further instructions. Forkis had no idea what to do with the girl planted on him, since he was chained. Several times, with tight muscles and clenched teeth, he tried with all his power to tear them out of the wall, but it proved to be as effective as trying to move a Kiritian corvette with a stick, by the way his favorite type of ship. The hounded, totally mentally disturbed fellow prisoner didn't seem to be someone who would have liked to harm him. Apart from simple, ragged clothes, she had nothing else with her, and therefore no weapon.

After a time, difficult to determine due to the constant intensity of the lights, the robots came again and took them one by one to the bathroom.

After they were dragged to that place, armed Sefiroth with two bowls entered the cell. One, filled with food in the form of mush with pieces of vegetables, he placed next to the girl, who tried to blend in with the corner of the room, terrified by his presence (then Forkis found out why - earlier the android had been playing with her unequivocally).

"You must be thirsty. Bon appetit, you won't get anything more." The artificial man splashed the contents of the entire bowl on the emperor's face. For him, he only brought water. Luckily, Forkis also this time during the forced visit to the bathroom, drunk a little in the shower.

A muffled sigh came from the loudspeaker, announcing words of discontent:

"You were supposed to put it next to him, not pour everything on his head."

The android huffed, walked over to the wall and leaned his back and foot against it, having folded his arms.

"What the hell are you standing here for?" Forkis asked a few minutes later, irritated that Sefiroth was looking at him like a scientist at a rabbit.

"I'm to see that the girl doesn't give you anything to eat. Why are you staring at that bowl?" He asked the prisoner. "Eat it!"

The girl sobbed, didn't take her eyes off the food, so as not to look at the android, but finally began to eat with her fingers.

"What about me?" The emperor snarled. "I'm not an android or a robot."

"You'll just watch what you can't do, and drink to be alive as long as possible." Sefiroth gave him a mean smirk.

Forkis was furious that everyone there referred to him as to an ordinary man, without respecting him as the emperor, even if he had been reduced to a prisoner role, nonetheless he hid it under a cover of mockery or contempt. He would do his best not to give satisfaction to these straw men in any way.

When the girl finished eating, the android took both the dishes and left the cell guarded from the outside by the robot.

Forkis began to suspect what the plan of the crazy woman who had imprisoned him here might have been about. And he didn't like it at all.

***

Unfortunately, he was right.

During the days that had probably passed, he was weak due to hunger, felt dizzy. He thought less and less rationally, usually about food, hoping to fill his belly to the brim. Increasingly, he had to fight the Onkalot Jun Kame, who wanted to take over his human mind. It even happened that he violently and thoughtlessly jerked the chains towards the girl, as if he hadn't been himself, as if he had been out of mind for those few seconds.

The pattern repeated itself: the girl was fed, he was forced to look at it, to inhale the smell of food, and only water was given to him. The woman from the intercom, when preparing the kidnapping, actually had had to learn a lot about him, because she hit the jackpot choosing that torture.

The situation was getting more and more dramatic.

An ordinary man would have just gotten tired, in the impulses of madness demanded from the girl to throw him food, not worrying about the guarding android. Perhaps he would have tried in a pathetic attempt to reach for something with his foot. The weaker-minded one would have screamed at them to release him, that he would cooperate, do anything for a stale piece of bread that in normal circumstances he would have so carelessly thrown into a waste basket.

Forkis didn't care what the prisoner had in the bowls.

He wanted her. And by no means in a sexual way.

Unlike the average person, he was turning into a beast, he was afraid that he would eventually lose control of himself. Had it not been for this captivity, Forkis wouldn't have learned that he was capable of such a thing, for he had never been in such a situation of hunger for so long. And the degenerate was probably waiting for this moment to unchain him.

And it finally happened.

"Come on, Forkis, tear her to pieces now," she said cheerfully, enthusiastically. The Kiritian even imagined her clapping at this command center of hers.

And he actually pounced on the girl. She could run with a screech only a few meters before he grabbed her and knocked her to the floor. Although he rather fell on her with weakness, when there was only blackness before his eyes, and his head seemed to be filled with humming bees. He fought for a moment to maintain consciousness, as well as with the thrashing, though immobilized, victim.

He couldn't do that.

Not out of pity for the defenseless, scared girl - the strong urge to survive dominated the human reflexes that were distorted in Forkis anyway - but he didn't want to give his tormentors the satisfaction that he would dance to their tune. It is possible that everything the cellulas of the seclusion room recorded would have been sent to the entire Universum, and in an instant billions of people would have seen what the Kiritian emperor had been so painstakingly hiding from his achijes for centuries. It is not known how the nation would have behaved, but a lot of oders collaborators would have certainly turned their backs on him.

He felt such a terrible hunger ...

There was some bullshit coming from the intercom that he had been ignoring for some time. Only some of the messages penetrated his mind: "Come on, tear her, eat her."

Yes ... he could do that. Why not? The fellow prisoner was dead anyway because she had seen too much. Humanity would witness an unimaginable horror in his performance, but he would worry about this problem later when he was full.

The terrified, trembling girl looked into his eyes as if at the eyes of death itself announcing the final end.

Those who watched him on the cellula receivers must have had a lot of fun following his struggle with himself.

Forkis decided.

"Sorry," he whispered.

He grabbed the girl's head with his hands and broke her neck in a flash. Then he corrected it to be sure, smashing it against the floor.

The streaks of blood flowing onto the smooth metal nearly drove him mad and squandered his resolution made with difficulty.

Forkis, screaming in anger, returned to the wall with the chains on and lay down in the half turtle position - cringing and touching his forehead to the ground. At least he won one victory in this pandemonium - he defeated the inner Jun Kame. It was Forkis who decided how, whom, and when to kill, usually punishing in that way.

"Er, look what you've done, Mr. emperor." There was no hint of falsehood in Laureta's disappointed voice. "You've ruined everything. And it was going to be great."

"There's only one person I want to break apart." Forkis saved scraps of his dignity at least a little by adopting the sitting posture. "And it will be you."

Although she was hundreds of meters from the Kiritian, in a safe place, Laureta felt uneasy as Forkis turned his cold, unforgiving gaze towards the cellula.

"And they say the Immortals don't lie. Unless you can kill with your mind through walls," she replied with less carelessness than she intended.

Forkis had no idea for, and no desire to exchange retorts. What he wished most was that they would quickly take the unfortunate girl's body away from here, because he was afraid that he would go mad again. To see the Kiritian emperor on all fours, with his face immersed in the corpse and the insanity visible in his eyes would have been the most pathetic sight in the age of space colonization.

The tormentor didn't turn off the intercom and there was an argument probably about the corpse - the guard robots were not built for manual work, the android didn't want to clean, and other people present in the control room didn't intend to approach the Kiritian ruler despite the assurances of security.

Finally, a consensus was reached, for Sefiroth appeared in the cell with the indispensable guards behind his back, who waited in the corridor. Taking a step over the corpse, he attached Forkis' hands to the wall again, threatening him with a gun.

After the android left the prison, he entered it ... Forkis was stunned to see the Onkalot with an anti-gravity disk and primitive

329

cleaning equipment, as if the complex had lacked intelligent cleaning machines or been saving energy. He no longer remembered the last time he had seen a humanoid jaguar alive, they were probably the Jun Kame slaves of the rebels, whose fate didn't interest Forkis.

This one belonged to a different tribe; his characteristic feature was a golden hoop in the middle of the tail. Forkis lowered his head so that his hair fell over his face.

"I haven't seen either of you for so long," he began to speak in Onkalotian; he didn't expect to be moved by the words of his native speech coming from his own mouth - especially from the Che'ab'aj tribe, the Stone Tree.

Now was speechless the Onkalot which, having loaded the corpse onto the disk and pushed it into the corridor, froze with a piece of material soaked in water and cleaning agent. He straightened slowly, turned his head just as slowly, and stared at Forkis in disbelief, ignoring that someone in the control room might have not liked his interaction with the formidable prisoner.

"What's the trick? How do you know our speech, Forkis?" He replied in the same language.

"Do those," the Kiritian made a sparing gesture with his head towards the nearest cellula, "understand the Onkalotian?"

"No, we can talk freely. I speak Anglo-American here with everyone."

"Translator?"

"Be quiet!" Android pounded his fist on the door from the corridor. "Clean up."

The Onkalot grimaced, but didn't care too much about the order.

Wiping the floor at a snail's pace, he eagerly continued the conversation.

"They don't have the pattern," he replied. "The language of the Onkalots is insignificant for the oderses."

"You don't like your employers, do you?" Forkis remarked, reading curses against Sefiroth in his mind. The humanoid jaguar wasn't surprised by this statement, for he thought the strange man had guessed everything from the expression on his muzzle.

"I've been working here for a long time, but employers have been changed. I don't care who they are, it's important that I have a goal."

"Washing toilets and floors?" The ironic conclusion of the Kiritian ended with an unfavorable glare from the other side. "What's your name?"

"Sinaj. Can you tell me how do you know what tribe I belonged to?"

"I will, but first a few questions. Please," Forkis added in a weak imitation of pleading, because he wasn't familiar with humility. "I need to know the answers."

"We shouldn't talk at all, I'll be in trouble," Sinaj said, against his desire. He would have liked to talk in his native language all night and day, no - a week, a month! Even if the interlocutor was a human.

Forkis made a point of using what he had just 'heard' telepathically. Mrs. Big Brother didn't interrupt them (whatever that forgotten joke from the distant past, still in use, meant), so maybe she didn't follow the conversation or walked away from the receiver.

"What is this place?"

"They didn't tell you?"

"If I'm asking, no."

"Shut up, damn it!" The android called again.

"Procent Lab," informed Sinaj. "Far north of Proxima e. The land of snow, storms and permafrost."

Forkis whistled. He knew the name, apparently political prisoners had been brought here in the past, but he didn't know the location of the facility.

"And what are you doing here? Wouldn't you rather go back to Chulimal?" He asked, genuinely interested in it.

"What am I to go back for? Anyway, what's the difference?" Sinaj snapped back.

"Do you know who's in charge here?"

"Temporarily that woman, but I only hear her like you. I haven't seen her; I don't even know her name. I don't have access to the sector with the control room, in the sense I could go in there if I wanted to, but what for. Let the arrivals clean up the dirt themselves."

"You are done now, Sinaj, so get out," Sefiroth didn't let go.

Forkis was running out of time. Although Sinaj belonged to the Stone Tree, a tribe that respected someone else's words, even enemies, and was able to firmly keep the secrets entrusted to it, the Kiritian didn't know if he could trust him. His old views, based on his tribal affiliation and upbringing, might have long since fallen to pieces. Nevertheless, Sinaj's dislike of the people in the facility and interest in the prisoner worked to his advantage. He had to go for broke! Perhaps this was the only chance of survival; about rectifying his situation, should he have made a fatal mistake, he would worry later.

"Wait, you gotta help me. As a Kiritian, I will only tell you the truth now, but I'm asking you in return, as a child of the blood of the Stone Tree, to keep everything to yourself. Look, I know this is gonna sound ridiculous, but I'm an Onkalot too," Forkis started to speak quickly. Sinaj looked at him this time as if he had been insane. "I'm Xajb'a Kej of the Chiq'aq tribe, Place of Fire."

"How..."

"Q'umaraq, a golden mouse, and really advanced alien technology that we didn't understand. The artifact turned me into a human. Yes, the ruler of the Kiritian is an Onkalot, and all I did was dictated by vengeance for killing our species off. I was kidnapped from Provelkava Grihorsk and I don't know why and by whom. The person who did this wants to cruelly amuse themselves at my expense and of everyone else's I will probably have to kill. I will die here too." Noticing the shock on the humanoid jaguar's face, Forkis decided to bring him down even more to finally convince him to be truthful. "I saw your leader Tumulkan several times. Every time he thought he was alone during making important decisions, he walked in circles and mumbled to himself. He also raised a finger when something dawned on him. Hardly any of the outer tribes knew about it, certainly no human. They didn't even know the name of the Chief of Che'ab'aj."

"I've heard you're a telepath. You could have read it from my head!"

"I inherited my telepathy from my Onkalot father, Awamajik of Jun Kame. It was also transferred to the human body thanks to q'umaraq. I only see what a person currently thinks about, and all you think about now is that I've gone mad from starving. I really am an Onkalot, Sinaj. You know the complex and the standards that prevail here. Help me break free somehow, and I promise I'll set you back on Chulimal or I'll do whatever you want, within my abilities, of course. The word of the Kiritian."

He said it chaotically and, in a hurry, trying to win Sinaj over in the time limited by the android. If the cellulas operator had seen what was currently going on in the seclusion room, it was possible that he would have personally and immediately ended this unbelievable meeting.

The Onkalot, shocked and with a distant look, left the room without a word. The door slammed shut behind him hollowly.

Forkis could only hope that the humanoid jaguar which had a mind more open to unexplained phenomena than a man (because he came from the polytheistic tribal culture, where technology was considered mysticism) would decide to do something in his case. The chances were close to zero, but they existed. As long as Sinaj didn't say anything he heard here.

\*\*\*

Forkis gave up hope of getting out of here alive. He no longer was stuck wretchedly in his chains, but lay sadly with them, not even having the strength to think about the future. Nobody had spoken to him for a long time, either visited or watered him.

And this is what would result from his status and immortality - he would die of hunger, lonely, in the unpopulated, forgotten part of the planet. It was all he thought about now, regretting his fate and the fact that he had confided in the random humanoid jaguar with the naivety of a child. Should have the situation with the girl in his cell repeated itself, Forkis would have not hesitated to eat her body. Who would have seen it, where it would have travelled, it wouldn't have mattered at all. And he would have still had the strength.

Immersed in lethargy, he didn't hear any footsteps in the corridor, and slowly raised his head only when the cell door opened with a slight click.

In the clearance appeared Sefiroth with Sinaj standing behind him.

"Are you still alive?" The android asked sardonically. He entered the room with the Onkalot, who folded the arms over his chest and stood at the entrance. "Good, I'll have more fun."

From the head of Sefiroth as a machine, Forkis couldn't read anything, while his companion had an empty mind, a serious expression on his face and he was looking at the prisoner with judgmental eyes.

The once mighty emperor had forgotten what the shadow of fear he began to feel when it finally dawned on him that he was about to be dead was.

Having interlaced his fingers, the android crouched down beside him, out of reach of his legs, with which Forkis wouldn't have been able to kick him anyway.

"Laureta flew away on some urgent matter," the Kiritian heard from the android's mouth the name of his torturer for the first time. He had come across it somewhere, but his indisposed brain wasn't now conducive to associating information. "There was an argument over who should have been in charge of the outpost while she was away, and eventually power passed into the hands of the robots."

"Then where are they now?" Forkis could see no figure or shadow in the opening from which the draft was flowing into the room.

"'By chance' they failed, and so did cellulas," replied the android with a nasty smile.

For a brief moment, a hope flashed in Forkis' heart that this was a salvation, and not an execution, which, for some reason he didn't understand, was to be arranged by the humanoid jaguar.

For a very brief moment.

"What do you want?" He snarled.

Sefiroth's finger transformed into a needle-tipped pistol.

"To spite Laureta," he replied, examining his hand. "That messed up bag has bossed the show here too much lately, has humiliated me and the indigenous base crew, has given me orders. And the machines from the Procent Lab must not be treated like this, just because we clean humanity of the weeds that are delivered here. I'm an executioner and guardian, and I rule here while my rightful owner is out. So the honor of killing the Kiritian emperor will be mine. However, I wish to keep it to myself. It will be my personal triumph - the killing of the most eminent prisoner of all time. Lauret's gonna be pissed when she gets back here soon and sees another dead body in the cell, but she can only give me an earful."

"Android with exuberant ego, traitor," Forkis glanced angrily at the Onkalot, who seemed to be focusing on something, possibly he was praying, "psychopath, rebellious machines, people unable to tame them. I must admit, you have a happy gang here." He wondered himself that in such circumstances he was still capable of joking.

"Just a moment more, be patient," Sinaj's confusing words, which Forkis unexpectedly heard in his head, surprised him very much.

"This poison is my favorite form of killing." The android jumped to Forkis in a flash and grabbed him by the neck with his left hand, lowering his head towards the floor. "I'm going to inject it into your veins in a moment, I'll seal the wound quickly with molecular glue before you die, and it'll be very fast, in about a minute. After three, the foreign chemicals will break down in your blood. In short, no trace will remain. The prisoner will officially starve to dea..."

Sefiroth slumped to the ground with a metallic thud, as it turned off or at zero energy reserve.

Sinaj approached the prisoner, took the android's hand with the needle away from him to a safe distance. Moments after he concentrated on something again, with his eyes closed, both exagon hoops opened.

"Forgive me for taking so long." The humanoid jaguar was helping Forkis get up in a hurry. "It was terribly difficult to get the right opportunity. Did you hear my mental message?"

"Yes: 'Just a moment more, be patient.' I was totally confused ..."

"Me and Sefiroth are friends. I persuaded him to kill you and turned him off in due time; he will be lying so for at least an hour. I wanted to do it as soon as he opened the door, but I was out of practice. I couldn't take care of the cell door itself, because apart from the electronic lock, it also has to be opened manually, and only reliable robots dealt with this forceful activity. Now fast! The guards can be here at any time."

Forkis rejected his neighbor's helping hand as he went towards the exit, staggering. But after he fell and saw only darkness again before his eyes, he slammed the last of his pride deep inside his mind and let himself be guided like a wounded man.

"So, you are a great buddy."

"You have to hang out with someone in order not to go crazy with loneliness. And the choice between a machine and a human is obvious."

"And how did you turn him off?"

"Sinaj stuck his head out into the corridor, nosed for a moment and listened.

"It's clear. Just like you are a telepath, I can disrupt the operation of electronic devices to a minimal extent."

"Can an Onkalot do so at all?"

"I was taken from Chulimal when I was a kitten. I had not yet developed any psionic skill at that time. It didn't develop until I found myself in the Procent Lab; it turned out to be phenotypic, not genotypic, i.e., dependent on the environment in which I had grown up. What now? Sorry, but my plan was short term."

Outside the cell, Forkis had to lean against the corridor wall for a moment to avoid being caught by weakness again.

"I need armor and some weapons, also to eat something ... Urgently."

"I know where your Kiritian armor is kept. It's not far."

"Why did you decide to help me? Did you believe everything I said?"

"I had to think about it. Too many things indicated that you were telling the truth, without detracting from the eighth point of the Kiritian decalogue. Moreover, Onkalots of Che'ab'aj and Chiq'aq have always been sympathetic to each other, even if you also have Jun Kame's blood in you."

They soon turned into a side aisle. Sinaj disrupted the action of subsequent cellulas, which still had the same effect, as if they had been working properly, because their location was indicated. But at least the operator didn't see the details.

"How many people does the staff consist of?" The emperor asked after the humanoid jaguar had finished talking about the distribution of the more important cellulas.

"Currently five mercenaries, a prostitute, me, the android and ten combat robots. Wait ... I think Lakin Chan has stopped favoring us ..." Sinaj uttered the name of the god of his old tribe, when deeper and more regular steps could be heard behind the coign.

***

Zimba, the mercenary commander, entered the control room after a long absence for inspection, and froze. As he ran to the nearest holographic projection, he poured nearly half of his drink from the mug, which he hurriedly set aside just anywhere.

"Oh fuck ..."

Something disturbed the vision in Forkis' room, but the image quickly returned to standard settings. Zimba saw Sefiroth lying motionless on the ground, empty chains and the cell door ajar. The disturbances appeared in the following sections of the monitoring, as if someone who was moving along the corridors of the local sector had wanted to maintain discretion.

It couldn't be said that the mercenaries had done their job badly, since they had been sitting in the cafeteria at comfortable tables for several hours playing gambling games - it's just that since Forkis had been imprisoned, days ago, absolutely nothing had happened. The temperature outside of the outpost at this time of day was minus seventy degrees, which was the standard on the planet's north pole, so it didn't seem wise to go for a walk to pass the time. Zimba had hoped Laureta would come up with at least some spectacular set of death torments for the prisoner, but she had chosen only boring hunger strike. When she had been leaving, she had ordered them to keep an eye on Forkis, which meant looking at the dispatch room's holographs several times a day and checking the outpost's technical parameters, which, anyway, did her AI. In general, while Laureta was away, the android and robots were supposed to take care of everything.

"Fucking lousy cat!" From the beginning, Zimba liked neither Sinaj nor Sefiroth, members of the permanent staff of the Procent Lab whom Casijo chose to stay. Seeing the state of the android and knowing about the skill of the humanoid jaguar, often helpful in repairing faults, the mercenary had no doubt that he was behind the failures. After the conversation of the Onkalot and Forkis in the foreign language, he came up with the idea of locking him up until the death of the Kiritian, but the rest found him paranoid. The argument in favor of Sinai was that he had never done any harm. "But I warned!"

343

Zimba grasped the rifle beside the mug with both hands and hurried out into the corridor. When he was in front of the cafeteria, he kicked at the automatically opening door, behind which his colleagues were still having fun. Mirella was sitting on the lap of one of them.

"Move your asses, the prisoner has disappeared from his cell!" He roared, making them jump.

Without waiting for a reaction from his comrades, he walked towards the sector where the prisoner had been held. After analyzing the disturbances in the cellulas' work, Zimba figured out where he was going - and he had to get there first.

He was, however, cut off by two combat robots, blocking the corridor like huge statues delivered anyhow by a vendor. He went immediately to the side aisle, but here too was another machine.

Running past the confused mercenaries the other way, he headed back to the control room to begin the fight against the blockade imposed on the guards.

Since he could no longer count on the machines and theoretically, he was now in charge of the facility, he decided to activate a completely different program.

\*\*\*

The Onkalot managed to turn off one robot, successfully standing with its back to them, when he and Forkis almost ran into him from around the corner. The machine kept its balance, standing on two pillar limbs with extended cantilever fingers. As its hull drooped and partially folded away, the arm with the attached automatic grinder also flopped.

Despite this minor success, Forkis and Sinaj were chased into a trap as soon as Zimba regained control of the facility. The other intelligent robots cut off their escape route through all possible corridors, so the two were left to lock themselves in the warehouse at which they were stuck.

The Onkalot removed the blockade of the door, which, unlike those in the cells, was less secure. Forkis went in first. As soon as the two-side gate shifted to the side, the lights activated as well. The cubbyhole turned out to be a storehouse of broken appliances, spare parts and redundant interior furnishings; it wasn't an arsenal, but the Kiritian saw his armor in a cabinet.

A screaming cannonade played on the corridor walls. Several large-caliber bullets from the robot's rifle entered the magazine - passing through Sinaj's body as if through air alone. The bullet weapon was old-fashioned by Kiritian standards, and in addition, it did a lot of damage in closed rooms, but it turned out to be deadly effective.

345

Chopped Sinaj, standing in the doorway, slumped down the exagon door frame, leaving streaks of blood behind him. Forkis cursed. If he had been standing in the line of fire, he would have looked identical, and the bullets would have also savaged all the storage equipment behind him. In the gap he noticed a robot standing in the distance, which began to walk clumsily towards the warehouse.

Struggling with the weakness, at some critical point even to maintain his consciousness, the Kitirian lumbered to the cupboard with his armor and fell onto its side. Fortunately, a stray projectile damaged the door cover. Hearing the sound of clanking metallic footsteps more and more clearly, as well as feeling the vibrations of the ground, Forkis grabbed a piece of metal in the shape of a crowbar and began to smash the obstacle separating him from the armor. He could only hope that the facility personnel hadn't deprived it of the element that at that moment was practically his only lifeline in the vast, raging ocean.

The oderses didn't use the glass-like puronax cover unlike the Kiritians, because if they did, even the concentrated fire of all the robots in these dungeons wouldn't have damaged the cabinet door, and Forkis was just deepening the web of cracks.

He reached his bracer before the nearest robot took the last steps to the open entrance.

The small device was in its place, it is possible that the staff had taken it for an ornament of the bracer or hadn't understood the essence of this technological novelty. Forkis was left with the hope that the Cortez inhibitor would now work as it had worked on the cellulas and city drones.

He activated it.

Sinaj's body, lying in a crimson puddle, was dragged towards the corridor, leaving a wide, bloody trail on the floor. It was lifted with the crunch of the bones being shifted. Forkis thought he heard the Onkalot's groan, which was impossible.

Scrapping a portion of the wall around the door, the combat robot climbed into the room, dragging scraps of metal with its body. It began to look around, move as much as his dimensions enabled it, spreading blood across the warehouse floor with his limbs. It stopped its arm with the blade extended, literally a centimeter in front of Forkis holding his breath, not identifying him by heat, biological or physical signatures.

To the electronic senses of the machine, the intruder was now immaterial.

\*\*\*

"What the hell is it about this time?!"

Just as Zimba had been eager to act a few minutes ago, now he definitely didn't want to step over the threshold of the control

347

room. He had managed to send all the unlocked robots to Forkis and chase the prisoner into a trap, but he hadn't foreseen that there might be some kind of failure again. The mercenaries watched the death of the Onkalot through the cellula of the warehouse sector, they also saw the prisoner hiding in the room, but they got totally confused when the target suddenly vanished as if he had dissolved into thin air. He wasn't visible on the facility's surveillance, nor in the robotic level preview.

Zimba knew nothing of the Kiritian interests in Provelkava. He had only been paid to stay here, guard the prisoner until his death, and secure the nether regions without asking questions. Laureta had flown out of Proxima e on some 'urgent matter' and it was impossible to contact her because of the only intraplanet communication available at the Procent Lab. So, the team had to rely only on itself.

"Go see what's going on there." Zimba waved at three of his four men. He looked at worried Mirella, who clung to the mercenaries.

"Go check it yourself," replied one of the chosen. In the unofficial, not-so-legal group, though effective on principle, prevailed casual relationships. "I don't give a damn, I'm staying."

"You know the deal. If we screw up, we'll have to give back the down payment and forget about the full wages. This Forkis is here alone, he runs almost naked and has no weapons, and in addition there are robots in the corridors. Zimba deliberately ignored the obviousness he had just discovered that, for some reason, the machines had lost sight of the target.

The argument about money had always been compelling, and the men lazily rose from their seats. They took the second argument, fully material, in their hands. They had a subpoint in their contract that they were not allowed to kill a prisoner - however, it contradicted the fact that in the event of a life threatening the mercenary had the right to 'neutralize' the guarded or escorted target. Neutral, apolitical Zimba didn't care that the object of their deal was the Kiritian emperor. If not this one, then another would have been in power, and every man in power had always meant grunge, so what was the difference, who and with what views would hold it?

After the three men had disappeared from the control room, Zimba spoke to his neighbor:

"Watch this, Eric." Having withdrawn his fist pressed with the thumb to his mouth, he pointed in a holographic projection at a robot wandering around the warehouse.

"Have you seen it? It's leaning back suddenly, as if it were receiving acoustic vibrations. Oh, see now!"

"I've seen it. And what is that supposed to mean?"

"That Forkis is nearby, but for some reason he is electronically invisible. Walking robots don't have eyes like humans, so they can't detect him with the vision modes. Probably it's Sinaj's doing, who damaged something; good that he's already dead."

"Can't you tell the machines to just shoot an entire sector blindly?"

Zimba looked at Eric with pity.

"To generate even more losses? We already smashed the cat from the Procent Lab. If we also fuck up the equipment warehouse, then the six-month salary will go to hell."

\*\*\*

Forkis had to wait less than a quarter for the nearby robots to retreat to another part of the complex. Though they couldn't see him electronically, they reacted to sounds - they caught louder breathing, the rustle of pants or the snap of a joint. The Kiritian, who initially planned, with only the bracer in his hand, to avoid a closer machine and only then worry about escaping from the complex, was forced to stand still. The robot rotated every time Forkis generated a sound even at the threshold of human hearing.

The massive, tall armor cabinet was facing the corner cellula, so the potential observer couldn't grasp the moment when it was being emptied. The emperor hastily donned the armor except his boots (he considered what it might have looked like in the control room preview; Doris Kagawa told him that the inhibitor masked not only the body but also the active equipment presents at him). At least he already had some protection against the oder weapons, he just had to watch his feet. In weakness, he activated the exoskeleton intensification mode. He immediately felt lining plates and stabilizing tubes on various parts of his body — the muscles were exempted from the effort in favor of the armor that would do most of the work for the wearer. Forkis didn't synchronize it with his will, so he had to make very gentle motions to move, which he had no problem with.

With the X17A4 pistol in his hand, he went out into the corridor. The path formed by Sinaj's blood drops indicated the way taken by the guards; deeper into the complex, their muffled mechanical footsteps still rattled. Forkis then set off briskly into the other embranchement. He found a plan of the complex engraved in metal on the wall and immediately headed for the dining room. The move was predictable, but there was nothing he could do about the animal's obsession ordering him to satisfy his hunger.

Having heard a noise nearby, he withdrew and was forced to take a roundabout way.

The robot previously deactivated by Sinaj was still standing in its old place. Forkis had the crazy idea of removing the gunboat from his shoulder along with the magazine tape packed like Golgi's tanks. The Kiritian X17A4 was mainly used for personal defense against living targets, but it didn't perform very well against heavy Oder walking equipment, even if the light ammunition easily pierced the robot's armor. The gunboat, even if it used primitive bullets, fared much better here.

The machines' alertness to acoustic waves was increased, so Forkis' barefoot peregrination didn't help much, because as soon as he appeared near the cafeteria, the guards immediately came there and began firing. Bullets and energy from smaller carabiners rushed relentlessly to the metal box behind which the target was hidden. The door to the room was flooded and battered, making it impossible to get inside.

The Kiritian tried to open fire on the robots as the cannonade was weakening, but the automatons reacted several times faster than a human, so he couldn't lean out from behind the edge. The crate looked more and more like scrapped mash.

Forkis crawled back around the corner, taking care not to get his feet hit. The bullets rang hitting at the dhurnsteel and biometal of the armor, ricocheting, barely marking it with dents. But if one had hit his leg, it would have been ripped off right away.

Having no chance in the confrontation with these machines, he began to flee to the sector near the entrance, where the control room was located.

On the way he came across three mercenaries who immediately opened fire with their rifles. Forkis dropped to his knees to shield those goddamn feet again (he wished he hadn't messed with his shoes and had gone rogue). He also started shooting.

The result of the clash was predictable. The mercenaries hadn't received information that the target was already wearing the armor, anyway, no one had been able to observe when Forkis had put it on. 20 mm gunboat bullets, with a real purpose to penetrate the casing of oder vehicles, swept away men protected by barely tactical armor at the distance of many meters. Drops of blood and bits of guts splashed the entire corridor, even the ceiling.

A big problem was still the robots, whose sinister, monotonous footsteps, Forkis heard more and more clearly. He had to stop them somehow or make someone do it.

Not worrying about the slaughter, he had made, he immediately headed towards the control room.

\*\*\*

"I don't give a fuck, I don't do it," Zimba hissed. He had just seen on the holograph the slaughter by the Kiritian, which looked as if the mercenaries had opened fire on a ghost, and it had repaid them with a taste of their own medicine.

"Me too," Eric echoed. "We won't stop him now. Let Perez take care of it herself, since she went to hell."

"I agree."

Zimba hastily turned-on defender guns that leaned out of the covered wall recesses at tactical points on the way to the control room. Even if Forkis dealt with them, he would waste a lot of time and not meet mercenaries in the sector anymore.

The men put on helmets, which immediately encapsulated their armor. They left the control room and headed for the oval gates on the first floor.

"Hey, and what about me?!" Mirella, with fear written in her eyes, clung to Zimba's arm just before leaving the facility.

The mercenary had no idea what to do with her. The most convenient way would have been to shoot her dead, which would, however, have been recorded on surveillance, and Mira was reportedly some close friend of Laureta, who had influence and could have later caused them trouble.

"Sorry, honey, but nothing was said about you," he replied. "Lock yourself up in the control room or something, set all the robots towards it."

"But I can't operate any of the equipment here!"

"You will probably get along with Forkis, you already met," Eric said sweetly.

"When the gates started to open, Mira, wearing light clothes, had to withdraw as quickly as possible, because through the open space, came a breath of snow and air, currently almost minus ninety degrees Celsius.

Wading through the snow to the thighs and with nearly zero visibility, the mercenaries reached the anti-gravity transporter without nozzles and flew away a moment after entering the cockpit.

\*\*\*

Forkis had a sudden thought to grab a piece of a mercenary's body in a hurry to satisfy his hunger, but his internal resistance to eating male flesh proved too strong. Even in the case of extreme starvation. Perhaps he would have forced himself to do so if the mechanical guards hadn't been hot on his heels.

However, soon after he had cleared his way of rotating heads trying to chop him up, he found a solution to his culinary problem.

In the control room, the blocked door of which he had to shoot at with a gunboat in order to get inside, he found a familiar, terrified person.

"Hi, Mira." Smiling mockingly, he folded his helmet down and embraced her with a gaze far from mild.

He approached her with a quick step and, acting with the force dictated by the exoskeleton, tore the left arm from her shoulder. In his state, he could have done the same, and without armor.

He cauterized Mira's wound with the energy of the pistol, but she didn't feel it anymore, because she had fainted from fear and terrible pain.

Meanwhile, the Kiritian began voraciously gnawing at the hand that was separated from the body.

\*\*\*

The robots were set to 'find target and destroy' mode, that's why they persecuted Forkis, trying to break into the control room. He managed to break the escaped operator's security, decode the guards' settings, and de-escalate them in time before the massacre of the walls reached a critical state.

When Forkis could finally breathe a sigh of relief, he scanned the object from the control room and learned that apart from him, Mira and an unidentified person in the infirmary, there was no one alive in the nether regions. Having chained the girl to metal ventilation ribs near the floor, in case she came with the idea of tinkering with the robots after regaining consciousness, he went immediately to check it out and look for medicines.

The spacious infirmary turned out to be decently decorated, which wasn't surprising for a facility once linked to research and then to government and prisoners. He was surprised, however, at keeping a living person in a refrigerator capsule intended for the deceased. He was shocked to find out that it was not about a human, but Sinaj. Somehow, he was still alive. The robots had had to put him here at the behest of the operator who had found the humanoid jaguar dead. Forkis thought so too when the guard had shot at him. Sinaj had been very lucky - the employees could have thrown his 'carcass' outside the building at extremely negative temperature.

Humanoid jaguars were adapted to the warm climate, tolerated only moderate coolness in the tropics; if Forkis had showed up at least a quarter of an hour later, Sinaj would have been dead this time for sure. However, on the other hand, the reduced temperature had helped to stop the bleeding from several deep wounds. Walking robots were not designed to attack people, the distance between the missiles fired was considerable. The machine must have been firing at Sinaj with the sight positioned exactly in the center of the body, that's why he hadn't been hit in the organs, but in the sides of the torso and the legs. The bullet brushed his head as well, without embedding in the skull.

Forkis took the Onkalot out of the refrigerator and dressed all his wounds, dosed him up and put him into a pharmacological coma. It still looked bad, Sinaj needed a blood transfusion urgently, and the emperor found only a human blood in the refrigerators. He took advantage of it and drank a liter. In a Kiritian medical center, in a quarter of an hour it would have been possible to produce the necessary amount of artificial blood with identical chemical and biological properties to that of Sinaj, but unfortunately Forkis couldn't use the privileges of advanced medicine of the Immortals. So, he left the Onkalot in the infirmary, as there was nothing else he could do for him.

He went back to the warehouse for the shoes, then went to the dining room, this time to find out in peace that after the cannonade it had become unavailable.

He returned to the control room.

Freed from the chain, Mira regained consciousness and sobbed no longer from the pain, because she had been given a painkiller, but at the memory of the terrible harm. So unbelievable, so hard to comprehend.

"Why are you whimpering?" Forkis turned with his chair, taking a break from trying to make contact with the Kiritians. "It doesn't hurt you anymore."

The girl was unable to look at the bloodied bones stripped of flesh, lying next to him on the control panel. There was no trace of the hand - Forkis had eaten it along with the phalanges. When she accidentally glanced at this place, seeing even a bit too much, she immediately looked down in horror.

"You ... you ate my hand," she stammered out. She was constantly clutching the blackened wound, trying hard not to look at it either.

"So?" Forkis finished nibbling on peanuts he had found in a drawer.

She couldn't believe what she was hearing. In her reality, she had already become a cripple. Although it was possible to reconstruct a limb by growing tissue from modified stem cells, the procedure was beyond her financial capacity. For Forkis, however, basking in modern Kiritian technology, such a procedure lasted a moment and every achij could benefit from it. As a fighter constantly dealing with physical injuries, he didn't understand the girl's suffering and lack of resistance to temporary inconvenience.

"Let's make a deal." He bent down, folded his hands between his spread legs, and focused his full attention on Mirella. In the state she was still in, he couldn't get any information out of her mind, because she was focused only on suffering and referring to Forkis as all synonyms for 'despicable' and 'psychopath'. So he still didn't know how much she was involved in the conspiracy to kidnap him, but he had no reason to be kind to her either. "You will focus carefully now; I will ask you questions and you will answer them honestly. But no hedging, or I'll catch a lie and then I might want to reach for the rest of your body."

The panic fear appeared immediately, restoring the girl to a state of full sobriety more effectively than the pleas that many didn't take seriously. For the full effect, it was necessary to add a prize:

"If you cooperate with me and it turns out that you didn't take an active part in the abduction, I will recreate your hand up to the last tattoo, hair and mole, I will take you from here and leave you wherever you wish. However, you won't be allowed to tell absolutely anyone what you witnessed here. Probably the Kiritians still keep my disappearance a secret. I won't come across well at the Zodiac Universum if my kidnapping and then torture come to light." Forkis leaned against the headrest. "I don't think I need to inform you that if you hurt me in any way, I will find you everywhere and you know what I'll do to you then."

Instinctively, Mirella glanced at the bones and felt on the verge of fainting again. "From the beginning, then," said Forkis. "Tell me who Laureta is and how I got here."

\*\*\*

He was sure he would learn much more, but the prostitute turned out to be the same category of stooges as Zimba and his mercenaries. She hadn't known anything about the action, she had just been told to take care of a small piece of the puzzle. But the remembered, nameless faces from Mira's mind were all that Forkis needed.

He managed to connect with the Kiritians still near Provelkava. As he had assumed, no outsider had found out that the emperor of the Immortals had disappeared, nor had any idea why Kiritian squadrons were still stationed on the outskirts of the city. Achijes searched them meticulously, terrorized whoever it was needed. Thanks to interrogations as well as geodetic and geological notes from the city archives, they found natural tunnels underground, with fresh biological materials in them, as well as traces of machines passing through there. Further searches were abandoned when Forkis contacted his subordinates.

"No, I'm fine, just get someone to pick me up," tired Forkis conveyed laconically to worried Kiret, who had just been on his way to the planet. "Get a paramedic with equipment as well, we'll make fake blood and recreate a limb. Calm down, not mine. Moreover, the team with sensitive nucloindectors, let them secure all biological traces. Oh, and take a lot of food with you. They have terrible cuisine in the Procent Lab."

***

Many inhabitants of Proxima e looked anxiously at the sky as the squadrons from the place near Provelkava joined in orbit with the next ships that had emerged from subspace.

As promised, Forkis took Mira from the north, recreated her arm (no one dared to ask what had happened there; the emperor got rid of the bones before the achijes landed at the outpost) and ostentatiously released the girl from the corvette into the city. After such a show, no one should have teased her, it would probably be easier for her to find a better job. She belonged to that class of timid people whose memory didn't need to be erased.

Sinaj lived to see the arrival of the Kiritians. He underwent a successful transfusion, then all the damage to his body was repaired except for permanent partial memory loss. Forkis found it even a good thing: the Onkalot had forgotten the emperor's secret and that he hadn't really wanted to leave the Procent Lab. Instead, he remembered Chulimal and his abduction, and that then, out of nowhere, the Immortals had appeared. So, he associated them with the kidnappers and hated them. Not understanding Forkis' favor, but also not intending to dwell on it, he ordered to transport him to H14 forests.

On board the corvette already in space, a medical technician paired Forkis' brain with a capripod so that he could mentally sketch portraits of people Mirella had told him about. They then searched for them in a central and secret database where there was a census of all people except those with the unregistered birth.

"Lauret Perez. It's that bitch," Forkis pointed a finger at the image of a woman on a holographic screen with lines of data displayed at it. Kiret Biffter, Captain Milles, Major Ivester, and several other officers also attended the meeting. Corporal Wiktor Shane and Rasmus Darkoris were on guard at the entrance to the bridge. "There is agreement with the traces found in the tunnels under the city, as well as those from the Procent Lab. I also saw two werewolves of Provelkava's elite."

"And Laureta was contacted interplanetarily by another of the torturers," completed Necron. "For my taste, he did it deliberately to make her stuck in a cesspool like the others. It is possible that he thought she had washed out and escaped from the north, shifting all responsibility onto the rest. And the woman is not just anyone - she is a guru of one of the more advanced fractions of lycans, rich thanks to her followers."

"Hence, she had the money to rent the facility and pay the mercenaries so that the permanent human staff of the Percent Lab wasn't involved. Lauret was only sure of Sephiroth and Sinaj, but no one considered that the humanoid jaguar would be willing to help me. Some details of that event, Forkis naturally kept to himself."

"But what did she want from you, sir?" Milles wanted to know.

"I don't know, but I'll figure it out. She probably already knows from Zimba that the plan failed and now, fearing for her skin, she will try to hide well."

"And what about those mercenaries, sir?" Ivester asked.

"They're harmless. Ordinary dogs of war, agreeing to do anything for money. Anyway, for now I don't want to look for them, let's deal with the big fish first. Necron, so now show the rest."

Laureta was replaced by Lord Tisamo and Casijo.

"The first is officially an industrialist, unofficially he is a criminal from Proxima Centauri e, involved in the illegal trade and smuggling of unregistered technologies in the Old Zone. The second man is also associated with the criminal environment. He bought a dilapidated state prison, and before that, a laboratory. Privately, everyone can keep their enemies there and do with them as they wish."

"Do they have connections with Calvary?" Forkis preferred to maintain a reasonably good relationship with the gangsters there, but only because of the numerous benefits. All in all, he asked the unnecessary question, because since he didn't know these people, they must have been irrelevant.

Kiret only confirmed his assumptions, flipping through the next data:

"No, Tisamo and Casijo are associated only with the planets and moons of the Old Zone. Compared to Calvary, they are very small players."

"Then we'll smash them both," Forkis decided immediately, For him, the best solutions had always been the simplest ones. "We will raid their headquarters right away; we will kill their families and related people. We need to remind the oderses from time to time what we are capable of."

For only half a second Kiret showed by a frown on his face that he felt consternation. In the past, he also hadn't shied away from forceful solutions, when nothing could be achieved in another way, but with the creation of the stable empire, he preferred the Kiritians to handle matters more sophisticatedly. These were the norms of civilization; no power was based endlessly on violence. Of course, there were exceptions, like Velkee Warfighter, who would have gladly endorsed Forkis' idea, but the general luckily didn't attend this intimate meeting that couldn't be called a briefing.

"Can I suggest an alternative solution?" He asked.

"Speak." Forkis was always eager to listen to ideas of the Second Galactic Dignitary, as he had a different approach to matters.

"Let's arrange a little machination. If we succeed, the bandits will save us trouble and will go for each other's throats."

"I would just execute them. I don't know why you want to play such a masquerade."

"I'll make it quick."

Forkis didn't like the idea. All Kiret and his pacifist inclinations recently. More than once he wondered if it was a good idea to appoint Biffter as his possible successor, even if he had the longest practice among the Kiritians. "But let the man have something from this trip," he thought, "since he covered such a long part of the galaxy to get here practically in vain."

"Alright, they are yours. I would like to take care of Laureta as soon as possible, but this time my way. I presume, Kiret, that you already have a specific idea allowing us not to waste our time?"

Biffter smiled slyly in response.

\*\*\*

Casijo knew it was over. The plan, about which he had doubted from the beginning, turned out to be a flop. And yet his damn gambler's soul had made him take part in the crazy game of Lauret, because the chance of success had been high. Moreover, leasing out the Procent Lab scored points on his account, which was already bulky, but you could always have more.

Zimba was reasonable enough not to contact him electronically, but to send Eric in the transporter so that he described what had happened. Forkis escaped, and Casijo would be the first person the Kiritians would turn to, as he officially owned the facility. Every day he looked anxiously toward the orbit in which there were the ships of the Infected, and no one knew what they were there for or why they were not departing. It was as if they had been waiting for something. Maybe they excluded him from the circle of suspects? Patience wasn't Forkis' strong suit. When he had certain information, he acted immediately, but so far no one had come to Casijo or tried to contact him. The uncertainty was overwhelming.

He decided not to take any protective steps, but to function normally in one of his villas on Proxima e, because escaping would have been useless anyway. And surely in case of the Kiritians. Sooner or later, they would have found him everywhere, even if he had gone to Andromeda, and it would be especially suspicious if he decided to leave now.

"Honey, why are you so pensive?" The young, fifth wife lying in the bed with him, played with his curly hair with a concerned expression on her face. "I see you forgot again."

"About what, darling?"

"I was supposed to go on a girl's trip and see Olympus Mons. It is the highest mountain in the solar system."

"Right, this on top of that."

"Since it was said, I will keep my word." Casijo kissed her forehead. It was going to be the same again. The former wife, whom he had kicked out, at the beginning also had been beautiful and assured him of her love. And then ... In short, it was cheaper for him to pay five good whores a month.

He stretched his arm towards a dresser and reached for the holonot, wanting to transfer a few thousand uinals for the trip to this wallet-sucking vampire.

After a minute, he sat up as if he had been tied with a rope lying, and yanked forward with great force. He thought it was a bank failure, but in the second and third, it was exactly the same! Not only money had disappeared, but also the reserves of its ore. He couldn't pay for anything even with the blood signature, DNA, dermatoglyphs, or scans of the eye's retina. In any way!

Nervous, he went out onto the terrace, ignoring the android bodyguards wandering around the garden. He immediately contacted his first bank, where he had reportedly paid himself all the uinals. When the bank transfer receipt was sent to him, it turned out that it had been made for his residence in a town three thousand kilometers away. But Casijo didn't own any real estate there.

After a few hours, the gangster's men not only found out that the cottage belonged to the son of one of the agricultural machinery restorers, but also learned that his father had a one-shot matter with Lord Tisamo.

"And that fool thought I wouldn't discover and associate it?" He growled to himself.

Casijo and Lord Tisamo knew each other from the criminal underworld, but were not friends. The action with Forkis was the only one they had had to deal with together. Casijo concluded that Tisamo probably had thought that he had been a dead man and had decided to appropriate his fortune. Maybe he had gotten along with the Kiritians. Or with Laureta, who, as the guru of the satanic sect, allegedly had had to fly in the middle of the action to Calcaris to prevent a civil war between the two lycan clans.

One thing was for sure - this boar had to pay for such a daring theft.

***

He made an appointment with Lord Tisamo for a casual business conversation, saying that he would have liked to cooperate with him. Strangely, the Lord also stated that he was just planning to meet him.

After dark, two groups of several people met in a small, sterile, high-tech city, where blue lights prevailed. They sat down at an outside table of a cafe; there were vehicles flying and lots of people moving around. It made no sense to check each other's weapons for safety, because there was always someone smuggling something or setting their armed man at a safe distance.

The conversation about nothing, with allusions and false smiles, quickly turned into fisticuffs worthy of assassins.

First attacked an android, which was one of Lord Tisamo's bodyguards, in a sparing move of his arm, firing a small, voiceless weapon at Casijo's neck.

"This is for kidnapping and killing my brother," the Lord said coldly, with his eyes no less cold as the blood-spitting thug fell on the table.

Seconds later, the Lord was shot dead by Casijo's man, sitting at a dessert in a restaurant across the square.

"And that's for the misappropriation of someone else's property," Casijo managed to say.

One of the passers-by realized there had been a gang battle in the square and started screaming. Other people massively joined the clarion call as the herd instinct came to the fore.

Losing touch with reality, Casijo didn't manage to establish what brother the Lord was referring to - like him, he had never heard of any of his money.

\*\*\*

Laureta Perez was furious with Casijo for communicating with her in the interplanetary way. The signal ported by the satellites called intermediaries, located in the space of the Universum, for the Kiritians was like a luminous arrow stretching through the cosmos and ending with the inscription: "Here is the organizer of the attack". At least a good thing was that when Forkis broke free, Laureta was several hundred light-years away from Proxima e. Unless the emperor had already dispatched the closest units to the planet, she had time to react.

371

That the Immortals would start snooping around Calcaris was as certain as sooner or later they would catch up with anyone who had taken part in the kidnapping. Laureta had to disappear and believe in a miracle. From the information gathered about Forkis, she knew that for an undefined reason he avoided the planet H14, which was officially explained with the chulimal nature about to recover. When, after exterminating humanoid jaguars, the colonists had taken root there and created metropolises, strange things had begun to happen. There had been even talk of an Onkalot curse. People had been decimated by natural disasters and previously unknown plagues, it even had happened that communication with the city had suddenly broken off, and when people had flown to the place, no inhabitants had been found there. Apparently, it had been similar with jaguars earlier - some tribes had suddenly disappeared, leaving houses, pyramids and tools, and the forest had devoured other traces of their civilization existence. The Kiritian attack, resulting from hatred and the possibility of competition, had turned out to be the most severe for the earthly colonies. The cities had become extinct, whoever had survived, had either moved out of H14 or begun to engage in mundane professions that hadn't attracted the attention of usurpers. Villages and self-sustaining farms had proliferated, orbital trade had also flourished. Already oblivious to the future threat of these apolitical peoples, the Kiritians had stopped coming to Chulimal — quite the opposite of the looters and treasure hunters who had believed in the existence of hidden Onkalot artifacts and valuables.

On H14 had also nestled primitive lycans wanting to live in the wild in forests, and it was they who now interested Laureta. She would easily assume sovereignty over them as a higher-caste guru, wait in hiding, and figure out what to do next in the case of Forkis.

After selecting a handful of Lycan aides, she secretly chartered a transporter that wasn't in a register of machines leaving Calcaris.

Flying into the atmosphere of feral H14, unattended by anyone, should have been no problem.

\*\*\*

After settling the matter with the gangsters, the emperor decided to go to H14 first and leave Sinaj there as he wished. He canceled some of the redundant ships.

Forkis had avoided the planet since leaving it with the construction team with whom he had later come to Earth. There were too many personal monsters from his past on Chulimal. He entrusted his people with all reconnaissance missions aimed at looking for suspicious changes and activity of enemies. However, he hadn't sent any patrol to the planet for decades, as Chulimal appeared to be stable. As the Kiritians emerged from the final subspace jump and found themselves several hours of a traditional flight from the planet, Captain Milles picked up in the area an unidentified electronic activity that quickly dispersed. Something they hadn't dealt with before. The phenomenon was closest to locating new types of machines in the exo-atmospheric space. The squadron crews remained vigilant, but the electronic signatures didn't repeat themselves.

The entry into the atmosphere was smooth. Machines flew over the jungles of the equator to the place indicated by the emperor. Kiritians sometimes passed lonely farms and villages where the inhabitants were experiencing moments of terror. The planet had changed a lot since most of the colonists had disappeared from it. It took on its original character again, the traces of both civilizations were almost completely absorbed by nature. "Perhaps that is a good thing," Forkis, silent, thought sentimentally, staring at the blurry canopy of trees through the cockpit cover.

The city of Che'ab'aj, as was called also the tribe of Sinaj, suffered the same fate as the rest of the humanoid jaguar legacy. The houses had long since fallen into decay or were torn down, only a part of a road with a waist-high grass remained, as well as a pyramid overgrown with moss and ivy.

Sinaj, however, didn't seem to mind such an image of destruction, at least he tried not to show his feelings before the

Kiritians. He had known beforehand what he might have found there. When he was released from the corvette after landing, he plunged into the forest without a word and looking back.

Forkis sighed; that's it. He hoped that Sinaj would manage somehow, since he had refused any help and forbidden the Kiritians to look for him. To him, Forkis was just a bad man, like the rest of them.

Seizing the opportunity, the emperor took courage and decided to go somewhere else. Alone, he only agreed to be accompanied by a guard orb - except for animals, the area was deserted anyway.

When the corvette and escort settled in the designated region, he climbed his skulak Firley, and flew over a bit.

He reached Chiq'aq, the Place of Fire.

Forkis' pulse quickened, as if he had run this section from the ship, not flown a few meters above the ground.

The primal natural sight slightly soothed his nerves, moreover numerous birds chirped so carelessly. The orb whirled in the air. As in the case of Che'ab'aj, also here practically only the pyramid remained, and the rest of the city had been devoured by erosion, soil and vegetation. In the former square, grew trees tens of meters high.

There was no trace of the bones of the murdered inhabitants, which brought the emperor a strange relief. He supposed they had either broken up or someone had cleaned up in Chiq'aq, maybe some surviving humanoid jaguars or a group of them. Forkis wondered if it could have been Q'ualel. They had never met after that quarrel; it is possible that the humanoid jaguar had been long dead.

His grim contemplation was interrupted by the signal from his PDA.

"Can I, sir?" It was Milles.

"I'm listening."

"The spy orbs released into the field detected new activity."

"The details."

"There are a lot of people in one of the ruins, a few civilian vehicles are stationed nearby. It looks like a meeting of local people, only some of whom have come from far away, because there are not many machines."

"Thanks, Milles. I will come back to you soon. Do we know the name of these ruins?"

"Yes." The captain paused for a few seconds to correctly pronounce the bizarre onkalot word: "This is Ajb'atenaja temple."

\*\*\*

A biological and physical scan of the masked orb provided another unbelievable piece of information - Laureta Perez was in Ajb'atenaja.

After Forkis returned aboard, the Kiritians flew there immediately.

Another of the temples remaining after Onkalots differed from most of the classically erected buildings. It was not a pyramid with a simple arrangement of corridors, but a large geopolymer complex full of halls and passages, built without taking care of symmetry and order. In the courtyard, statues depicting achijes and priests of humanoid jaguars as well as bowls-hearths surrounding the road leading to the stairs of the main entrance had been preserved in good condition. In some there was fire, consuming the surrounding moss and wood. Forkis thought the Kiritian artificial fire from generators would have looked good in them.

"Let's check this place," he ordered.

As they looked for the landing area, lycans in astonishment looked up at the sky from the courtyard, other ones started pouring out of Ajb'atenaja. They were representatives of a faction of a satanic sect - a demoralized nightmare of the locals who had to constantly protect their farms from them. Most of them looked like taunters in skins and rags. They were far from being educated, gentle and rich lycans living in great cities on other planets. Forkis saw in a close-up the same two adjutant werewolves he had seen in Provelkava Grihorsk. So, he had further evidence that Laureta must have attended the local assembly.

Having found no suitable landing site, they released a logistic hyperdrone with a firing cannon to clear a square of land to the ground. Forkis with a few achij teams came to the temple, the lycans looked at them a bit like the Indians once at Columbus and his entourage. Almost everyone was drunk or stoned, paradoxically it was possible to talk logically not with people, but with the two werewolves guarding the complex.

It turned out that in Ajb'atenaya there was some sort of collective orgy, like a primitive version of harroweeng, where stimulants were not kept off.

"So, sir. Are we spoiling the party or crashing it?" Corporal Darkoris asked jokingly.

"I would crash hands down," replied playfully crude Private Tsar Seymour, who for some reason was on the team of Kiret flying to help Provelkava Grihorsk.

Forkis looked glumly at the building. It was definitely not a serious and sensible idea, but it was already so accepted that the executions were often accompanied by abnormal entertainment.

***

Confident of her safety, as well as wanting to de-stress among a gang of savages, Laureta started drinking dark green liquor made from a local cactus. Bucket after bucket. Amidst food, fire and stimulants, the lycans danced and made love in a great hall of the temple, while she sat on one of stone thrones of the old Onkalot high priests. She was pretty drunk when the Kiritians showed up at Ajb'atenaja, but still sober enough not to confuse the information about their arrival with a drunken delirium. The alcohol made the fear she should have felt at the moment barely smolder in her mind - even when Forkis entered the hall, with his helmet slid open, and surrounded by his achijes drawing general attention in the silence. Embracing the woman with his eyes, completely not surprised by her presence, he smiled unpleasantly and folded his arms over his chest. Laureta stood up, holding a not emptied bottle. Not thinking too logically, staggering, she moved towards the corridor leading to one of the side exits from Ajb'atenaya, wanting to escape into the forest. Forkis stood and just watched her.

After a few minutes she saw the darkening sky and the star K'ajolom.

"Good evening, Private Kazuo Shimizu is making a curtsy. Where are we going?" One of the pair of ahijes guarding at the exit asked. The serenity in the words was apparent, for Perez saw disturbing amusement in his eyes.

"It's very dangerous in these jungles at night," said his companion thoughtfully, but with words tinged with sarcasm.

She realized that the guards wouldn't let her pass, knowing something she could only guess.

They also didn't stop her when she was withdrawing into the building, remaining at their posts. Laureta wanted to use a different exit, but the situation with the guards repeated itself. And not lycan ones.

Forkis had set his achijes around the entire temple complex in advance.

The woman had no choice but to confront him, which he had probably counted on.

Still holding the bottle in her hand, she returned to the main chamber. Forkis had already sat down nonchalantly on her throne, and tapped his fingers on the headrest, on which he threw his arm. His people mingled with the lycans as they joined the party. The sectarians didn't know the reason why Laureta was on Chulimal, so they thought that the presence of the Immortals was her idea, and that's why they showed no hostile intentions towards them. Anyway, no one in the drunk company cared about such things at all.

Forkis was following Laureta with his gaze the same way as before when she had been approaching him.

"This is my throne," she said. "Sit on the smaller one."

He looked at her seriously, playing with his fingers until on his face appeared a sly smile.

"Won't you even give such an important guest something to drink?" He asked pleasantly. Like her, he dispensed with a welcome chatter that he would have most gladly orchestrated with a gun to bring the matter to an end quickly. However, he promised Laureta something else - and he felt like something else.

She raised the bottle slightly, the Kiritian took it with a firm grasp and quickly emptied it, then tossed it onto the stones of the ground. It was made of a biodegradable, horny structure produced by certain bacteria, so it didn't break up, but rolled into the hall with a clatter fading away in the tumult of the surroundings.

The situation was too neurotic. Laureta had to drink more so as not to think about anything at all, especially how screwed she was. She went to the table, grabbed a large mug, and poured the entire contents of a transparent decanter into it. And then she started pouring the liquid into herself.

Forkis also didn't idle and use the benefits obtained from a wide range of local flora.

381

"And wut noo?" Perez muttered as the drunken Forkis took his throne again, and she swung from side to side beside him like a lake plant in the bottom current. She looked around and noticed half-consciously that the emperor was constantly being watched by the achijes who were not playing until they were replaced. They probably had an eye on her too.

"And what is supposed to be? I came here to have a good time. So I hope you will satisfy me properly."

This was what she was familiar with, she was quite pretty and didn't hesitate to use it to manipulate people. She sometimes did this even with androids. She got what she wanted and completely dulled her logical thinking, so she was no longer able to catch Forkis' nightmarish allusions. But on the other hand, he couldn't probe her mind since it turned into a total drunken mush.

Smiling alluringly, she straddled the Kiritian's lap, placed her hands on his shoulders, and gave him a firm, imperious kiss. She hated Forkis, she wanted to kill him, but she wanted to find out just as much how truth a rumor was that he was the fulfillment of every woman's erotic dreams. Anyway, what woman wouldn't have been tempted to take advantage of the opportunity, having at her disposal the emperor of the Immortals himself?

Forkis pulled her to him and started kissing even harder, all over the face and neck, hinting that he was dominating the game, he was the winner.

His mouth alone was enough to make her tremble. Alcohol and drugs in Laureta's blood had a similar effect - she had no chance of winning against these three mighty kings. She succumbed to the dark temptation.

The sensual struggles of two killers hating each other didn't belong to frequent romances.

Forkis undressed her partially above the waist and started caressing her heated body, mainly with his tongue.

At one point, Lauret, morbidly wanting more, looked with a smile at his eyes with a similar expression. She reached for the alcohol from the large supply they had arranged on the table next to her, and for the next time she took a few decent gulps, pouring most of the liquid on herself and the Kiritian.

Then she totally spaced with her memory.

*** 

She only recovered in bed, lying in it with Forkis. She wore only a white negligee, but the Kiritian retained some of the armor, while the rest knocked around the room, as if he had been throwing it off anywhere in a hurry. Laureta realized that she was in one of the private rooms at the rear of the complex, separated from the corridor by a synthetic fiber screen. In a brazier functioned an artificial fire generator of an excessively intense orange color. They probably were alone there, but when the woman looked at the gap under the cover of the entrance, she was convinced that she saw the hands of a crouching child who quickly withdrew them.

The alcohol must have still wreaked havoc in her mind.

"Oh, you've already come back to me. Alright. So we can move on to the next stage," Forkis said in his baritone, resting his arm on her chest, and his head on it. He was stiff too, but unlike Laureta, he was able to form intelligible sentences in his state. "I'm really surprised you decided to come here with us. It is as if a sheep was hanging out with wolves."

"Wait, what flight? Has she made a flight? What the collapsed star was going on here?"

Clarity of mind quickly began to break through to her shattered self, as if she had been given a drug to neutralize all stimulants. And she certainly had put a lot of them inside herself. It's possible Forkis raved and mistook Laurent for some other whore. Her memory began to come back to her as well, revealing terrifying facts as if hidden behind a curtain.

The Kiritians, however, found her.

And apparently, they decided to take their time with their designs.

Meanwhile, she totally freaked out and started hitting on Forkis!

"So, will you tell me why you wanted to kill me? What do you hate me so sickly for?" He asked ingratiatingly, though with a cold look in his eyes.

She knew that the jokes and the time of pathological relaxation were over. Now came the time for the specifics and putting all cards on the table.

"Do you remember the village of Dharsa Pass?" She had no problem confiding. "My grandmother was a girl then, you ordered her to be taken aboard your ship with the rest of the children. She saw her family executed on your order. When it turned out that she didn't qualify for being a Kiritian, you gave her to the orphanage. She was supposed to go to a foster family, but in fact, she was taken by a pimp and she ended up being a whore in a brothel. Her whole life was hell, and so was of my mother, whom my grandmother had given birth to at eighty-three; she also became a prostitute. They both suffered, they were consumed by their antipathy to you, but also too passive and delicate to do more than sink into regret. They hated their fate no less than you did, but took no steps to improve the situation. Only I dared to do it, I wanted to make this generational revenge. I was born a woman of action, evil and cruel, I gained power and wealth, and when I was ready to act, I began preparations to avenge my family. I almost did the impossible, but

385

that stupid cat and the mercenaries screwed it up. If I hadn't flown from there ..."

She was surprised when Forkis only smiled half-arsed.

"So, revenge. How perfectly I understand it."

She was expecting everything oscillating in anger and torture, but not that he would kiss her! He did it in a way she had already known, as if he had been going to absorb her through his mouth, turning Laureta into something like a flame creeping alongside, but redder. She couldn't take it any longer.

She attacked him, desiring more and wanting to postpone the judgment moment as much as possible. Forkis had done this more than once - first he indulged in a sensual game with the victim, and then he killed her.

They began to play passionately with each other, as then in the chamber among the achijes and lycans.

Damn, what should she have done now? How could such a coincidence occur at all?! It was rather unlikely Forkis would find her that soon. Probably it was because of that fool Casijo or the others who got scared and started ratting. Or the charter didn't went as it should have gone.

She had already realized that running away was out of the question since the entire complex was guarded. Forkis came here to kill her. She had to think, and fast!

"You got a detox," he confirmed her earlier considerations. "It's not proper to punish a drunk, is it? What's the fun when the victim is not fully aware of what is happening to them?"

"I got it!" She came up with something!

Laureta touched her hair and breathed a sigh of relief as her fingers felt a few bone clips. Three of them contained needles soaked in a poison recently developed on Proxima e - for which even the Kiritians couldn't yet have an antidote - but only one dose was enough to kill a man the weight of Forkis. All she had to do was unscrew the cap of the primitive-looking ornament.

The woman had no choice but to pretend that she was having a good time, and then finish the plan begun on Proxima e. After that, she didn't care what would happen.

She glanced worriedly at the Kiritian hanging above her, who was trying to bite her ear. She leaned back feistily. Could he read everything from her thoughts? There were no signs on his face that he had figured out the intentions of his victim. Perhaps Forkis' skill was weakening when he was drunk?

"Aren't you scared?" He asked.

"No, Forkis," she replied, smiling alluringly.

"And you should, you really should." There was also a smile on his face in a similar tone, but really predatory.

Then she gave herself again to him for long minutes, screaming with pleasure as he filled her sometimes. She would have lied to herself if she had said that this relationship wasn't hellishly pleasant. Although very specific, because Forkis' behavior was usually similar to that of a tiger examining a freshly hunted deer with its tongue and teeth, with which it was going to play for a while. Laureta felt uneasy as she remembered what she had so badly wanted to witness in the Procent Lab. The good entertainment ended when the observer was to experience the hard way the desired horrors affecting the third parties. She was even more terrified as she recalled the words of the promise that Forkis had made while being chained; it had seemed so funny then. Now he started to talk some idiocy about consumption, the woman answered in a similar tone, continuing the sick game, keeping her nerves under control with increasing difficulty.

She had to act first. She only needed a few seconds.

As she turned her head to the side, being kissed on the neck, she could have sworn again that she saw the baby behind the screen.

"There's a girl there," she announced.

Forkis glanced towards the exit, something must have been wrong, because he had lost interest in his lover for the time being. Frowning, he seemed to strain his mind as if he had been using telepathy.

And she took advantage of it.

She pulled the hairpin out of her hair, tossed the cap onto the floor, and plunged the needle into Forkis' arm.

The poison should have acted immediately, paralyzing his muscles within a few breaths. And soon after, killed when the target became incapable of breathing, especially speaking and calling for help via the communicator.

But none of this happened.

She must have felt the wrong hairpin!

Surprised, Forkis turned to face Perez and pinned her hand firmly to the bed with his mighty grip as she tried to reach towards her hair again.

He understood what had happened when he saw the needle in a wrapper between her fingers.

They had so much in common. He considered forgiving Laureta for everything she had done to him, paying tribute to her courage, strength, and most importantly, that she was not indifferent to the family grievances of two generations ago. He would have come up with something so that the people didn't find out or accepted it - a similar dilemma he had already experienced in Aytar's case. Forkis had respect for strong people who were not afraid to fly very high. He could have mended her mind, by force, if she hadn't wanted to voluntarily.

389

The woman, however, signed her death warrant.

The emperor saw in his mind the unfortunate teenager, whose neck he was forced to break. No, that was definitely something he couldn't pardon for.

He jabbed his jaws into her throat and, successfully for Laureta, killed her before he set about stripping the flesh off the bones and drinking her blood.

\*\*\*

When he looked, all bloodied, towards the screen, he did see the baby there. A girl, seemingly four years old, scared to death because she was pale and stiff. It would have been a phenomenon if it had happened otherwise.

"Where did the brats come from?" Forkis managed to think before he fell straight onto the partially eaten corpse. With a blurry glance, through the bloody veil, he saw that an older boy had come running for the girl. Her name was Ania - so much he managed to register before the poison took over his body.

\*\*\*

"God gave up his happiness. He went among his beloved people, sharing with them hardships and strenuousness," Kiret mocked him more than once with these words, when he acted like an ordinary achij who risked his life.

Forkis couldn't do anything about the upbringing and mentality he had been taught in Chiq'aq. There, the chiefs sat on thrones for solemn meetings when their rank required it, but on a daily basis they actively participated in the life of the tribe, living like every inhabitant. A ruler was considered a true ruler only when he knew the needs of his people inside out. When he knew what blood, pain and tears were. And this couldn't be achieved by constantly staying in the Chief's House, which was considered contemptible.

This collided with the attitude of people who had a different view of the security of the autocrat.

Forkis agreed with Kiret about his daring willfulness, but he knew perfectly well who he was, so he had always protected himself properly. But even the best security works like a lottery - nothing happens for a long time, and suddenly good numbers are drawn.

He had the misfortune to draw such numbers twice in a row - first kidnapping and now poison.

He decided not to inform anyone about the events in the cubbyhole, so that he wasn't accused of his irresponsibility as an emperor who neglected his safety. About what he had been doing here, not to mention. He had really been sure he had been completely safe. The entire temple had been controlled by the achijes - apart from the corridor that had been supposed to ensure him intimacy - the lycans had had no weapons that could have harmed him, and Laureta had gone to bed with him almost naked, capable at most of slapping his face. Forkis wouldn't have figured out that a woman's hairpin could turn out to be deadly.

He was lying face down in the springy, slippery gut, with his head between the rib cage when he was awakened by the sound of the PDA communicator. He felt horrible, as if the ceiling had fallen on him, in addition he had a high fever and could barely encompass reality. Amid the crunch of the bones and the plopping of the guts, he rolled over from his back to his belly, which ended up with falling from several dozen centimeters. He immediately vomited up the human flesh, blood, and the remnants of his last carousal.

"What?" He asked wailingly, turning on his PDA. He didn't have the strength to support himself on his elbows and he fell to the floor again, miraculously not landing in his own puke.

Milles took his word as an expression of dissatisfaction.

"Sorry, sir, but this is urgent. We suspect that the rebels sent child spies to Ajb'atenaja, who had to enter the temple area at the time of the changing of the guard. In addition, they flew in an unknown type of carrier. We detected enemy activity, but only because they temporarily removed the covers of their buildings, probably not expecting us on this planet. The opposition has its base on the H14, and worse, their technology has advanced significantly. We had made the mistake of ceasing to monitor them in this sector as a threatening opponent. It's not looking good, sir. Shall I send all the ships and fire at their positions?"

Great, new varieties of poisons first, unknown to the nano-detoxicants circulating in his blood, and now this. Forkis put his hands over his face. In that state, he couldn't think logically. Despite the fact that by Laureta's mistake, he had received a dose that didn't threaten his life, which, moreover, the body began to get rid of, he still felt terrible and he was going to experience another round of vomiting.

"One of the boys is Beliar Drunkenstein," the captain continued to outline the situation without receiving an answer, "probably the son of Carlos Drunkenstein. That's what the other escaped children called him. The senior is a renowned rebel aircraft builder and supplier of new technologies to the opposition. If he is on the planet, there probably is Aveo Lacetti, a commander of the 3rd Rebel Fighter Regiment, who has gotten under our skin more than once. If we attack immediately, the rebels may be completely excluded from the game."

"What do you mean the turds ran away from you, Milles, to Argens[18]?!"

"I contacted you on this, sir, to find out if we had to catch them, but you had your PDA turned off. So, what's the order, sir?"

What did they even expect of him? Let them leave him alone. All he wanted now was to sleep, even on that bloody, acidic stone, and get up after a few hours, then tidy up, wash, get cleaned up, and communicate to all and sundry that he had settled Laureta's matter. Now he was clearly not suited to making difficult decisions.

"Let it go. Without spontaneity." He felt Laureta's hairpin with his hand. No wonder no achij had paid attention to it; the scanners didn't detect a piece of bone as something dangerous. Forkis tried in vain to open the wonder, which looked like a homogeneous mass. The woman must have been familiar with it. "If the rebels gained technology that we missed, we could fall into the shit up to the ears if it turns out that they are hiding a fleet on H14. We stay in Ajb'atenaja. Unless something serious happens, don't bother me for the next few hours."

He was furious with himself. He had never made so many mistakes at once. Due to his sentiments, he had lost interest in his home planet, and rebel filth had flourished on it. He had to get a

---

[18] The equivalent of the 'hell' type. Argens are fictional evil spirits or demons that inhabit outer space.

grip in the end, because another wrong decision might have ended up miserably for him.

After Milles disconnected, he climbed onto the bed and lay down beside the corpse among skins stiff with clotted blood.

When he fell asleep, he dreamed of the girl with dark auburn hair and a fair complexion, peeking earlier from under the screen - but now she shot him down in a cosmic battle.

# Acknowledgments and Afterword

The idea was inspired by a humorous article on the Joe Monster website about specific human preferences. Some quite common, other bizarre and rather unusual. Particularly noteworthy was paraphilia discussed in the introduction. It was so strange and a bit scary that I thought why not take the risk and write a text on this subject, especially since there is hardly anything like that in Poland. Vorarephilia also fit perfectly into the character of Forkis/Xajb'a Kej, who almost two decades ago, in the original version of Onkalot, had vore inclinations as a pred.

The characters of Xajb'a Kej (the name in the Mayan language means Deer Dance Square) and his friend Q'ualel (Minister in

Mayan) were inspired by myths about the Indian brothers Ixbalanque and Hunahpu, who experienced various adventures. As is the case with the mythology of the Mesoamerican peoples, brutal, macabre motives prevail there. Vore is also there, and the Zodiac Universum series contains many references to ancient cultures of Central America. When I rewrote the old Onkalot, I planned to completely abandon these elements. Especially the scene with the rat, which I thought was scary and infantile, but it turned out that readers liked it. They suggested that I not only keep it but also make it more shocking. So the rat stayed, but so that the episode was not completely taken out of context and made sense, it was also necessary to change the character of Forkis himself. Thus, the scene that was to be thrown out not only survived and changed, but also entailed a complete psychological reconstruction of the character, also physical, because Forkis originally hadn't been able to perform certain activities.

After the release of Onkalot, experimenting with vore-themed stories like First Law of the Arena began. I read some foreign literature on this subject, and legally translated one of the texts into Polish, transforming the details for the Zodiac Universum. Then the short story Aytar was written - about the past of the supporting heroine from the trilogy. It turned out that what was supposed to shock and frighten, the beta-readers and reviewers found quite a good comedy. So, I decided to write more texts with both vore elements and a closer look at Forkis, and make a retrospective anthology out of it.

As for the question of whether the author is serious and the stories are not a non-canonical joke, I rely on the readers' interpretation. Conspiracy theories are welcome!

www.ingramcontent.com/pod-product-compliance
Lightning Source LLC
Chambersburg PA
CBHW031032030726
47497CB00004B/1109